Prai
Death of an

'A high octane jaunt full of laughter and wisdom. Funny, wise, with some deliciously sexy stepping stones... I adored Eve immediately.'

Judith Holder, star of the *Older and Wider* Podcast

'Gripping, atmospheric and pleasingly twisty, *Death of an Englishman* is a captivating and engrossing read: I loved it.'

Chloë Houston, co-author of
***The Book Game* by Frances Wise**

'Always entertaining... Anna Beer plunges the reader into Oxford's murky depths with the mystery of a missing manuscript and a cast of the eccentric to the obnoxious, even both...'

Amal Chatterjee, author of *Across the Lakes*

'An absorbing, intriguing read... Lovers of detective fiction will relish the witty references to other crime writers and characters.'

Dr Lynn Robson, author of *Early Modern Murder,*
Calvinism and Female Spiritual Authority

'Anna Beer constructs a riveting, often amusing narrative around conflicting cultural ideologies, revealing her characters with warmth and humanity.'

Helen Carr, author of *Sceptred Isle*

MORE PRAISE FOR
Anna Beer

'Beer pulls no punches, and her history is complex, nuanced, and fascinating. This feminist corrective sings.'

Publishers Weekly on *Eve Bites Back*

'A delightful, and challenging, read.'

New York Journal of Books on *Eve Bites Back*

'A splendid alternative history of English literature.'

Guardian on *Eve Bites Back*

'*Eve Bites Back*... is shaped by the same principles [as Beer's earlier work] – feminist indignation, certainly, but also a drive to share ideas and observations about a diverse body of achievement, emerging from historical periods radically different from our own ... invigorating.'

Times Literary Supplement *Eve Bites Back*

'What brings the book to brilliant life is Ralegh's voice. In conversation with his writing, Beer's prose soars ... It's hard not to think Sir Walter would have approved.'

Guardian on *Patriot or Traitor*

'Beer's book is a rigorous and readable take on her subject – it captures the full scope of the character of Ralegh, one that remains frustrating, but endlessly fascinating.'

Times on *Patriot or Traitor*

Death of an
Englishman

An Oxford Mystery

Anna Beer

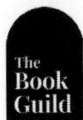

First published in Great Britain in 2025 by
The Book Guild Ltd
Unit E2 Airfield Business Park,
Harrison Road, Market Harborough,
Leicestershire. LE16 7UL
Tel: 0116 2792299
www.bookguild.co.uk
Email: info@bookguild.co.uk
X: @bookguild

The manufacturer's authorised representative in the EU
for product safety is Authorised Rep Compliance Ltd,
71 Lower Baggot Street, Dublin D02 P593 Ireland
(www.arccompliance.com)

This work is entirely fictitious and bears no resemblance to any persons living or dead.

Typeset in 10.5pt Adobe Garamond Pro

Printed and bound in Great Britain by 4edge Limited

ISBN 978 1835742 112

British Library Cataloguing in Publication Data.
A catalogue record for this book is available from the British Library.

For RJBR, EMBR and HSW
'the believers'

I am not I, pittie the tale of me.

SIR P.S. HIS ASTROPHEL AND STELLA

There is an uncanny stillness to an Oxford quad as midnight approaches. The modern world is held at bay. If you were to stand in the cloisters and listen, you would more likely hear the imagined footsteps of monks than the actual laughter of students. The thick medieval walls keep their counsel. Tonight, they hide the sound of a man's last rasping breaths while the darkness, and a dozing porter, allow a woman to slip out of the college, back into the present. But there is a witness to both the fugitive and the dying, a witness who hears the Oxford bells begin their midnight toll and chooses to do nothing. For now.

I

Spring was making a very uncertain advance upon winter. Eve studied the trees for signs of life, impatient for buds, glad of every daffodil, but also with the knowledge that April, a couple of weeks away, would still likely be the cruellest month. She was better at stoic tolerance of cold, grey, March skies than she was at the abundance of spring. Oxford station was grey, a bitter wind making the waiting passengers hunch into their winter coats, and the coffee she held had been a waste of money. When had she become such a coffee snob?

And yet, Eve still felt the surge of anticipation that any train journey generated. There was even an exquisite pleasure in choosing her route to London. Would it be the straightforward, quick and dirty speed of the GWR or the pleasure of arriving, after a meander through the Chilterns, at elegant Marylebone station? And even if the journey itself was prosaic, she could indulge in fantasies as the train passed suburban villas, shopping centres, and industrial estates. *Where next?* she would think in the full knowledge that her final destination, today, was a publisher's offices in Soho. But there had been enough times when she'd set off from Oxford and her London terminal had been merely a stepping stone to Mallaig, Cadiz, Narvik,

Marrakesh. Eve settled back into her seat. Once this job was out of the way, she'd head somewhere exciting. All was well. The train was on time. And the coffee wasn't that bad, really.

Eve had nearly missed the message from Jon that had brought her to this chilly platform. She had only dug out her phone in order to delete the ridiculous dating app she'd loaded up the previous Friday. Cursing Linda for being persuasive and the algorithm for generating a suspiciously large number of messages from eligible men over the weekend, she had spotted the old-style text from her boss. *Call me at 12.* Jon was a man of few words, which was ironic given his business. His ostentatious commitment to his dumb phone – no photos, no social media – was part and parcel of this, and, like the man, both admirable and profoundly irritating.

'I thought of you *immediately*. Just up your street. I need a safe pair of hands, and, well, you know Oxford, don't you?'

Eve relished flattery as much as the next person but had wondered why Jon was bothering with it.

'Did you see, that appalling man, David Morrow, died recently?'

Eve had seen. His passing had prompted a skirmish in the ongoing culture wars. On one side, regret for the sad loss of an honest, straight-talking man who was willing to take on the woke brigade. On the other, a weary acknowledgement of yet another older white man's ability to get media coverage, whether in death or life, by railing against cancel culture while not, in fact, being cancelled. A poor man's Farage, but literary rather than political. Actually, if Eve was being fair, Morrow had written some good stuff – what, twenty, thirty years ago? She had one of his books from the nineties and had found it on her shelves when she'd heard about his death, struck by how glamorous the man had been back then. The author photo was all cheekbones and floppy hair, a hint of a pout to the full lips, more than a hint of defiance in the eyes staring straight to camera. Now he was dead. Eve had guessed what was coming next.

'Heritage have been in touch with me.' Jon tried to sound as if this was an everyday occurrence, but his voice was thrilled. One of the big trade publishers was coming to him for help. 'You'll remember they paid a foolish amount for the rights – and he was due to deliver the manuscript this month.'

Eve did remember. *An English Hero* would be a biography of the courtier, poet and soldier Sir Philip Sidney, who lived and died in the first Elizabethan era, which happened to be Eve's own historical hunting ground. The book had garnered Morrow a six-figure advance. A while back, she thought, but the pandemic had made her and everyone else hazy about dates. What would she do with £100,000? She came back to earth, Jon in mid-sentence.

'...get the MS, tidy it up a bit, you know what to do, and Heritage will be happy.'

Eve worked for Jonathan Peck as a literary consultant. She operated as a kind of midwife to other people's books. Most of the projects came from publishing houses who didn't have the payroll employees to 'fix' a book, or sometimes an author, that had gone horribly wrong. Some came from individuals who felt they had a story to tell but not the literary skills to tell it. Sir Robert, who had made his millions in the pork products business and whose chapters she had returned to him transformed today, was a case in point. The job formalised (and provided reward for) something she had done for friends, and friends of friends, and even enemies, for years, even through her very messy twenties. Eve still took pride in the way she had emerged from that decade with a nine-year-old daughter, a doctorate, and a decent enough job in one of the new universities teaching literature in English. Her thirties had been spent producing the requisite book of the thesis and sticking out her teaching job until Rosa hit eighteen.

Free of parental responsibility, or so she thought, she had looked around her and felt a desire to do things differently. Eve knew she could fix things. Not plumbing, sadly. But narratives. Enter Jon and his start-up, and, to Eve's amazement and delight, the work had come in. Of course, she soon found out that Rosa reaching legal adulthood was merely the start of a new phase of parenting, but back then, three years ago, she had been optimistic. She had also swiftly discovered that with the freedom of the freelance life came a dangerous professional invisibility, and she'd therefore grabbed at an affiliation to one of the newer and poorer Oxford colleges, St Abb's. New for Oxford, that is, meaning nineteenth rather than thirteenth century. Poorer because it didn't have a deer park. Affiliation meaning there was no money in it, but she was no longer an outsider. For income, she needed Jon and his clients, which was why she was now sitting, freezing, on a bench at Oxford station.

Eve's good mood did not survive past Didcot as she read up on David Morrow. God, he would have *hated* the thought of her finishing up his lucrative masterwork. It was not merely that Morrow had railed against the corrupted humanities departments of 'the West', with their hand-wringing post-colonial guilt, their critical race theory, their obsession with pronouns. No, Eve, as a woman, represented the monstrous regiment who had emasculated a whole generation of men (white, English, cis-gender men), taken their jobs, challenged their ideas, made it impossible for their sons to follow in their footsteps. Women blind to, and resentful of, men's natural right to be the provider, to open doors, to compliment women on their appearance. Women who refused to give men a free pass, failing to understand that the poor darlings were at the mercy of their desire to reproduce.

4

Eve had ambivalent feelings about reproduction and, more specifically, the man who had successfully impregnated her, early in her final year at university. The moment itself had been rather joyous, part of a riotous New Year's Eve, a pleasurable coupling to an only half-ironic soundtrack of Britney and Steps. However, the condom discussion had been brief and, on his side, duplicitous. The result had been Rosa, and Eve could not complain. But her lover, keen in pursuit of his essential drive to procreate, was not so keen on being a father. At the time, and ever since, Eve had not been able to afford, in any sense of the word, to indulge in her essential feminine nature of chaos. She had worked tirelessly and efficiently to provide for and to raise Rosa. Now her work was done. Kind of.

And so, in a very different sense, was Morrow's. Eve scrolled through the clips and images from a few weeks before. While receiving her instructions from Jon, something had nagged at her memory about the man's death. Now she was reminded that the discovery of his body in his college rooms came straight from the *Inspector Morse* playbook, prompting wild speculation from Morrow's supporters and enemies. Eve watched the head of his college attempting to spoil the media's party, standing outside a dauntingly impressive neo-classical building, a discreet slate sign identifying it as The Master's Lodging, and intoning that the 'world has lost an important voice, but we, at Dudley, have lost a friend.' Superintendent Bashir of the Thames Valley Police being challenged loudly by angry protestors spouting racist nonsense, claiming that the force was failing to investigate the sudden, sinister death of 'an English hero' because he 'isn't black'. Talking heads, and there were many, weighed in about the importance of robust, civilised debate. Most could not bring themselves to agree with Morrow's increasingly vociferous and controversial statements, but they defended to the death his right to express them. The man's family was notable for its silence.

But then, as the March days passed, the interest waned, and the clips dried up. The police decided, disappointingly, that Morrow's death was unexplained but not suspicious. The new chief constable used the moment to celebrate her hard-working officers who simply got on with their jobs, offering a not-so-subtle dig at those who'd watched too much *Morse*. The conventional respect for the family and university's privacy went more heeded than not, and only a handful of formal obituaries celebrated or castigated Morrow. Then, Eve calculated, the end of the Oxford term had come: dispersal and silence. Even the conspiracy theorists went quiet. The funeral – close family only, no flowers, no donations – barely made the news cycle. So different from Morrow's biographical subject. Back in February 1587, Sir Philip Sidney was honoured with the grandest of funerals; indeed, the grandest for any private Englishman until Sir Winston Churchill surpassed him. The ceremony created a national hero and inspired national lamentation. But Eve, who lived and breathed this first Elizabethan era, knew that it was not only the body of an English hero being interred that day. The queen and her courtiers used the pomp and circumstance to bury bad news: the military disaster unfolding in the Low Countries (Sir Philip's deadly skirmish at Zutphen was just one of many missteps); the execution of Elizabeth's cousin, Mary Queen of Scots, earlier in the month. It worked. Sir Philip's death refashioned him as a hero martyr to the Protestant cause and the English public were sold the policy of war with Spain. *Did David Morrow see this part of the historical picture?* Eve wondered.

No matter if he did not. Her job was to help writers over the line. She was good at it even when a writer (Sir Robert came to mind) needed quite a bit of help even to see where the line was. This time, the writer happened to be dead. Which might make things easier. The train swayed and rattled over a succession of points, heralding London. Eve settled back to enjoy the final minutes of the journey.

She had taken an early train so that she could walk to Heritage's headquarters, determined to feed off the energy of the London streets. Just after eleven, and slightly breathless (it was always a bit further than she thought from Paddington to Soho), Eve was being ushered into a room by a receptionist to be greeted by Toby Milton, Morrow's editor.

'We're so pleased you've agreed to take this on – it shouldn't take long to bring you up to speed with everything. Honey, coffee in five minutes, OK?'

Eve took just too long to realise that the receptionist was, in fact, called Honey.

Gesturing to the sofa and its occupant, Toby murmured, 'Josephine, this is Dr Eve Brook – do sit down, Eve, do sit down.'

This was presumably Morrow's agent. For some reason, Eve felt uneasy. Josephine was distinctly cool, Toby distinctly anxious. Why had she been called into the offices and within twenty-four hours of Jon's call? Surely, all of this could have been done over the phone, maybe a Zoom call if they simply wanted to make sure she was presentable, at least from the waist up. Meanwhile, Toby was babbling.

'We're all devastated about David, of course, but the show must go on. I know Josephine feels the same way. We're pretty confident we can get the book out on Super Thursday now we've got you on board, Eve. David was due to submit at the end of this month. Almost there. Almost there. He'd had a few distractions but perhaps you know about that?'

She did, although she thought those distractions occurred some time ago. Morrow had accused the grieving parents of a young Liverpudlian of weaponising their son's death with the aid of the socialists in control of the media. Morrow's dead seventeen-year-old was a criminal, whilst all the evidence suggested he was just a schoolkid in the wrong place at the wrong time. For Morrow, the intervention meant yet more television appearances. For the parents, a deluge of racist hate. For, yes, the boy had been black. Morrow's eventual retraction of certain words ('criminal', in particular), written, he claimed, when he'd had a 'bit too much to drink', received far less airtime than the original attack.

'But the last time I spoke with him, he was back on track. Goodness. I can't actually believe he's gone. Anyway, Jon Peck speaks very highly of your work, Eve—'

Eve had had enough. 'OK. What do I need to know?'

The relief on Toby's face was evident. Eve guessed that he hadn't been sure she would take on the job. And his mention of the Liverpool case had been a mistake, reminding any sane person that Morrow was an unpleasant piece of work. But Eve wasn't satisfied by mere daydreams of travel. Six weeks of work (they wanted the completed manuscript in May), and she could be on her way. Eastern Turkey, the Turistik Doğu Express; now, that would be something. She'd need four days to get to Istanbul, then a boat, a bus and a train to Ankara. If time was a problem, she could always fly home from Ankara.

Heritage's publicity materials, poised (optimistically, it seemed) to be sent out with the proof copies of *An English Hero*, tested her resolve. She read that Morrow's work was a dazzling takedown of 'wokeness', hung on a 'proudly traditional' biography of a great Englishman from the first Elizabethan era. Morrow, or so the publicity went, would sweep aside fashionable discussions of sexuality, imperialism, women, and refocus attention on Sir Philip Sidney's straightforward magnificence. The publicity material made a lot of the fact that no-one today knew the name Sir Philip Sidney, as true heroes were replaced by tokenistic and insignificant historical also-rans. We should be proud of our English heritage and history. No more shame about writing about dead white men. Those dead white men had made England great again.

Eve could see why Morrow, an academic who had never fought in a war, never even done national service, might fetishise a man who was both intellectual and warrior. And she also knew that the story of Sidney's death was an absolute gift to any biographer. Appointed Governor of Flushing, the man had volunteered to fight in the Netherlands. No 'one rule for political leaders and one rule for the soldiers' for this guy. It got better. One Sir William Pelham, newly arrived from England to fight the good Protestant fight, had forgotten to bring his leg armour. Sidney, insisting that he must fight on equal terms with Pelham, took off his own. What a man! There was yet more. Wounded in his heroically unprotected thigh, gasping for water, his servants scurried to get Sir Philip drink. But 'as he was putting the bottle to his mouth', he sees a poor soldier, close to death. He stops drinking. He sends the bottle over to the man, with these words: 'Thy necessity is yet greater than mine.'

Yes, Eve understood Sidney's appeal for Morrow. But she was enraged by his biographical take on the man. Where were the special friends, the men 'who never married', as the euphemism went in the older history books? Where was Sidney as the champion of pan-European humanism? The man had been valued far more highly beyond England's shores than he was at home. Even Catholics admired him. Above all, where were the women? Not just the man's wife, Frances, but his sister, Mary, a profoundly significant literary figure in her own right. And what of his great love, or muse, or – what, in fact, was she? – Penelope Devereux. Eve had done the hard yards, the research.

She had the notes. Boxes of them. Labelled 'Penny D', each one accusing her silently of abandonment. But she'd had to earn her living and worthy academic monographs on minor Elizabethan female courtiers were not the way to pay her fuel bills.

Eve reminded herself that she had not been brought in to provide a more nuanced account of the late-Tudor period, let alone the complexities of Sidney's life. It was time to go. Just a few practical questions to sort out.

Toby's response finally explained his nervousness. 'It's a little complicated, Eve. We both have every right to the manuscript – I'm the publisher, Josephine the literary executor – but because David's death was so sudden, we don't actually have it on our desk. And, out of respect, tact, you know, we thought it might be better for you to have the necessary discussion with the widow. She's quite near you, actually, Cotswolds. You don't mind, do you?'

Eve did mind, but it was too late to back out now.

She used the train journey home to learn about literary executors, trying belatedly to make sense of the silent, watchful presence of Josephine in the meeting. Eve learnt that if you wanted to be sure that your papers were handled with care; that any future income went to the people you wanted to receive it (rather than your publishers); that any income from already-published works was maximised for your heirs; that copyright matters were sorted properly; then you would be wise to appoint a literary executor. The more so if there was any chance that your family, well-meaning or not, might intervene.

Eve paused in her reading. She knew of Cassandra Austen, sister to Jane, Harold Owen, brother to Wilfred. Both had taken great pains to curate – or, put more crudely, destroy – their famous siblings' legacies. All her unease returned. Was Morrow's widow well-meaning or hostile? What had she let herself in for?

II

Fortunately, Eve was easily comforted. It was one of her strengths. Stationery and food would almost always do it. The next morning, when Milos appeared, she was looking with delight on a brand-new notebook on which she'd written, in bold letters, *An English Hero* and onto which she had stuck a postcard showing a rather fine portrait of Sir Philip Sidney. It would do for now. An Ordnance Survey map was spread across the kitchen table. Milos and Eve ignored each other, as usual, and Eve returned to her route planning: the train up to Kingham or perhaps Moreton-in-Marsh, then a four or five-mile bike ride through the country lanes to the Morrows' Cotswold home. She wasn't quite sure what to take with her, feeling frustrated, and not for the first time, at the way in which Toby, watched by Josephine, had sent her on her way.

'The wife is, well, she's quite a difficult woman by all accounts – of course, she's grieving – but we hoped, well, we thought Betty Morrow might find it easier to deal with a woman.' Eve had tried to get a bit more insight into this difficult woman, but to no avail. And why wasn't Josephine – who, by all appearances, was a woman – making the journey herself? Eve thought, unkindly, that she probably rarely moved outside of a one-mile radius of literary London and would lack even the most basic social skills, let alone the empathy, to cope with a prickly, traumatised widow.

The four or five miles proved surprisingly taxing, since Cotswold lanes made a point of descending steeply to every tiny stream, usually with a blind corner at the bottom, and then offering a nasty ascent to regain the height lost. Eve had already passed signs to Much Frogford and Frogford Parva and was reviewing, not for the first time, her stubborn refusal to own a car, and cursing, also not for the first time, a particularly aggressive four-by-four driver who seemed determined to send her into a hedge when at last she spotted the sign she'd been looking for: Cozens Lane.

There were two houses. This was the full visible extent of Little Frogford. The first, closest to the turning, was immaculate, white-painted stone, new thatch complete with sculpted owl, window frames renewed but so tastefully and authentically that they enhanced the overall effect, a tidy front garden poised for spring, with hosts of daffodils clustered around the entrance to the path and a few tulips bravely emerging. One word came into Eve's mind: money. Further on, the second house was not exactly decrepit, but clearly there had not been much money to spend on keeping on top of the maintenance. This was the Morrows' home, 'Sarsens', with its sad patch of unhealthy lawn and a few shrubs at the front. Eve knew enough to realise that judging any garden in the middle of an English March was a mistake, but the car in the lane, a shabby once-silver VW Polo, didn't look as if it had been taken out in years. Eve's hard-won but usually robust professional confidence collided with a visceral sense of sadness. She didn't want to meet the widow. She didn't want to have to deal with grief.

Pulling herself together, she reminded herself that she was here to do a job and knocked at the cobweb-covered door, bike held at her side, her comfort, her steed. The seconds passed, and she felt almost relief. The widow wasn't in. Eve could cycle back to the station, be home in time for lunch, get back to Sir Robert and his triumphant pork products. Just as she was going to turn, the door opened.

A small, pallid woman, grey hair tied back from her face, looked up at Eve then at her bicycle.

'Yes?' she said.

'Hello, I'm Eve Brook – Toby Milton will have told you I was coming…'

The woman seemed confused. 'Toby Milton?'

'Your late husband's publisher? I thought you were expecting me – I am so sorry if that's not the case – and,' (since she was embarked on apologies), 'I am so sorry for your loss.'

Still silence. Eve wondered if the woman had some form of dementia or was simply suffering from shock. Either way, this wasn't going to be easy. She decided to take charge.

'Mrs Morrow, is there somewhere I can put my bike? Then perhaps I can come in and we can have a cup of tea?'

The woman abruptly began to focus. 'Yes, yes. Behind that hedge. You don't need to lock it; no-one comes down this lane.'

Eve discreetly disobeyed her host, since bitter experience had shown that bikes could be nicked from the most unlikely of places by the most ingenious of thieves, and then she was across the threshold, following Mrs Morrow into a kitchen which felt a little more encouraging. An Aga threw out some welcome warmth, and there were interesting prints on the walls: bold lines of colour that hinted at landscapes. Something warned her to approach this conversation slowly, so she asked about them.

'They are striking, aren't they? My son's husband did them.'

When she said 'husband' there was a hint of supplication

to the word, as if asking Eve not to judge, but also undeniable pride – both in the art and the relationship.

'David didn't like them; in fact, he was rather unkind about Raphael, but the kitchen is *my* territory and so here they are. He can't complain, really, can he? Every other room is his.' Did Mrs Morrow not know her husband was dead? Eve was again chilled, despite the warmth in the room.

After ten minutes of desultory conversation, Eve went the direct route. 'Mrs Morrow, I have been asked by your late husband's publisher and his agent – who, as you are aware, I am sure, is also his literary executor – to prepare his last book for publication. I understand Professor Morrow was due to submit the finished manuscript this month and so, despite his tragic death, they believe that the work should reach its public. I won't change a word, just tidy it up so that the publishers can send it out into the world.'

'Why not just leave it?'

The widow's question was a good one. The publishers could recoup the first instalment of the advance from Morrow's widow and avoid paying out more on delivery of manuscript and publication. Morrow's agent would lose out, but only on her fifteen per cent commission on advances and sales. So, why *were* Heritage so keen to make sure the book came out? Eve assumed the simple answer, as it so often was, was money. David Morrow dead would (probably) make them both more money than David Morrow alive. That was what they were gambling on.

Eve felt unable to say that but decided to risk another answer. 'Mrs Morrow, it may be in your interests for this book to be published. Your financial interests.'

Although the conversation so far had been utterly banal, Eve had begun to understand that the woman was neither demented nor, it had to be said, particularly grief-stricken. She just seemed remote, detached, uninterested. Whether this was a result of her husband's death or a more long-standing approach to life was another question. Eve was beginning to suspect the latter. The look Mrs Morrow gave Eve was clear-sighted and cold as glass.

'Perhaps they didn't tell you. My husband's literary estate has been, I think the phrase is, diverted away from me. I do have this house,' she said, looking around her, 'although currently I do not have the means to maintain it.'

Eve was furious, with Toby and Josephine primarily for sending her out here, with herself for not asking more questions, and with David Morrow for his testamentary decisions. It should, legally, have been almost impossible for him to disinherit his wife, but he'd come pretty damn close with this 'diversion'.

She was also at a loss. Who would receive the hundred thousand? And, more relevant, who, in fact, had possession of the finished manuscript? Because she was beginning to realise that it was unlikely to be Mrs Morrow.

She was on the point of asking these questions when a male voice called out, 'Elizabeth? You in there?'

Whoever it was stopped short at the door, clearly astonished to see Eve. He was probably around Mrs Morrow's age, mid-sixties, maybe older, although with the energy of someone much younger. Complementing his attractively greying hair, his skin had the healthy glow that only a winter activity holiday could bestow on an Anglo-Saxon, probably skiing or a spot of sailing in the West Indies.

The man pulled himself together quickly, smiled warmly, and thrust out a hand: 'Charles Mallam, live next door.' He oozed the confidence and wealth and, yes, complacency of someone with a beautiful house. 'What brings you here?'

It was charming, but Eve knew she was being vetted. Before she could reply, Mrs Morrow (Betty? Elizabeth?) answered for her.

'Dr Eve Brook,' (so she *had* looked at the business card Eve had placed on the table between them on her arrival), 'is here to take David's manuscript. She is going to prepare it for publication. Toby Milton, the publisher, sent her. I was just on the point of telling her that it really is nothing to do with me, given the terms of David's will.'

'Ah, I see.' It seemed he did see.

Mrs Morrow's neighbour pulled a chair out and joined them at the table. He placed his Range Rover fob, attached to a large RAC Club keyring, in front of him. His need to have his totems within sight and touch was the only indication that he was at all uncomfortable.

Eve experienced the full force of Charles Mallam's correction, feeling a little like a schoolgirl: 'Dr Brook, I think your London people have sent you on a wild goose chase. Elizabeth is not the person you need to see.'

She was being dismissed but risked one more question, 'Presumably, you know who *does* have the manuscript, if it is not in this house, Mrs Morrow?'

Elizabeth looked towards Charles Mallam. He duly answered for her. 'After the funeral, Elizabeth was in no state to deal with David's literary estate – and, to be honest, I don't blame her for putting that all to one side since her husband had taken active steps to exclude her from his professional life. All we know...' Mallam seemed to regret that 'we', making Eve wonder about just how close this man was to the widow Morrow and just why he had a house key and could walk in at any time. He paused, looked at the woman he called Elizabeth, but the rest of the world knew as Betty, hinting she should take up the story.

'It was all too much for me. I lost track of who was coming and going, who was taking what and where. I mean, it's not as if I was consulted when David was alive.'

It was Elizabeth's turn to pause and look round her kitchen. Her eye lighted on a small picture in a corner of the room. Eve's eyes were drawn there, to a small sketch of what might be a human head, all dark lines and charcoal smudges with one strange jag of deep yellow cutting across it.

'I think you'd better go back to your London people.'

Eve returned her attention to this odd couple, whilst weighing up the chances of looking at the portrait more closely, different as it was to the cosier, more colourful, prints in the room. She was getting desperate and sprayed her questions at them.

'How did Professor Morrow write? Am I looking for his computer? Or notebooks? You must know that, and it would be a great help to me to know.'

Again, the exchange of looks.

'I used to help David with his books, in the early days of our marriage. We all did it then – the wives, I mean. Typed up notes, did the background research, edited, copy-edited, indexing – that kind of thing. I'd pretty much know what was on every page. I was one of the few people who could read his handwriting.' There was no wistfulness or pride in the statement, but nor was there bitterness. 'But this book, no. He had probably found somebody else to help him.'

Charles Mallam showed Eve to the door (he really was at home here), then walked with her round the side of the house to stand over her as she retrieved her bike. Eve's curiosity got the better of her. Her question ('how long have you lived in Cozens Lane, Mr Mallam?') was a polite version of what was truly running through her head: how long had this man had free run of David Morrow's widow's house?

His response was bland and uninformative. 'Quite a while, Dr Brook, quite a while. It's a lovely spot. How far have you got to go now?'

She reassured him that she had only a few miles to Kingham station and plenty of time to cover them. Mallam wished her '*bonne route*' and half turned back towards Elizabeth Morrow's door before deciding to follow her wheels as she headed past his immaculate cottage. She looked back and he was nowhere to be seen.

Eve's glimpse of Morrow's private life had merely confirmed her dislike of him. She knew about the public man, transformed into a celebrity by his stay in the USA at the time of Donald Trump's ascendance. He'd been approaching sixty, resting on his (faded) academic laurels whilst enjoying all the pleasures and perks of a post at Oxford, when an American university with more money than sense had offered him a year's fellowship. Whilst there, enjoying a different set of pleasures and perks, Morrow had become, as he put it, 'disgusted with the out-of-touch London elite, the chattering classes living in their echo-chamber.' No matter that he existed in two extremely rarified bubbles: an Oxford college and a Cotswold hamlet. No matter that he himself was solidly upper middle class, a product of a northern grammar. The fact that he had been born and raised in Yorkshire proved that he must be gritty and working class.

Returning to the UK, he'd embraced his new identity. Grumpy, anti-woke before woke was invented, a besieged white man in a world out to get him. The camera loved him, and his visibility grew with each passing month. He had retained the hair (tousled) and the waistline (slender) of his younger self. With make-up to conceal the effects of his more mature self's lifestyle choices (bourbon and lots of it), he looked good. And he didn't just look good. He was able to destroy people in argument, live and in the studio. After all, he'd had years of practice in the privacy of an Oxbridge book-lined study. *And perhaps at home*, thought Eve.

As Eve let herself back into her terrace in Oxford, Milos seemed quite pleased with himself, although 'fifteen minutes' was all he said. She only needed ten to shower and change. He had surpassed himself: ordinary leeks transformed by something called tarator with a drizzle of burnt butter and molasses. Milos poured her a surprisingly small glass of wine.

'It's a manzanillo from a unique micro-climate.'

None the wiser, Eve sipped, bit into her charred leeks, and was completely happy. Milos took cooking very seriously. Which was fortunate, because Eve took eating very seriously.

She knew better than to speak with Milos about her day. He simply wasn't interested and though, when under pressure, he could fake a form of social competence, the cracks showed within minutes. To Eve, Milos was a perfect lodger: he was a superb cook, cleaned up after himself and his personal boundaries were very, very clear. She was a private, solitary person herself and apart from the evenings when Milos had the time and energy to cook meals like this, they co-existed in a space that happened to be her house, rather than having any meaningful human interaction. Which was just how she liked it. Eve headed to her room as soon as she had eaten her final mouthful. Milos would never ask her to tidy up because she would never do it to the standard he required. Which was also just how Eve liked it.

Only when she lay on her bed did she realise just how disconcerted, disturbed even, she had been by the day's encounters. She was still puzzled as to why Toby and Josephine had sent her to Elizabeth Morrow. They must have known that, at best, they were sending her to meet a woman who had very, very little to do with her husband's life as an author and, at worst, a woman who had been treated shabbily by that author. *Was* there something they believed that she could find out, as a relative stranger? Or were they simply plain wrong, assuming that *An English Hero* would be at the house, and it would be a straightforward, a more pleasant, way to do business for Eve to collect it over a cup of tea? Eve needed some answers.

Morning came, and with it an apology from Toby. He had heard rumours about the state of the marriage – 'but one never knows, does one?' He just didn't understand the legal side of things; 'you can't just disinherit your spouse, can you?' he asked, somewhat querulously. Eve, who had done a quick search that morning on the very subject, explained that you could, though you had to have a good reason and even then, said spouse could challenge the will. But Toby was missing the point.

'That's not exactly what's happened here. Elizabeth Morrow,' (strange: she had not warmed to the woman, but she felt she was owed the respect of using her given name), 'has, as far as I know, inherited the house – although she said she didn't have the money to keep it because, for fuck's sake, Morrow's literary earnings have been directed to someone else. She says she doesn't know anything about the book manuscript. Anyone could have taken it, she said, and right now, Toby, I don't even know what "it" looks like. A laptop? Notebooks? A pile of A4 typed sheets? A memory stick?' Eve's anger was speaking now, blinding her to the fact that she'd only just met Morrow's publisher. 'Come on, Toby! What did you hope to get from sending me down to Little Frogford?'

Even before Toby answered, Eve knew what he would say.

'To be honest, I wondered if Betty was being completely straight with us. I'll come clean. We knew that the marriage was...' he paused, 'not a happy one. And that Betty might, for her own reasons, wish to put a spanner in the works of what would have been David's capstone achievement. We hoped that, seeing a friendly face, she might mellow and pass on the manuscript.'

And so this was how the whole 'against the family's wishes' thing played out, was it? But Toby had not met Elizabeth Morrow. There was a curious and chilling detachment in her eyes. Eve believed that she had closed down very thoroughly and very successfully and was way past any revenge on her husband for using her as unpaid labour decades earlier. Then again, Eve did not know precisely why the marriage had not been 'happy'. Mrs Morrow may have had powerful motives for thwarting her husband in death in ways she could not in life. Powerful motives to seek comfort, and more, with her kindly neighbour. But the overall impression was of a woman who just didn't care anymore and didn't have to pretend to care anymore. Eve believed her when she said she didn't know where the manuscript was. She recounted Elizabeth's precise words to Toby, consulting her notebook: 'It really is nothing to do with me, given the terms of David's will.'

'I think Josephine owes us both some answers, don't you, Toby?'

Eve emailed Jon while waiting for Toby to call her back. He texted her immediately, a choice set of expletives. She could imagine him typing them, one-fingered, into his tiny handset, each word spelt out in full. Eve was strangely comforted by his comprehensive outrage. If she – and it was looking like Toby Milton – had been duped, then so had he.

When Toby called back, he was all charm and business. 'Eve, first of all, *thank you* for going to Little Frogford. We had no idea it would be a wasted journey, and Josephine is keen to make sure you are *fully* compensated for your time. Do get Jon to invoice us appropriately.'

Eve was taken aback. There was no longer any pretence as to who was in charge.

'Josephine is still *really* keen to have you on board – and wants to have a one-to-one, completely frank exchange as to how we can all achieve our goals.'

Eve doubted whether Josephine knew what complete frankness even looked like and ran a quick calculation. Dealing with such blatantly manipulative, insincere people was the price she would pay if it meant not worrying about just how much her buildings insurance would be this year, whether she could even *get* insurance this year (floods and more floods), and travelling on the Turistik Doğu Express.

And now she was sitting in the dark, sipping a rather superb cocktail, trying not to slide off a deeply uncomfortable bar stool. Josephine was the picture of poise. Pilates, undoubtedly, or years of ballet training.

'Eve, first of all, I'm sorry. Complete disclosure. I should have been open with you from the start but, well, you know how it is.'

Eve didn't, but she was too busy calculating whether it would be appropriate to attempt to retrieve the olive from the bottom of her glass to bother with an answer. Why didn't places like this provide snacks? If this was Italy, there'd be a table laden with profoundly unhealthy nibbles. All for the price of an Aperol Spritz. Eve forced a smile and waited to hear what line Josephine would spin to bring her back into the project.

'As you know, I am David's agent *and* his literary executor.'

Eve struggled to remember what she'd read about literary executors. This was one strong Martini.

'It is therefore my duty to ensure this book sees the light of day. I remember when I secured the contract for David how much it meant to him. He said, "It's not about the money, it's about striking a small blow for intellectual freedom." He had no idea that he would die so soon, so suddenly, but there's a reason he appointed me. He knew his family would do everything in their power to thwart him. My God, they made his life a misery – that dreary wife was a millstone around his neck; his son, well, his son was full of the kind of politically correct nonsense David detested. Future generations will, I feel sure, laugh at all the fuss around taking the knee, veganism, trans rights,' (Eve could hear the quote marks), 'as if any of that will make a difference to the real problems we face, that ordinary people care about.'

Eve recognised someone parroting, and not very convincingly, the pieties of the tabloids and kept quiet.

'He relied on me, he expected me, to act for him. And I will.'

'So, if you are his agent and his literary executor, how come you don't know where the manuscript is? Surely Professor Morrow was in regular communication with you?'

'Well, that is precisely the problem. I secured the deal for *An English Hero* shortly after David's return from his time in the States. But then the pandemic made things tricky – David wasn't one for Zoom – and even in the last year or so, when life was getting easier, I had only heard from him a couple of times, and in both cases about other matters.' Josephine seemed distinctly happy to recall Morrow's racist outburst and its aftermath. She almost smiled. 'He was a professional. He didn't need hand-holding. Perhaps I was naïve,' (Josephine seemed less pleased about this), 'but I assumed he would deliver the manuscript to Toby Milton at the end of this month and that would be that.'

'Let me get this right. You have had no communication with David Morrow about the manuscript since...' Eve left this hanging.

Josephine stirred her cocktail. 'I am trying to tell you. I wouldn't have *expected* to have discussed work in progress with him.'

'So you hoped that, faced with a neutral stranger, Mrs Morrow would hand it over. But she doesn't know where it is, and she doesn't care. Where do I come in?'

'We were hoping—'

Eve interrupted. She'd had enough. 'Who is *we*? Who would I be working for? Toby Milton, as Morrow's publisher? Or you, as his literary executor?'

'I suppose, technically, it would be me.'

'OK, technically, what would like me to do?'

'Find the book.'

Eve decided to buy time by going for the olive. Either that or she would faint from the combination of an empty stomach and strong alcohol. God, she was a lightweight these days.

'I will think about it and get back to you with my daily rate for this kind of work.'

Eve was rather pleased with herself, although she suspected that Josephine saw straight through her. She'd never done anything like this before in her life.

III

By Monday morning, Eve had her contract. She had thought of an outrageous fee then doubled it. Josephine Levine didn't even blink. Eve celebrated, alone, at her kitchen table, taking a moment to appreciate the light on the trees across the meadow while she sipped a cup of freshly made coffee. It was another reason she appreciated Milos. After getting himself breakfast, he left the house at the same time (five minutes past eight) and in the same way (quietly) every weekday.

Eve silenced the small voice that asked, *why would the agent be willing to pay this much?* and turned her mind to the most important consideration. Did she need a new notebook? *Reason not the need*, she answered herself, but then had a better idea. She went to her desk, rifled through her stash of postcards, picked out a Nicholas Hilliard miniature of a young woman, all lace ruff, golden curls and flowers in her hair. She fixed it to the back of her notebook. The case was flipped. She wrote on her new front cover *Looking for Mary*, a private acknowledgement of her very different take on the Sidney family and their importance to English history. It was time to get to work.

There were two people Eve needed to see. One was a short cycle ride away across the city, sitting in the Master's Lodging of Dudley College. First, then, the Master's Lodging and then, if that proved a dead end, she would try to reach Morrow's son, Michael, who – she consulted her notes – lived somewhere near York, presumably with his artist husband.

Eve was surprised to learn the Master was willing to meet that very day. Perhaps it was the effect of the Easter vacation. Life was quiet in the quads of Oxford. Like most of the older Oxford colleges, 'Dud's' did not bother to identify itself. One either knew one's way around or one didn't. Eve was struck, yet again, at how much of the university's beauty was hidden away. It had taken her years to find one college's deer park, another's secret graveyard, yet another's exquisite walled garden. Now, she walked past groups of tourists milling around the medieval Leicester Quad and ducked into a dark passageway, ignoring a series of private signs. She emerged, as the porter said she would, into a vast neo-classical courtyard which Eve had last seen in her quick and dirty search for online information about David Morrow.

Eve was greeted on the doorstep of the Lodging by the Master's secretary and ushered inside to a warm, comforting room, lined with the expected books, although here they did not feel like mere window-dressing. Rachita Solanki, descendent of northern India's ruling class, a woman whose given name meant creative genius, and whose titles, Dame Professor and now Master of Dudley College, put her firmly in the ranks of the British establishment, needed no help from props. Papers and journals were piled haphazardly, a gown was draped over the back of one chair in which a cat lay serenely claiming its place.

'Come in, come in – it is chilly out there, isn't it?'

Eve felt at ease in a way she rarely felt at the university and delighted at the sight of a tray piled with everything required for afternoon tea, including a substantial fruit cake.

'We've got tea, but I can ask Michelle for coffee if that's what you'd prefer – or a fruit tea?'

'No, no – proper tea suits me well, and that cake looks delicious.'

Having insisted that Eve take the place of the cat ('oh, she'll reclaim it as soon as you've gone') and poured her a cup of tea ('how do you take it?'), the Master sat back and appeared to take a deep breath. Only at that point did Eve realise that Dame Professor Rachita Solanki was buying time. More than that, she didn't know where to start. She rearranged, not for the first time, the deep-crimson rough-silk scarf over her shoulders.

Eve was confused. The conversation was, she thought, merely a formality. It would do no harm to remind the Master of that fact.

'As I think you are aware, I am here acting for David Morrow's literary executor. We know, as you also probably know, since you worked with him, that he was due to submit the manuscript of *An English Hero*,' (the two women exchanged glances that spoke volumes – Eve needed to learn to keep the ironic quote marks out of her own tone when talking about the book), 'this month. His literary executor is, of course, keen that it be published and has asked me to finalise the manuscript. Unfortunately, Dr Morrow didn't share his work in progress with either his agent or his publisher, and his widow has no knowledge of the book – or even what form it took.' Eve was watching Solanki carefully by now. How much of this was news to her? Was that a grimace when Elizabeth Morrow was mentioned? 'Which is why I am here. I have the authority of the literary executor to make a search for the manuscript and, if it was not kept at his home, it makes sense that it would be here, at his college. I have been advised...' Had she? Josephine had been slightly vague about the legal niceties. '...That this is a perfectly legitimate search, but I thought, out of courtesy, I would speak with you first.'

Rachita Solanki appeared to be weighing up what to say next. More time passed, time in which the Master took a gleaming silver pin from her head, allowing her long, grey-black hair to run free for a moment, before, in a deft movement, securing it in place once more. Even though Eve could see the woman's tension, she was astonished at her first words.

'Eve – I loathed David Morrow. I despised both the man and his work, and I thought it was a travesty, a mockery, of everything that we do that he got a "six-figure" advance for what was going to be a quite terrible book. No, I was not looking forward to the publication of *An English Hero*. As far as I knew, and he rather delighted in telling me all about it, Morrow was peddling a tired, jingoistic, not to mention scholarly inept, view of English history, framed by the kind of shoddy, shock-jock, clickbait crap that made his name in the States.'

Eve was about to comment when the Master continued, with, if anything, even more bitterness.

'There was, however, more to my animosity than mere academic contempt. You may know that, although I was appointed well over a year ago, I only became Master in Michaelmas.'

Eve did know. The same search engine that had yielded information about the significance of Solanki's names and roles had also reminded Eve that she had delayed her arrival at Dudley until she had signed off on a controversial, ostensibly government-led, investigation into abuse in the House of Commons. Which meant that she began her job on the back end of Morrow's dalliance with inflammatory racism, and in the midst of the alleged de-platforming that had so delighted Josephine. Solanki was a highly intelligent woman and was in no doubt of the connecting line between Morrow's populist racist dog-whistles and his allegedly scholarly historical work. For her, his English history was a white English history, a natural outcome of his casual, cruel, racist tweets.

'This coming term will be only my third here at Dud's. I have been very careful, conscious that I was the first woman to lead this college, and the first person of colour. But not careful enough. Morrow, from the first meeting of Governing Body, sought to make my life difficult.'

Morrow. Eve was reminded of something that his widow had said, in the gentle voice of a kindly teacher. 'He was never a professor, you know. At least, not here. In America he may have been, but everyone is, over there, aren't they?' But Solanki did not even use his correct, if lowlier, title: Doctor.

'Over Michaelmas, he gathered his supporters – you know how it works, a barely hidden world of man-to-man conversations. "Probably a lesbian. But you can't say that anymore... Tokenism – doesn't actually help the Blacks, does it?"' Solanki's impression of Morrow was uncanny. She was a good mimic. 'I think it was third week of Hilary when he lit the touchpaper. A vote of no-confidence tabled at GB. I remember sitting in the Cavendish-Bentinck Chamber and thinking, *fuck!* To think I'd just finished the public inquiry – only the seventh woman in thirty years; there were more inquiries led by people called Anthony and William – and now to be blindsided by a bunch of misogynist racist dinosaurs. I'm sitting here now, so clearly their coup failed. But only just.'

Eve was conscious that Solanki had moved into Oxford-speak, not bothering to gloss the names of terms (Michaelmas and Hilary) or GB, Governing Body, the college's ruling committee. Eve was being tacitly welcomed as an insider.

'Ostensibly, their grievance was directed at my discussions with the Nangadef Foundation. You'll know they are doing a lot of work with various organisations, including a number of Cambridge colleges, examining how institutions have contributed to, benefited from, the Atlantic slave trade. There is definitely a form of restoration, of acknowledgement, perhaps even reparation, to take place here in Oxford, at Dudley. What I believe Morrow got hold of – and I still don't know how, since I was not broadcasting this widely – is that the foundation were interested in making a very, very substantial donation to the college. In return, our main quad would be named for Kofoworola Ademola, and we would commit to actively promoting applications from BAME pupils. It appears that his outrage at these discussions – which, I might add, were at the earliest stage – drove the no-confidence vote.'

Rachita paused. She was a charismatic, eloquent speaker, wrapped up in her story. It was almost as if she had forgotten Eve was there.

'But, as I said, I am still here. Morrow is not. I am not going to pretend grief. And, before you think I am going to try to stop you finding that bloody manuscript, I am not. Contrary to the popular media, and their hysteria about no-platforming, I welcome plurality, debate, conflict, even, in our intellectual life.'

There was another pause. Rachita was collecting her thoughts, so Eve improved the moment by slipping another slice of deliciously moist fruit cake onto her plate, whilst offering the Master a top-up.

'Yes, thank you,' she replied distractedly, only belatedly realising that her mug was hardly touched. 'Eve, I know your work.'

Eve smiled. Her 'work' had fizzled out long before Solanki arrived in Dudley.

'And you know Oxford. I think, I hope, I can trust you.'

Eve did know Oxford. Only too well. She put on her most

sympathetic face and wondered why she was being buttered up. She felt quite sure Solanki did *not* know her work.

'The actual circumstances of David Morrow's death were… awkward. If the media got hold of them, well, it would not just be my job on the line, but the college's reputation. If the Nangadef Foundation became aware, the opportunities they are offering would disappear. It's a funny business being head of a college because we are not in any meaningful way heads. First among equals. That's what they call it. I had no real authority over Morrow. He could do what he liked, and he could do it in his college rooms.'

Eve felt slightly sick. What had happened on the first night of March? St David's Day, she realised with a shudder.

'Before I continue, can I ask you to treat what I tell you in strictest confidence?'

'I can't make any promises until I hear what you have to say. But I will do my best.'

'The death certificate for David Morrow, signed by our own college doctor – a close personal friend of his – says he died of a heart attack. It uses fancier language, but that's what's there. What it doesn't say is that he suffered the heart attack while attempting to fuck his very young research assistant. I know this, because she came to me a couple of days later and told me what had happened. Morrow was forcing himself upon her when he seemed to have a seizure of some kind. The young woman took her chance to get away, leaving him struggling to breathe and in a cold sweat. She did help him to his bed (which is more than I might have done in the situation), which is where he was found in the morning. Dead. This young woman, unaware of the seriousness of the situation but traumatised enough by Morrow's sexual demands, had wisely headed back to her family that same day. When the news of his death reached her, she came to see me. I am not entirely sure why.'

It was a miserable story. The girl's vulnerability. The loneliness of Morrow's death. (Why didn't he call someone?) But it had nothing to do with the manuscript. Which Eve pointed out.

'Ah, but I think it might have something to do with it. The young woman came as his guest to the Formal Hall that night and, I have to say, held her own. She was, she said, Morrow's research assistant and she seemed to know her stuff. I know, I know – that may have been a euphemism for a far less salubrious connection, but if she was working with him, for him, she might be your best bet to find your *English Hero*. All I would ask is that you keep this focused on the manuscript. The girl has been through enough, and, as I said, one word of scandal would be red meat for the red-tops.'

Eve sat for a moment. Something in the story didn't quite add up, but she couldn't quite work out what it was. She was sure, however, that her task had just become even more unpleasant. The Master seemed exhausted. Her cat, in a rare moment of feline compassion, leapt onto her lap and as Eve was dismissed, all Rachita's attention was now focused on stroking the rich, caramel fur.

IV

If Eve had secretly hoped that there would indeed be a big folder duly labelled 'My New Book' on Morrow's desk, she was to be disappointed. Watched over by Michelle, she looked around the spacious but strangely impersonal room, with its books on their shelves as in the Master's Lodgings but little of its warmth, and definitely no cat. What was strange was that there was no evidence at all of *An English Hero*. No scattered reference works to be consulted as one checked through one's final draft. No marked-up printouts of chapters. No lists of things to do in this final straight before pressing send and hoping that your editor liked it. Eve had asked Michelle if anyone had come to clear out the room and been told that, apart from the scouts tidying away some personal items, nothing had been touched. In itself, this felt strange and sad. The room was as it was a few weeks ago, on the night of David Morrow's death. Only later did Eve wonder at Michelle's failure to mention the police, who must surely have conducted a search. Or perhaps Rachita Solanki's powers extended to keeping even the police at bay.

Eve couldn't even be sure that Morrow used the room to work in. She realised she had voiced the thought out loud because Michelle answered her.

'You might be right. My sense is that he saw students here when he did some teaching, which wasn't that often really these days. He slept in there, of course, if he'd been to one of the dinners.' Michelle gestured towards a rather bleak alcove dominated by an austere stone fireplace, the only furniture a single bed, small wooden table, metal desk lamp. 'During the day, he was more often in the SCR – there's a wonderful coffee machine in there; it was one of the best things that the Master did when she arrived, improved the college coffee! And not just in the SCR.' Michelle, like her boss, assumed that Eve spoke the language of Oxford: the Senior Common Room, scouts not cleaners.

It was another dead end, which meant speaking with the young woman who had been, it seemed, the last person to see David Morrow alive. The phrase made Eve feel as if she had wandered into a murder mystery, except she was no Inspector Morse or even Harriet Vane. More Inspector Clouseau. She smiled ruefully to herself. *Keep it simple, Eve.* Her job was to find the manuscript, prepare it for press, and then buy her ticket for the Turistik Doğu Express.

Dame Professor Rachita Solanki messaged her the next day to say that the young woman they had been discussing was willing to speak with Eve but would prefer it to be in person and on her home territory. Could she pass on Eve's phone number and the woman would contact her to arrange the meeting? Of course.

The text arrived soon after; an unknown number. Eve was suddenly conscious that she didn't even know the name of the woman she was going to see. It was a calendar meeting invitation, the next day, 2.30pm, with a Google Maps link to the venue, somewhere in Sheffield. Eve checked in with Josephine Levine, not going into details but making clear that she was following up a strong lead and reminding the agent as casually as she could that she had agreed to pay all expenses as well as a daily rate. Morrow's agent seemed distracted, keen to get off the phone as soon as she could, which meant that Eve didn't have the chance to spell out just how expensive it was to travel by train to Yorkshire without booking months in advance. No matter: Eve was on her way to a coffee shop in Hillsborough on a ridiculously priced return ticket with almost no idea as to what to expect from her meeting but determined to enjoy the expedition.

She'd taken the precaution of getting into Sheffield a good hour before her meeting and she was glad she had. Eve didn't know the city at all, and quickly discovered it had hills, steep hills. It also had some very unfriendly traffic junctions, or perhaps Google Maps was simply not telling her the local shortcuts. The intertwined warren of paths and small streets (later she would learn they were gennels) meant that if you knew your way around, great. If not, it could all get very confusing. There was not much time to look around her, but Eve was as interested in and excited by this new city as she would be, and had been, on arriving in Prague or Salamanca. Hillsborough, her destination, had been only a name until today. She'd been in her last year at primary school when the tragedy had happened, one of the grim markers in her loss of childhood innocence. Death could and did come suddenly. And adults didn't always tell the truth.

Escaping the unprepossessing centre, Eve warmed to the city. The sheer diversity of building styles within a small area, even within one street of terraced houses, was intriguing. There was a sense of multiple neighbourhoods, different Sheffields. Along with the betting shops, discount stores, and pubs that had seen better days were the businesses directed at the local students or expats from London: Zero Waste and Bargain Booze, vintage clothing and vinyl stores, craft beer and sourdough pop-ups, and, yes, boutique coffee shops.

Eve arrived with a minute to spare and grabbed a table with a view of the door. On the other side of the café, two white men in their thirties sat across from each other, one balancing a baby on the table, the other holding his cycle helmet. Eve pondered the rise of the new man: hands-on fathers, cyclists, responsible. Both wore check shirts, both were carrying a bit too much weight around their middles, one wore glasses that were a decade out of date. These were men who did not care about what they looked like, happy to talk about how tight the harness should be, how the baby liked to be carried. Eve eavesdropped shamelessly, wondering at how the world had changed. And how the hell anyone managed to cycle in this precipitous city. And why weren't the men at work on a Wednesday? Behind the counter, another, younger, white man, with dreadlocks, examined his phone with an intensity that suggested either porn or football. Some things did not change.

After ten minutes, Eve began to get restless. Had she come all this way for nothing? Just as she reached for her phone to fire off a passive aggressive *I'm here* complete with smiling emoji, the door of the café opened and a very young woman, barely out of her teens, Eve guessed, walked in, scanning the room. Could it be? Eve regretted not agreeing on some form of identification, but since, apart from the check-shirted Professional Dads, she was the only other person over twenty in the café, she suspected none was needed.

'Hiya. Eve?' The woman was striking. She had very pale, slightly freckled, skin contrasting with the crimson of her lips, shaped with artistic precision. She took off her beret, revealing a jet-black buzzcut from which a shock of red hair rose, clashing appallingly, gloriously, with the lipstick. *Such confidence*, Eve thought, but then quickly revised her opinion. The girl, she really was a girl, having sat down opposite could barely make eye contact with her.

36

What did she really know about this young woman? She seemed an unlikely candidate for a research assistant, but Eve chided herself for judging on appearance. Coffee would help. She forced the guy with the phone to pause whatever he was looking at and make them a couple of cups of coffee. A macchiato for Eve. Latte for…

Who was she? Eve said as brightly as she could, 'I don't even know your name!'

'Phoebe.'

'Great. Well, thanks, Phoebe, for speaking with me.' Eve heard the patronising tone in her own voice. She was not dealing with a toddler, for God's sake. She changed gear, now adult to adult, explaining succinctly what her job was, and why the Master of Dudley College had suggested this meeting. As Professor Morrow's research assistant, Phoebe might know where his almost-completed book could be found.

The words 'research assistant' appeared to rouse Phoebe from contemplation of her sickly looking latte.

'Is that what the Master said?' Hearing the title said with a northern accent gave Eve, a Londoner by birth, a jolt. The word seemed more oppressive, more coercive, conjuring up steel mills and plantations, men whose bidding was done. By young women like Phoebe.

'I wasn't his "research assistant". I was his sugar baby.'

Phoebe looked Eve in the eyes, daring her to judge. Judgement was unlikely, since Eve had absolutely no idea what a sugar baby was, though, with a sinking heart, she was beginning to guess.

Like many liberal-minded women of her age and class, Eve talked the talk of sex work as empowerment, but the industry nevertheless made her uneasy. That uneasiness grew into full-blown horror when, later that day, she explored a hinterland of websites on which (allegedly carefully vetted) men offered to fund the 'passion project' of their 'girls'. Men and girls. The former had to prove their financial worth. The latter had to show their faces. And sometimes, often, more. Eve didn't know whether to be more dismayed at the gendered abuse of power or the loneliness to be glimpsed. So many of the men claimed that they were seeking a soulmate. That was what drove them to pay out thousands of pounds for GFE. Girlfriend Experience. That experience encompassed a certain number of texts per week, a phone call, photos, a good morning and a good night. Youth was at a premium.

At first sight, it looked almost innocent. The menus included 'non-sexual' or 'basic vanilla' agreements. With these, the women might have to support a man's mental health in various ways, but only the occasional sext would be required. But this was a mere sideshow to the real business. Eve tried to laugh at some of the more ridiculous offerings (cock worship?) but couldn't. Richer men, the ones with genuine power, were looking for sex with a veneer of romance (the GFE), the GF in question readily available when required. And if the GF didn't deliver, things could and did get nasty. Even a quick search found plenty of cautionary tales from women abused in various ways by coercive clients.

But Phoebe's own account of her deal with Morrow revealed a transaction that was not quite so reductive.

'It's not what you think it is,' she had said.

Over their surprisingly bad coffees, Phoebe explained that Morrow paid her an allowance to support her own writing, her poetry. He was like one of those angels. As the young woman continued, occasionally spiking up her already almost vertical hair, Eve recognised that Phoebe had, in fact, been, in her own way, her patron's research assistant. She had listened to Morrow. He had talked to her about the book he was writing, how it reflected the real world. Phoebe was scornful, although whether the scorn was borrowed from Morrow, Eve could not know, of what she called progressives who go on one demonstration and think they're changing the world. She had enough money to rent a room in a shared house in East Oxford: 'Posh twats but nice enough when they weren't coked up.' She'd done, 'Two sets, not slams,' she reassured Eve, who wasn't quite sure about the difference but heard the pride. 'It were jammy.' For a moment, Phoebe was animated, remembering a back room in a pub off the Cowley Road, being up on stage, owning her words.

The moment passed. As if compelled to speak, Phoebe told Eve about the first of March, that evening in college. She confirmed that things had 'gone wrong'. She wouldn't go into details, but Eve could guess. By morning, Phoebe had decided that the deal with Morrow was over (*yeah*, thought Eve, *he was after only one thing*) and she headed back to Sheffield. What struck Eve was that Phoebe called the man DM. Who else did? And she sensed that the young woman's sadness and anger was directed at the loss of the relationship rather than, what? A sexual assault?

'I thought that might be why you were here. Hashtag metoo and all that shit. I mean, if he'd been a problem for other women, and they had come forwards, then maybe I'd have my say even though it changes nowt. No-one's going to believe me when I say it were about my poetry.'

Eve kept quiet. There'd be time later to sift through Phoebe's words.

'I didn't want to have sex with him. He was my way out of here,' gesturing to Sheffield, outside the doors of the café, 'I had my own room.'

Eve wondered, with some humility, where and how Phoebe lived now. This was the second time she'd mentioned having her own room. On the basis of less than an hour, Eve was rather liking Sheffield, but there was something driving Phoebe away from her own city.

'DM could be quite funny. At least, he weren't always miserable. It was, like, everybody stressing out all of the time about climate change and pronouns and he would be, like, chill out. None of this is new.'

Yes, Eve thought, *none of this is new. Men with power had been imposing themselves, their bodies and their ideas, upon women with less power for millennia.* For all the confessional, Eve felt Phoebe was holding something back. She didn't want to push too hard; the girl – no, the young woman – had been through enough.

'I know you said that you were not a research assistant to David Morrow,' (she couldn't bring herself to call him DM), 'but hearing you talk about your…' (what was the right word – relationship? No) '…dealings with him, I get the sense that you were important to his creative process, just as he hoped to help you with yours.'

Eve couldn't tell whether Phoebe was flattered by this idea or whether she'd already, somewhere, realised that she had been more important to her patron than it seemed from the outside.

'I promise that I will not bother you again after today, but you might be the key to unlocking the mystery of the manuscript's location.' Again, Eve felt she'd wandered into the pages of a novel, but the very real signs of distress on Phoebe's face and body brought her back to reality. 'His wife,' (and immediately Eve kicked herself for mentioning Elizabeth Morrow), 'well, to be honest, everyone who one would have thought would know where he kept the manuscript, they don't. Know. Do you?' Eve wasn't making sense.

Phoebe stared at her coffee for far too long. 'Do you really, truly promise to leave me alone? If I answer.'

Eve held her breath. It was only two days ago she had made another promise that she wasn't sure she could keep to the Master of Dudley.

'Yes, Phoebe. And I am so sorry to have reminded you of your trauma.'

'OK. I'll tell you.'

Eve hoped she kept the triumph out of her face but allowed herself a fist pump under the table. Triumph was short-lived.

'It's not what you think it is.'

V

The sad story of David Morrow's final weeks emerged in broken sentences. Eve pieced it together later, writing up what she was now calling her case notes. An English hero indeed.

David Morrow had been struggling. No-one was quite willing to say it out loud, but having been a functioning alcoholic for decades, he was getting less functional by the day. And he knew it. He worked in worlds – academia, media – that facilitated his drinking, encouraged it, normalised it. College dinners were binge drinking by any other name: four to five drinks in two hours was just the warm-up act. But it was taking its toll. He was perfectly capable of writing an op-ed (Phoebe used the term with pride, revealing just how dazzled she had been by Morrow's place at the heart of the right-wing media establishment, his status as the irresistible bad-boy for the left) or arguing with some pompous dickhead on the telly – but he could not get anywhere close to the 100,000 words of coherent historical and cultural analysis his publishers had commissioned. In one of their earliest conversations, around new year, Morrow had talked about how he was going to speak with his editor (Phoebe couldn't remember Toby's name) and make the case for something shorter. Because nobody read big books these days. *An English Hero* would work far better at 50k. Even as Eve felt uncertain that the conversation ever took place, Phoebe confirmed that, when she met up with DM in mid-February, he admitted he had not spoken with Toby. He was ashamed, she thought. He'd just got drunk more often, and alone. Which was one of the reasons she agreed to come with him to a college dinner, as his research assistant. It had been their joke. She even wore glasses to appear more of a geek, smoothed her hair down so that it looked like a short, neat bob – concealing the shaved patches above her ears. She rather enjoyed being suitably vague about exactly which college she belonged to or who was funding the research fellowship, both implied by her presence at High Table with Morrow.

And then, afterwards, both of them drunk, DM had suggested they go back to his rooms.

'And he told me…' She seemed unable to continue. Coming back to the present, to Eve, Phoebe said, with venom, 'This fucking manuscript you're looking for, it doesn't exist.' The story came out in fits and starts. 'Jesus, he looked awful. He kept saying, "I can't do it, I don't know what to do."' Self-pity was followed by anger. 'I'll tell them all to fuck off.' Morrow began ranting at people – his publisher, his agent, the head of his college – who weren't in the room. 'He was really out of it, spit coming out of his mouth, his eyes kind of weird.' Phoebe stopped again.

Eve sat silent, willing her to continue – not because of *An English Hero*, which meant precisely nothing to her, but because the young woman was obviously so distressed.

'I tried, I tried to calm him, suggesting that he lie down. I was genuinely worried by now. He was sweating; his skin was grey.'

Eve stayed very still, the scene vivid in her mind.

'He… misunderstood me. I think. Mebbe he thought I was asking him to fuck me.' Phoebe's voice was a monotone.

She described Morrow getting a burst of energy, rummaging in his desk, maybe taking a tablet of some kind. Eve looked Phoebe in the eye. She was joining the dots. This was no time for euphemism.

'Was it Viagra?'

'I dunno. Never been with anyone who needed that shit.'

'Then what happened, Phoebe? How did you leave him?'

'He kind of collapsed. I left him lying on the bed. I tidied him up a bit. I don't know why. He was out of it by then.'

'Did you take anything from the room?' Eve blushed. *God,* she thought, *you really don't trust her, do you?*

Phoebe looked up and, for only the second time in the conversation, stared straight at Eve.

'No. There was nothing to take.'

Eve remembered this woman could stand up on a stage and deliver, improvise, dazzle with her poetry.

'Do you want another coffee?' Eve was surprised at how shaken she was by their conversation. She didn't want another coffee. She didn't even feel like cake. But she had a strong sense that they needed to have a break and ordering drinks would offer a chance to regroup.

'Yeah,' said Phoebe.

Eve brought the cups back to the table, having glanced back at Phoebe (was that even her real name?) throughout the transaction. She had a sixth sense that the girl would disappear on her. But she sat there, a touch of her bravado back. She spiked her hair once more. They hardly spoke in the time it took them to drink their coffees. Eve reflected on the fact that the second cup was never as good as the first. And the first, in this case, had been pretty poor. Phoebe's phone went off a couple of times. She ignored it. And then she simply walked out. She didn't even say thank you for the coffee.

For all the ostentatious rudeness of her departure, Eve felt she had failed Phoebe in some way. Maybe she had. Eve had handed her a business card.

'If you ever need anything, if you need help, get in touch.' It was a ridiculous gesture. Phoebe already had her number. And if she needed help, she wouldn't be calling Eve. But she didn't want to leave things as if getting the manuscript was all that mattered.

'Bye, Phoebe,' Eve said to the now almost empty café.

Once again, she was aware how quickly this simple task had drawn her into a complicated and distressing web of relationships, how many unhappy people she had encountered in the previous week. Was it only last Thursday she'd been savouring Milos's charred leeks? She forced herself to focus on the past weekend's mundane, but not unhappy, pleasures: a decadently expensive visit to the cheese shop in the Covered Market, a long tramp along the Oxford Canal, a chat with a neighbour about the council's plans to stop cars using their road as a rat-run. *Positive thinking, Eve, positive thinking. Turn that frown into a smile.* She liked her solitary life. She really did. And at least, in Sheffield, there were trams to discover. Eve had had enough of walking.

The journey home to Oxford, longer, slower, more crowded than the train up, offered little balm. Eve tried to make sense of Phoebe's relationship with Morrow. In some ways, she had most in common with the young men who found older women (sugar mummies?) to support them. In chat rooms, and Eve forced herself to find out about them, these men, apparently blissfully unaware that the very women they were writing about could see their words, reassured their fellows that the dynamic was completely different for them, since there was so much less possibility of a purely financial powerplay shading into a sexual one. These young men, in a massive self-awareness fail, congratulated themselves on their virtue, saving their wrath for the older men who would 'power dump' on young women. One wrote, smugly, of his sense of being in control. *I didn't have to sleep with her. Didn't even kiss her. She just wanted to spend time together.* The assumption was, of course, that she would have liked to have sex with him, because who would not? The young man received '500 a week'. Whether this was pounds or dollars (Eve secretly hoped it was Kyrgyzstani som), it seemed the going rate, which explained a lot. Eve put to one side a question that nagged at her (why would a woman, with money enough to spare £500 a week, want the company of a man so arrogant and stupid?) and returned to the problem in hand. She had learnt more about that dismal evening, Morrow's last night on earth. But she had entirely failed to find the location of the manuscript. In fact, she'd been told that it didn't even exist. A lucrative job was disappearing in front of her eyes. It had been too good to be true.

Thank goodness for friends. One hour with Linda and the world seemed a better place. Objectively, nothing had changed. The job was over. Phoebe's career as a poet was over. The dream that was the Turistik Doğu Express was over. David Morrow remained dead and his book unfound – and possibly unwritten. But the prospect of April's cruelty (made even worse by the prospect of god-awful April Fool attempts) seemed less awful. A large glass of wine helped, but it was mostly being able to talk about things – including cock worship, which had induced an eruption of Barbaresco from Linda – with an older, wiser, woman. Linda was even willing to forgive Eve for deleting the dating apps.

Eve knew that she helped Linda too. One day, a few months previously, Eve had spotted her friend out in town. She looked terrible, with her helmet of bluntly cut grey hair, her ill-fitting, drab clothes. She had her husband Brian in tow. There was no other way to describe it. He shuffled behind her, dragged forwards by Linda's terrible energy compounded of anger and despair. Eve never told her friend that she had seen her that day. Looking at the attractive woman across from her, short hair styled away from her still-beautiful face, a bit of make-up, a joyous, bright ensemble of clothes, probably handmade by Linda herself, Eve knew that it was important to have these moments of escape. Here, in this wine bar, with Eve, Linda could be completely herself. Not merely Brian's carer.

Maybe that's what the escape to Oxford was for Phoebe. In her own neighbourhood, she could not be anonymous. Everyone would know her business. Coming south offered a fresh start, where no-one knew her name, where she was excitingly different in her accent, her appearance, even her way of walking.

Kindly, but with a wicked twinkle in her eye, Linda helped Eve to realise that she was projecting, wildly and potentially inaccurately, her own experiences onto Phoebe.

'Memory is a strange beast, Eve. You'll find that when you get to my age. Large chunks of life gone, oof,' (Linda gestured with her glass, and Eve could not help but notice the shake as she replaced it on the table), 'as if they never were, having loomed so large at the time, and for years afterwards.'

There was both comfort and sadness in moving on, in letting the past go. Linda suggested that Eve believe in Phoebe's resilience, stop trying to act as saviour to someone who didn't necessarily need saving. Eve remained uncertain. The fact was she carried the past with her. And why *should* Phoebe have to be resilient? But, yes, her friend was right, damn it.

Eve turned the conversation to a book she'd been reading. Novelist and travel writer Rebecca West, back in the darkest days of World War Two, had written in praise of the eastern 'Slav' over the people of her own western Europe. The Slav believed that to make life better, you 'add good things to it, whereas in the West we hold that the way to make life better is to take bad things away from it'. West went on to write of food, and hospitals, and passion, but Eve wanted to talk with Linda about her own austerity of clothing and dress. She was aware she didn't have the gift of adding good things. She sought invisibility. Phoebe was the opposite, also her daughter Rosa. Linda, too, on a good day, like today. Women who decorated themselves, added to their beauty.

Linda finished off her glass of wine, dropped a big hint about a new dating app for the over forties, insisted on paying (every time they went out, there was the same mock argument over the bill), and they parted ways, Eve to the right – and Milos, Linda to the left and her husband, whose Alzheimer's-ridden mind clung to the wreckage of his memories.

'Enjoy Milos!' Linda's parting salvo was delivered with a filthy chuckle. Eve could not convince her friend that her lodger had precisely zero romantic interest in her. Linda believed that Milos harboured a secret passion for his landlady, a passion which he concealed so successfully that it was invisible. Smiling, Eve walked home the long way, revelling in the evening light on the cherry blossom.

She called out, 'I'm home,' to Milos, whom she glimpsed in his usual Thursday night position, hunched over a chopping board, extremely large knife in hand, and headed upstairs. Whilst she was changing, her phone went. It was Rosa and Eve thought she had just enough time to catch up with her daughter before taking her part in the weekly dining ritual. Rosa was deep in an explanation of throuples – 'Isn't it a bit tiring, love – I mean, one person is knackering enough?' Eve had ventured, but Rosa had merely laughed at her weariness and said that perhaps monogamy was the problem, prompting Eve to remember her conversation with Linda about the so-called Slav approach to life; add, don't subtract – when Eve broke off. She'd heard a strange noise.

'Rosa, Rosa… you'll never guess!'

Rosa, with infinite tolerance, asked, 'What will I never guess, Mum?'

'I just heard Milos…'

'What? *What*?!'

'…laugh!'

'You *have* to go and see what's happening; maybe he's found *the one*.'

Rosa, like Linda, had a view on Milos. She was convinced he was gay but closeted. Eve herself veered towards viewing him as a happy-enough asexual, with a very occasional, and not very pressing, worry that Milos was one of those incels who would suddenly combust in sexual rage. Then again, if she was honest, she didn't think too much about Milos, let alone his sex life. If she'd had to describe him to a friend, she'd be hard put and that wasn't only because she wasn't the most visually observant of people. Her lodger cultivated anonymity. He was a generic white middle-class man, in his middle-thirties, average height, brown hair cut short but not too short, clean-shaven, no piercings, no tattoos, and, for clothing, a uniform of white shirt and dark trousers. Maybe Rebecca West had got the Slav temperament all wrong after all. Eve realised she didn't even know the colour of his eyes. She listened more attentively. Yes, Milos was with a man. In the kitchen. And there was the laugh again.

'OK, I am going in. Will text you later.'

She entered the kitchen as casually as possible, speculating as to what she might be interrupting. Milos was poised over various small piles of immaculately prepped vegetables. Probably colour-coded. Nothing new there. What was new was the man leaning against the back door, with his nose buried in a glass of wine. The man who could make Milos laugh.

'Hi,' managed Eve.

Milos, irritated, it seemed, at the interruption, glanced up at Eve before returning to the real business of the evening with what sounded like a 'huh', but could have been a greeting. The man with the wine glass stepped forwards.

'Well, it looks as if I will need to introduce myself. Ayoub.'

'Delighted to make your acquaintance, Ayoub.' Bloody hell, she was sounding as if she was in a Jane Austen novel. 'I'm Milos's landlady. Eve.' Oh God, she was making it worse.

Milos focused, briefly. 'Ayoub knows a lot about wine.' This was high praise from a man who knew a fair bit about wine, and explained a lot, not least Ayoub's presence. 'I've brought a couple of bottles over this evening – would you like a glass, Landlady Eve?'

'I'd love to but perhaps with the meal? I've just had a large glass of wine on an empty stomach, and I wouldn't want to…' Eve was babbling. What was wrong with her? She was perilously close to discussing digestive tract problems with a complete stranger. An extremely hot complete stranger.

Milos intervened, 'Food will be ready in…just under twenty-five minutes. Come back then.'

'OK – see you in a bit, guys.'

Eve retreated to her room. She wasn't used to this. It wasn't only that the meal was going to be served at (she calculated) 7.43pm, which was thirteen minutes later than usual. And if she was honest, it was not merely that there was someone other than Milos in her kitchen. It was that she wasn't used to fancying anyone. Three rapid-fire alerts on her phone reminded her that she was supposed to report back to Rosa. *Still no idea whether he and Milos are an item – but he's staying for supper!*

A glance in the mirror reflected Eve's rather anxious, tired face back to her. She was slightly flushed from that large glass of red wine with Linda, her hair engaged in its usual chaos, and she was wearing a jumper that had seen better days. But it was a much-loved jumper with whom she'd been through a lot. Eve smiled briefly at her flicker of vanity being so quickly snuffed out by her affection for a piece of knitwear. Smiling, her face was transformed. She reassured her reflection: 'You'll do.'

Over the meal in her small kitchen, Ayoub did nothing to reduce his appeal. Eve reminded herself that she had vowed never to have a relationship with anyone, ever again, but that was not the same thing as a vow of chastity. Was it? Ayoub had gorgeous dark-brown eyes, curly black hair, was funny, he listened well, and (being fluent in English, French and Arabic) he enjoyed words as much as she did.

'Names are fascinating, aren't they?' he said, turning those eyes towards Eve, who just at that moment had a mouthful of food and could only nod. 'Ayoub is the Arabic form of Job. What a miserable bastard, usually right about life though. It means "returning to God".' He knew about her own name ('life, mother of life, giver of life') and was thoroughly charming about it: 'Eve, you are the meaning of life' was delivered with mock seriousness.

Astonishingly, Milos joined in, explaining in somewhat pedantic detail the various potential etymologies of his own name, showing a familiarity with Slav and Greek traditions that should not have surprised Eve, but did. Ayoub spoke about growing up in Beirut with his Lebanese Muslim father and a French Christian mother but spending large parts of his life in Paris and London ('it seemed safer, but… the crazy people are everywhere, aren't they?'), and then he asked Milos about his family. Eve received another shock.

'My father gave me nothing but my name.' There was an awkward silence. Ayoub was reaching for the wine bottle and refilling their glasses when there was the sound of a key in the door. Only one person had a key. Eve's heart sank.

'Mum! Milos! Hi! Oh, I didn't realise you had company!'

The lying little cow, thought Eve, but there was nothing for it but to draw up a chair for Rosa and make the introductions. The awkward moment evaporated under the onslaught of the young people's chatter. Ayoub was a good-looking man but, face it, he was ten years younger than Eve. Probably closer to thirty than forty. Which meant he was nearer in age to Rosa than he was to her. Having made the brutal calculation, Eve found it relatively easy to shut down any flicker of desire he had created and bask in the glory of being Rosa's mum. Because, yes, Rosa was flirting outrageously with Ayoub, which seemed a bit unfair since (as far as Eve knew) her daughter preferred women.

It turned out that Ayoub's interest in wine was, these days, strictly amateur. Just as Milos, at heart a chef, had thrown in his lot with a career of university administration, Ayoub had trained as a pharmacologist.

'First generation immigrant. My parents wanted me to have a job. They were probably right. But one day, I'll return to my first love, wine.'

Rosa was vague about her own work but forthcoming about her environmental activism.

Eve had not enjoyed an evening so much in months, and it was with reluctance that she left first, grabbing a quick hug with Rosa, thanking Milos for his cooking, and bestowing a warm, slightly drunken 'good night' on Ayoub. As she left the room, she heard Milos explain: 'Eve doesn't hug people. Except Rosa.'

VI

Her first thought the next morning, as she buried her head into her pillow and attempted to summon up the willpower to roll over and sip the glass of water by her bed, was that she really was out of practice. With the emotions as much as the wine. April Fool's Day indeed. Her second thought was: *Milos has grey-blue eyes.* Half an hour later, having forced herself to move, swallow a couple of paracetamol and two glasses of water, and impatient of her befuddled head, she decided to walk her hangover off and think through the problem of David Morrow's book.

With each step, Eve gained more distance from her encounter with Phoebe. It was on Monday that she had made a straightforward plan: first the Master of Dudley, then Morrow's son. But the trip to Sheffield had disturbed her: the antagonistic conversation with the vulnerable young poet, the glimpses of a sexual economy to which Eve would have preferred to shut her eyes, the image of a dying David Morrow, knowing his own failure. Had Eve been too willing to accept Phoebe's account of a book unwritten? Indeed, was Morrow in his right mind on the night of his death? Was he telling the truth to Phoebe? Maybe there *was* still something to find. Somewhere. Eve returned to her conversation with Elizabeth Morrow. Someone could have, and almost certainly did, take away her husband's notebooks, his computer, from his home in the immediate aftermath of his death. Which meant there was something to take. Only a limited number of people could have done so. It was time to go back to her original plan.

The house was peaceful when she returned in the late afternoon. Milos would be visiting his mother, Janice, in Essex this weekend, as he did every fortnight. His revelation about his father, the man – presumably Czech – who had appeared and disappeared from his mother's life, leaving a child as his legacy, preoccupied her for a moment, but not for long. That was another benefit of Milos as a lodger: he showed no curiosity about her life, and she had very little about his. Eve set to work.

She found it easy to track down the Reverend Michael Morrow. She considered a direct approach best, crafting a polite but assertive email informing Michael that, acting for his father's literary executor, she would like to collect David Morrow's laptop and notebooks from him. It was only the truth, she *would* like to get hold of them, even if she, in truth, had no idea whether Michael had them.

Michael replied almost immediately, which was surprising but welcome. His message was enigmatic. *It would be good to talk with you about my father's work. The literary executor, for all her professional expertise, may not have the full picture.* So, Michael knew about Josephine. And Michael was hinting that he knew more than Josephine. Eve was thrilled. She was on the trail again. A quick consultation of the train timetables, another email to Michael, another positive response, and Eve was all set for another superlatively expensive but thoroughly enjoyable train ride, this time beyond Sheffield to York, then east on the branch line to Malton, a short distance from Michael's benefice, Almthorpe.

The branch line did not disappoint, meandering along the River Derwent, with glimpses of a ruined priory, cows moving lazily, old signal boxes. Eve was briefly confused by the river. She and her train were headed towards the sea and Scarborough. The river was not. Another mystery to solve later with a map. Twenty-five joyous minutes later, the train drew into Malton, another delight in its dilapidated strangeness, its shabby Victoriana. Just her kind of station.

As Eve alighted from the train, she belatedly regretted not having paid more attention to the family photographs on display in Mrs Morrow's house. It was the woman's house, in her mind, even if Eve knew both the Morrows had lived there, even if it was more a prison or retreat than a home. Eve looked around her. The only man waiting was tall, wrapped warmly against the cold north-east wind (spring was definitely a distant dream up here), no dog collar, and Black. Not Michael. But the man waved to her as she looked uncertainly around the station exit.

'Eve? I thought so!'

Eve collected herself, understanding that this warmly smiling man had been sent to meet her.

'Raphael Agwuegbo – at your service. Michael asked me to nip out and collect you. I would say it is because he is busy, but actually it is because he can't drive!'

'Do we have far to go?' Eve asked, getting into a car that looked as if it belonged in the last century, a relic from a grainy documentary recording those who packed everything they owned into an underpowered vehicle and pointed their Skoda west from the collapsing Soviet bloc.

'No, only ten minutes or so by car. Michael usually walks it when he comes back from visiting his mother. He says it's therapeutic. Nothing therapeutic about the weather today, though, and I'm hoping you don't need an hour's walk uphill to clear *your* mind?'

Eve was quickly revising her view of Michael Morrow. Although Raphael's comment hinted at the tensions between him and his parents, everything else revealed a settled, loving, and purposeful domestic and professional – or should that be vocational? – life. Eve had made the assumption that Michael had joined the church as an act of defiance against his atheist father but was becoming aware that this had been her own secular outlook at work. You don't get accepted, or she hoped you didn't get accepted, as an ordinand, then work all the hours of the day for a paltry stipend in – and she was right about this – a cold, damp, ugly church-owned house just to annoy your parents. Apparently, even the more established priest with whom Michael looked after six parishes didn't get to live in the beautiful Old Rectory next door to St Bartholomew's, the largest church in their portfolio. The Rectory had long since been sold off to swell the church's funds. She shouldn't have been surprised. Even in their short drive from the station, across the river, up a steep hill and on into and through a sprawling village, Eve had noticed elegant signs for The Old Forge, The Old School House, The Old Post Office. Presumably the pub, boarded up, to let, sign flapping in the chilly wind, would go the same way, converted into luxury apartments or a large family home. The Old Black Lion.

Michael, in person, turned out to be a plain man, tall, prematurely balding, sallow and very thin. A man who had little or no interest in the clothes he wore on the evidence of the misshapen jumper he was wearing. Raphael, in contrast, was rather good-looking, with an effortless style about him which Eve suspected was not effortless at all. She remembered his art on the walls in Betty's kitchen. Husband and husband were quietly affectionate towards each other and Eve realised that this was the first time she had seen two people, a couple, comfortable in each other's company for a very long time. There was love and kindness here.

But there was also wariness. Michael had a tendency to clear his throat before he said anything, but this was just one of the reasons that conversation did not exactly flow. Over lunch, a hearty soup mopped up with bread, all homemade by Raphael, she learnt a bit more about the life of a priest, from flower rotas to sitting with the dying, from Messy Play to marriage ceremonies. Michael's only resentment was the vast amount of meetings and paperwork around safeguarding, although he stopped short of saying it was unnecessary. He seemed genuinely grateful for having been brought to these scattered parishes, proud of ensuring that there was a service on Sunday in every church, something that had been impossible before his arrival.

They talked about their village, and Eve learnt that the soup tasted so damn good because Raphael used a West African leaf called uziza. Available in all good Peckham food stores. Which was Raphael's tactful way of pre-empting Eve's potential question about where he was really from. But nothing more about David Morrow.

As Raphael made them all a cup of very good coffee – 'Priorities, Eve, priorities,' he said with a chuckle, gesturing towards the sparsely furnished house and the small two-bar heater – Eve felt it was time to go direct. Michael drew a deep breath, gave one of his anxious coughs, but then, with the assurance of a man who could and did preach from the pulpit every Sunday, made his pronouncement.

'I wanted to meet you, and I suppose I wanted you to see me in my home, in my life as a priest, and as husband to Raphael. I thought then you might understand me when I say... there is nothing here for you.'

Raphael sat extremely still, looking at Michael rather than Eve. She paused.

'Nothing?'

57

'Nothing.'

The next question was the important one. 'Nothing for me? Nothing for Josephine Levine? Or nothing at all for anyone?'

'Since it is my father's literary agent who is seeking the book, and you are working for her, I think she is the significant person here.'

Michael had avoided the third choice, making Eve even more certain that he had something.

'What if I wasn't working for Josephine?'

'Ah, but you are.'

Raphael stepped in. 'My understanding is that a literary executor has very few actual rights. The family's wishes take precedence. And the family, in the person of Michael and his mother, say there is nothing for you.'

Eve looked at Raphael. 'Your understanding?'

'Well, I'd like to have announced dramatically at this point that I am a lawyer, but since I'm not and I can't, I suggest that a simple Google search will confirm what I have just said.'

Eve was defeated. Surprisingly, she felt relief rather than disappointment. She had tried, more than tried. Two trips to Yorkshire in a week. She could invoice Josephine, write a report, perhaps she'd get paid enough to take that train journey after all. Her brain moved quickly, whether because of the coffee or because she felt back in control. It was time to be honest with Michael and Raphael.

'I have to report back to Josephine Levine. What would you like me to say? She is quite a determined woman, and despite what you say about the legal rights of a literary executor, if she thinks you are hiding or withholding her author's work, she will come after you.' In for a penny, in for a pound. 'Off the record,' Eve said, smiling at Raphael, knowing that there was no such thing. 'I am quite happy to go away empty-handed. But Josephine needs managing.'

Michael thought for a moment then suggested he and Raphael talk further and send Eve an email setting out the official, 'on-the-record' position. She could then pass this on to Josephine on Monday.

Business completed, the three of them relaxed. So absorbed had they been, first by the food and then the chess moves of their conversation, none had realised what the icy wind had presaged: snow.

'What time is your train, Eve?'

She double-checked her ticket on the app and confirmed she needed to be back at Malton by 3.30pm. It was approaching three already, so they said their farewells swiftly, and Raphael brought the Skoda round to the door in an act of chivalry. The snow was swirling around Eve as she jumped into the icy car.

'Sorry, the heaters don't really work.'

Eve was well aware of that fact as she sat, hunched and frozen, as Raphael drove in increasingly poor visibility, and with one hand clearing the windscreen.

'The demister doesn't work either.'

It was a long ten minutes, but the Skoda ploughed on relentlessly. Eve didn't know whether to be grateful that it was mainly downhill.

Raphael dropped her off – 'I'd better not get out – might never start again,' he offered, with a wry grin – and Eve explored her options. The café was very closed, and there was no-one in the ticket office. She was disconcerted to hear music, something classical, vaguely patriotic and bombastic. It was coming from the speakers on the Victorian-era platform, muffled by the continuing snow. Delightful, but she needed to get inside. A couple of other people huddled in the corner of a decrepit waiting room, which smelt of urine and something else Eve didn't want to think about. Sometimes she wondered about her devotion to train travel.

She peered out at the departures board, which was disconcertingly blank. She checked the app that was tracking her train and saw it was halted at the first station out of Scarborough. The minutes ticked by. The other two travellers seemed stoical in the face of the wait – maybe it was normal for this line – and Eve determined to make the best of the situation and dug out a book from her bag. It was really too cold to concentrate, however, and after another thirty minutes and the departure of her two waiting-room companions, she decided she needed to do something. What she could, in fact, do was another question, since there were no staff around and she knew better than to try to contact a rail company directly. She stepped out of the waiting room to a world transformed. The snow continued to fall gently, huge, single flakes casually drifting down to join their brethren, and there was a stillness and peace about the station that caught Eve's breath.

VII

Seconds later, however, she understood for the first time that she was stranded. She checked her phone one more time, hoping for a train. Any train. The app burst into sudden life. All services had been suspended. There were the usual fulsome apologies for the inconvenience and a blink-and-you'd-miss-it mention of the possibility of a refund. And then Eve's phone died.

There was only one thing to do. Walk back to Michael and Raphael's and throw herself on their mercy. Eve felt defeated, overwhelmed. It was not the prospect of a two-mile trudge uphill through deep snow that made her feel like weeping. It was the thought of turning up unannounced, of being an inconvenience. She realised the absurdity of her social anxiety, but that didn't make it less powerful. In the end, the walk itself pushed her fears to one side, requiring all her stamina and focus as she attempted to remember the route. At one point, feeling that she had strayed into a disaster movie, she had to reach up and wipe a signpost free of snow so that she could read (hurrah!) *Almthorpe 1 mile*. She'd found the turning. That would be a twenty-minute walk on an ordinary day, but, dragging her numb feet through banking snow, it took Eve nearly an hour.

Leaving Malton, the occasional car had struggled past her, and Eve had toyed with the idea of flagging one down. But her fear of hitchhiking was stronger than her fear of hypothermia. In any case, there was no guarantee the cars would get up the hill to Almthorpe.

At last the village loomed. Thank God it was April, not January, or she would be doing this walk in the dark. As it was, twilight was descending when Eve stumbled up to Michael's door.

His astonishment was real, but so was his immediate assessment of Eve's needs.

'Come in, come in. We have a fire – you can warm yourself. Rapha – put the kettle on, we have a visitor!' And Michael, blessed Michael, ushered Eve into the sitting room, helped her out of her sodden outer clothes, boots and socks – 'Rapha – warm socks! We need warm socks!' – and settled her in an armchair. Raphael appeared moments later with a tray of tea things, a towel and an enormous pair of socks. A plate of toasted crumpets arrived next, completing Eve's restoration if not renaissance.

'Thank you, gentlemen, thank you. The train didn't come. No information, nothing, and then my phone died and, well, I thought I'd come back here.' Only then did she think to try to find her phone and start recharging it. Until that point, her only thought had been warmth, followed by tea and crumpets.

Raphael glanced at Michael, a silent message. 'You are going to have to stay here, Eve. I've just checked and all train services to York are suspended. Even if we could get you there, it's the same for the cross-country route to Oxford. The snow's easing off now, so they are hopeful that things will be running again in the morning.'

Eve didn't know what to say. The heat and food and kindness had brought out her latent exhaustion.

'You look shattered – have a snooze on the sofa, then join us for a bite to eat. I'll make up the sofa bed for you later – you'll be in the warmest room.'

Eve did just that, drowsily hearing Michael leave the house (Raphael was worried about him in the snow drifts, but Michael dismissed his concerns – 'this is what I do, Raph'), the sounds of dinner being prepared, a burst of BBC Radio 6. She was properly asleep when Michael gently nudged her shoulder to say that food was on the table. Slowly, she came back to life and tucked into a delicious, sweetly spiced casserole ('Rapha is *such* a good cook – he can make things taste cordon bleu when it's just leftover veg') and changed her mind about a glass of wine.

'Just one, though, or else I'll fall asleep on you.'

'It wouldn't matter if you did, Eve,' said Michael, although he, she noticed, wasn't drinking.

Later, as she lay on her sofa bed, warm, snug and full of food, she tried to identify the moment when the wariness had disappeared. Raphael was now Rapha to her: as he had joked, 'Like Nadal, but without the talent – or muscles, for that matter.' Perhaps it had been her genuine interest as the men talked about their discovery of their local area during Covid. Rapha showed Eve the series of charcoal drawings created by David Hockney, completed over a spring season nearly ten years earlier, pointing to the artist's phrase, 'the Chinese say black and white contains colour, and so it can'. You just have to look. Rapha was honest in his assessment of his own artistic talent, wishing he had even a tiny fraction of Hockney's genius.

'And your mum's, of course,' he added affectionately to Michael.

Perhaps it had already been lifting when she had shown no desire to pursue David Morrow's book, shown she was willing to accept Michael's 'nothing'. Perhaps it was her return – exhausted, vulnerable, grateful. Or perhaps it was the pleasure she took in Raphael's food, the questions she asked him about the spices and vegetables he used (it turned out it wasn't just leftovers), trying to remember so that she could tell Milos on her return. They hadn't even made a big deal of her vegetarianism. Or perhaps it was, dare she think it, because they liked her, and she liked them. Human friendship.

Eve had felt it was not her place to ask, but she had learnt from Michael of the need to conceal his sexuality from his church as he sought sponsorship from the diocese on his journey towards ordination.

'But here you are?'

Michael explained just how precarious his position was, dependent on a supportive bishop, on treading carefully at every step. Eve had not realised that although the Church of England tolerated, just about, same-sex couples, those couples' lives were hedged about with restrictions. Michael and Raphael could not marry in a religious ceremony. Their civil partnership came with the promise to remain celibate and the real threats of being disciplined and never getting another position in the Church. Michael had known all this when taking the path to ordination. He laughed, but with little humour.

'I relied on two things. One was that, although I knew I was gay, I had convinced myself that I could live a life of celibacy. Remain single. Meeting Rapha blew that one out of the water. But I also relied, and continued to rely, on the gulf between public pronouncements and private practice.' Michael told an anecdote about a recently married gay priest who was summoned to the Bishop's Palace. On arrival, he received a formal letter of discipline and then, shortly afterwards, the bishop and his wife were toasting the groom and groom with a round of gin and tonics. Eve seized the moment to offer her own toast, filling Rapha's glass with the last of wine, checking to see that Michael still had what she had discovered was his Lenten water. The men seemed both pleased and distressed.

'But we are still not married.' Even their civil partnership, just over a year earlier, had been a very discreet affair, a formalisation of their living arrangements. 'We became a bubble. Covid had its upside. Two single men, living alone. It was just common sense that I should move in.' Rapha actually giggled when he said this.

Eve risked a question about David Morrow. Making a gesture that could encompass the church house and Raphael, Michael's vocation and his marriage (no, his civil partnership), she asked what his parents thought about 'this'. Michael's answer went back seven years.

'Mum was already closing down by then, so I honestly don't know. There was no change, really. Nothing negative. But nothing positive either. I suppose she was happy if I was happy. Dad, David, went off to the USA around the time I was ordained deacon.'

Eve had no idea what this meant but knew that Morrow had headed for the States in 2018.

'I think he was far more thrown by my Christian faith than by any hints that I wasn't your conventional hetero guy. I'm not sure he thought about me much.'

The two men exchanged a glance. Eve had no idea what had been said to occasion it.

'I guess you'll understand more than most people why I didn't take the obvious path, which would have been ministerial training in Oxford. It would be like pissing on Dad's patch. No, I found what I wanted here in Yorkshire, was able to escape for a while into a different family. I know it sounds grim but compared to Raphael – who lost his entire family – I was quite lucky. And I have hope, now that my father is dead, my mother might return to herself, as it were. I might get my mum back.'

Eve must have looked aghast at Raphael's loss. He stepped in quickly. 'They're not dead. Michael is referring to my family's beliefs about homosexuality. You'll find my parents (and aunts, uncles, cousins, so many cousins) alive and well in Peckham. Mum and Dad came here from Nigeria in the eighties, seeking a better life, but brought with them their fundamentalism. I don't think they're going to change their mind anytime soon.'

Eve found herself talking a little about her own parents, the father she had hardly known, the mother whose bitterness and helplessness (and alcohol intake) corroded her childhood, her own determination to do things differently when she found she was pregnant with Rosa.

VIII

The bottle of wine was long gone. Raphael was sipping a glass of brandy, Eve and Michael herbal teas, when Michael took the conversation in an unexpected direction.

'Eve, I said there was nothing for you here. I think you picked up on my carefully chosen words – after all, you are a writer.' (Hell yeah, she *was* a writer, just not writing anything right now.) 'You probably guessed that there is something. I didn't lie; my words were truthful. They were not the full truth. I'd like to tell you that now.'

Eve nodded, grateful.

'I took some notebooks and his computer from my father's house. I knew about the will, but I also knew – thanks to Raphael – that I had rights as family. Rapha and I spent two days going through the stuff I took. I will only talk about what is relevant to this book.' Michael's face appeared distressed. Eve guessed that he discovered things on David Morrow's computer that he would prefer not to have known about his father.

Crucially, Michael's story appeared to confirm Phoebe's. In the folder simply titled 'The Book', the two men found reams of angry bile, a collection of clickbait tweet-style observations on contemporary culture and its war on white men, working-class white men like him, rambling attacks on queer readings of history. Had David Morrow even bothered to seek out the many and various – and, to Eve's mind, fascinating and plausible – queer accounts of Sir Philip Sidney's life and work? Those special male friends for starters. The fact that Sidney's prose masterpiece, the *Arcadia*, was packed with beautiful cross-dressing men having feelings for other beautiful men that no woman could inspire, 'a love much more vehement'. After all, in the end, women were women. How much could you expect of the faulty model? Then again, if every male writer who celebrated friendship between men at the expense of inadequate woman was outed, there'd hardly be a straight guy left in the literary room.

Michael was more preoccupied with class: 'Since when my father was working class, I do not know,' he said, wearily. What was clear was that David Morrow had a thing about 'real men' who got things done, a fear that there was a whole generation growing up without knowledge of the achievements of the great men of English history. Instead, minor figures were being elevated to significance, and those great men being blamed for everything. Not for the first time did Eve wonder just how much of Morrow's take on history was fuelled by his own sense of being overtaken and undervalued by the next generation.

All this was fascinating, if hardly surprising given what Eve already knew about the man. But more importantly, Eve heard that Michael and Raphael failed to find any historical research, let alone a coherent, almost-finished narrative.

'I, we, felt in the present of hate. Nothing, nobody, would be served by this bile coming into the world.'

Raphael added, laconically, perhaps to calm Michael, who seemed gripped by powerful emotion, 'It wasn't even well-written hate. Then again, racist, homophobic, misogynist prose tends not to dazzle the reader with its literary merits. It doesn't need to.'

'It's OK, Raph. I don't need calming down. I need to tell Eve the truth.'

So there's more, thought Eve. What *had* he seen? But, no, Michael's confession took a different direction. He had destroyed the notebooks and wiped the computer out of horror at his father's political and social beliefs.

'Did I do wrong?' he asked, hardly seeing Eve or even Raphael. 'Legally, no,' Michael answered his own question. The words were well-rehearsed. As Morrow's son, he owned the books and computer. Unless the will expressly said that the literary executor owned the materials, which it did not. Michael recited the words as if it were the litany: 'My agent, to do as she should think best, and if necessary, ignore the wishes of my family.' As Eve already knew, that *if necessary* had very little legal force. 'Morally, I wonder. But I cannot, in all faith, add to the misery and hatred in the world.' Michael bowed his head, his speech done.

Raphael got up from his seat, stood behind his husband, and encircled him in his arms.

'It's OK. You did the right thing. It's over now.' And then, looking at her: 'Eve understands. Don't you?'

And she did, or she thought she did.

Michael appeared to pull himself together. 'Would you like to see the video of my father's funeral?'

Eve wasn't quite sure that she *did* want to, but she was so grateful to this kind couple for taking her in for the night – and for trusting her with the truth – that she assented, if rather weakly.

'Did you officiate, Michael?' she asked, then immediately wished she had not, given the pain and shame that appeared on his face.

'No. I could have done. But my father left clear instructions that in the event of his death he was to have a humanist, secular funeral.' He smiled ruefully, attempting to soften the profound bitterness his voice had shown. 'It was actually quite a small affair. I think the college are talking about doing a big memorial service but, I don't know, maybe because it wasn't term time by the time the funeral took place, maybe... I don't know.' Michael paused, began again, something that sounded like 'the police needed to...' then broke off again. It was too late in the evening to push Michael to say more and, after a moment, he spoke again, clearly putting the subject to bed. 'I didn't have much to do with it. I don't think Mum had much to do with it. The GP guy – Dr Goode? – he gave the eulogy. It was on 16th March – a Wednesday – I remember being thankful that I wouldn't have to miss any Sunday services. My father died on the first day of March, but you know that. The news came to me on Ash Wednesday.'

Eve had known the date but had not even considered its significance to the Christian calendar. She belatedly realised that Morrow had died after a feast in Formal Hall, on Shrove Tuesday, his final Mardi Gras, Fat Tuesday. And now Rapha was saying just how brave and determined Michael had been, leading the Ash Wednesday service, smudging his congregation's foreheads with black crosses, when he was so exhausted, so shocked.

'He'd only had a few hours' sleep – I'd picked him up at close on 2am at York – some problem with the trains. You were only just leaving the house when your mum phoned – I don't know how you carried on.' His husband's praise was making Michael uncomfortable. Rapha, sensitive as ever, went silent and pressed play on the computer.

The video was not exactly premium quality. Michael explained that the crematorium had a Zoom facility born of the pandemic, and even though there were no restrictions on attendance in person, they'd sent through the recording. A humanist officiant led the proceedings, which were brief to the point of perfunctory. A blurry Michael stood up at the end and read a poem. He did not read well, and the camera moved away from his face too often, but, catching the words 'the eternal note of sadness', Eve was sure she knew the poem and waited for its final, poignant lines, a plea for love in a world where there was 'neither joy, nor love, nor light, nor certitude, nor peace, nor help for pain', where 'ignorant armies clash by night'. Michael had done well to get it agreed, given the melancholy line about the retreat of the Sea of Faith. She was moved.

The hours spent together had changed her view of Michael. Her heart went out to this man who, somehow, through all this, had kept a flame of love for his father, despite that father's rejection and hostility. A man who could be honest about the pain and loneliness and hopelessness of his father. That his chosen poem was called 'Dover Beach' and featured the white cliffs of England was, Eve thought, not on Michael's mind, but you never knew.

The coffin consigned to the flames, the mourners, such as they were, left the building. Eve saw Elizabeth, comforted discreetly by her neighbour, Charles. She caught a glimpse of the Master of Dudley, wearing uncharacteristically sombre clothes, eyes cast down. Michael, of course, with Raphael. David Morrow's only real friend, the college doctor, in an expensive cashmere coat and an embarrassingly old-school combover. He had given the eulogy, singing the late literary titan's praises with, apparently, no irony. So that was Dr Nick Goode. Eve could now put a face to the name of the man Morrow had appointed as his conventional executor.

Josephine Levine had given the first reading, from one of Morrow's early books: a powerful passage of trenchant prose, which made Eve even more melancholy. Toby Milton was there, hunched inside a corduroy jacket that clearly did not keep out the cold, with a young, anxious-looking woman (one of his unpaid assistants, perhaps? A girlfriend? It was impossible to tell) at his side. They both left as soon as they possibly could. Everyone looked chilled to the bone.

Eve's eye was caught by another woman, of perhaps her own age, perhaps younger. White skin, dark straight hair cut into a very blunt bob, clothes as chic as Josephine's, slender, and with a way of carrying herself that Eve part envied, part feared. The woman left the crematorium without even a glance at the other mourners. The film sputtered on for another minute or so and then stopped abruptly. The whole thing had only taken twenty-five minutes, and from her own experience of crematoriums, Eve knew that the next group of mourners would be champing at the bit outside, waiting for their chance to say goodbye.

It was only a glimpse, but Eve was curious.

'Who was the young woman who walked out at the end, Michael?'

Another shared glance between the two men. But she knew Michael well enough by now to know that he could not lie. He was clearly toying with refusing to answer her ('you don't need to know, Eve') but thought better of it.

Wearily, and prefaced by the return of his anxious cough, he said, '*That* was Juliette.' Normally kindly Michael spoke the name with an exaggerated French accent and a bucketload of contempt.

'And Juliette eez…?' asked Eve, covering her relentlessness with an attempt at humour.

Another cough. 'My half-sister.'

'Oh.'

'Let's get some sleep.' Raphael had had enough. Eve could tell he was concerned about Michael, who seemed a man on the edge of a nervous breakdown, and she herself was once again exhausted. Not by the day's events, tiring though they had been, but by David Morrow's legacy. Where was the love? Right here in front of her, she reminded herself, and said her goodnights, changed into an enormous hoodie given to her by Raphael, before wrapping herself in blankets on the surprisingly comfortable sofa.

The blurry images from the ceremony refused to disappear. Her mind strayed, perhaps inevitably given her quest, to another death over four hundred years ago. Eve had seen, years ago, the remarkable visual record of Sir Philip Sidney's funeral, recorded on a manuscript at Christ Church College in Oxford. She was lucky. These days, she would have been pointed sternly to the online resource. The scroll recorded a procession, headed up by poor men, soldiers who had served Sir Philip in battle, servants of the great man's household. Only then came the friends, followed by nobility, men and women on horseback. Towards the back, the representatives of the City of London, the Company of Grocers, the Civic Guard. Finally, more horses, and more men of foot, representing the dead man's military command. Sidney's elite status ensured his burial place was St Paul's Cathedral but the breadth of his appeal, the range of people who honoured him, was evident in this record of his cortege. Examining it, all those years ago, the historian in Eve had questions. Was this rare and beautiful image all part of the early and ruthless myth-making of Sidney? Or was it a true and accurate record? Probably, as always, a bit of both. Lying cocooned on a sofa in Almthorpe, as her brain finally stopped churning, Eve asked herself just why Morrow had been so fascinated with Sidney. And she felt saddened that whilst so many had mourned the great Elizabethan, so few seemed to mourn David Morrow.

IX

Morning came, and there was no mention of Juliette. The three of them, as if acknowledging that yesterday had been a step too far for one and all, ate a companionable breakfast. Sunday was, of course, Michael's busiest day and Eve tried to make herself helpful as he rushed around collecting up his books and papers, all the time fielding countless WhatsApp messages from various church groups. Raphael reported that the snow was melting and he had high hopes the car would start. It had better. Michael's first service of the day was five miles away by car and involved some tricky hills.

A quick investigation of trains suggested that she would not be able to leave Malton until at least lunchtime, so Eve pottered around the vicarage while Michael headed off to do his job. She packed her few belongings. It didn't take long. She had not, of course, come prepared for an overnight stay; she didn't even have a toothbrush. Dental hygiene would just have to wait and, anyway, it was not as if she was going to be in any intimate situations which required fresh breath and clean underwear. She was, as instructed ('we have to run a tight ship on Sundays!'), standing outside the door when Rapha returned, and they walked together to the church in Almthorpe through the deceptively slippery sludge. He had already dropped Michael off.

Eve sat at the back of the sparsely attended communion service, the Lenten solemnity suiting her very well, and then, gathering around a table with a tea urn, cups and a plate of welcome biscuits, witnessed just how much Michael was liked and needed by the elderly congregation, and just how well Raphael filled his role as vicar's husband, if only in the eyes of the law, not his church. His impeccably knotted scarf was as much a sign of his calling as his husband's dog collar.

Drying his hands from the washing up, Raphael caught Eve's eye. He gestured towards the door and his wrist. Time to go. Eve was sorry to leave. There was time, just, for one final conversation at the station. Raphael sat staring through the windscreen.

'It has all been so hard for Michael. He didn't say last night, but when we were trying to get into his father's computer, we discovered that the password was Michael's date of birth. To think that he typed that in every day, well, it just made the pain different. As for Juliette. What can I say?' He paused, glancing at Eve. 'Another tough one for Michael. She's almost exactly his age,' (Raphael must have heard Eve's gasp), 'yes, Morrow had an affair whenever, back in the late eighties. She appeared last winter. A few weeks before Christmas. It was all very dramatic. "My name is Juliette Michel, and David Morrow is my father."' Clearly, parodying Juliette's accent was one of the ways in which the couple dealt with her existence. 'Betty didn't react, Michael just retreated even further into denial about his own relationship with his father, and meanwhile, Juliette and "Papa" became best mates. Or so I believe. We only saw them together for a short time, during our own visits. It's full-on for Michael, of course, up here, so we try to visit his mother before the actual Christmas celebration and then again in the New Year.'

Raphael sighed, glancing at Eve to see how she was receiving a story that seemed downright operatic: soap operatic.

'Morrow invited Juliette, can you believe it, to stay at Little Frogford for the whole of the Christmas holidays – being Oxford, that's a full five weeks. So she was still there when we came back. She'd taken over his bedroom; we were relegated to the sofa downstairs. Not good for my back.' Rapha winced dramatically. 'I think Michael hoped she might have disappeared. She hadn't and, in fact, she'd taken further steps to displace him. But I don't want to talk about that. Safe to say, there was no love lost between…'

But Eve would not hear between whom, seeing her train arrive. She hurriedly said her thanks and her goodbyes. Michael's plea for 'love' at his father's funeral, his plea to cling together in the face of darkness, was even more remarkable. And now, Eve was on the slow, crowded Sunday-afternoon train south from York with a headache called Juliette Michel. The very sound of the train seemed to whisper, 'Walk away, walk away.' Two people had now told her there was no book to find. One of them was saddened by this, the other was relieved, but neither had reason to lie.

But morning came and Juliette was still on Eve's mind. She found herself running back over her conversations with Elizabeth Morrow to see if she'd missed a reference to a long-lost daughter of her husband arriving and setting up camp in the family home for the duration of Christmas. No, Elizabeth had not mentioned Juliette, which was interesting in itself. Or perhaps just another instance of her tunnel vision, her refusal to engage with her husband, dead or alive. Phoebe also had not said anything about Morrow's daughter. Did she even know about her? And what about Michael? He must, somewhere, have understood that sharing the funeral footage meant sharing the existence of Juliette with Eve. Was he, consciously or unconsciously, pointing her towards his half-sister? And if so, why?

Eve had no answers, but she did have a sense that unless she followed her quest, however futile, until its end, she would not rest easy. With practised self-deception, she convinced herself that this was a win-win situation. If Juliette knew nothing of *An English Hero*, then Eve would not only prove Michael and Phoebe right but also justify the former's decision to erase Morrow's toxic outpourings, such as they were. The case would be closed. On the other hand, if Morrow had got much further with the book than either Phoebe or Michael believed, and if he had shared his work with Juliette, then Eve would have shown a praiseworthy tenacity and, with the manuscript in hand, could crack on with the job she'd been hired to do. Yes, Eve needed to see Juliette Michel. And she needed to let Josephine Levine know of her progress and get her permission to continue the quest for *An English Hero*.

Eve surprised herself by having no qualms at all about keeping the majority of her discoveries in Almthorpe to herself when she spoke with Morrow's agent and literary executor. She emphasised exactly how much of a dead end her visit to Michael had been, discreetly suppressing Michael's own part in creating the dead end. Eve then, somewhat disingenuously, proposed one final investigation, glossing over the fact that she had only learnt of Morrow's illegitimate daughter within the last twenty-four hours.

Josephine Levine was, to Eve's astonishment, forthcoming. Effusive, even.

'Ah, Juliette – now, *that* is a young woman to admire. David was thrilled at her arrival in his life. So witty, so urbane, so stylish. And she was dazzled by him, unlike his sanctimonious son and that happy-clappy husband of his. Juliette and David – it was lovely to see him so close with family at last. She even persuaded him to get rid of the appalling beard he'd gained during the pandemic.'

For a moment, Eve was speechless. Hardly trusting her voice, she ventured to ask why Josephine had not mentioned the lovely Juliette before, whilst scribbling other questions to herself: *how does J know J if no contact with DM? The beard?!* If the agent found Eve's voiced question awkward, she covered it well.

'I would have mentioned her when we first spoke, but, well, Juliette had inherited something of her father's spirit, and she seems to have gone off radar since the funeral. I couldn't see how she might be relevant.'

Eve smelt *un rat*. 'Off radar?'

'You see,' (and the relish in Josephine's voice as she embarked on her salacious history was tangible), 'Juliette's mother was David's great love back in the late eighties. Betty was, well, you've met her, haven't you? She was hardly a match for David, and it's just surprising he stayed as long as he did.'

The full implications of Raphael's comment about Juliette being a similar age to Michael hit Eve in her gut. She felt sick. Michael, she knew, had been born in 1990. He had told Eve, over the course of their long, snowbound Saturday night conversation, that his mother had suffered two miscarriages in the early years of her marriage, the second a full sixteen weeks into the pregnancy. Eve did the maths. Morrow had begun, continued, his affair with Juliette's mother through these terrible times. Did Josephine know this? Eve doubted it, or else she would surely not be so callous.

'Anyway, Michael the miracle baby arrived in 1990 – thank the Lord – and I suspect that Betty laid down the law to David.' (OK, Josephine *did* know about Betty's history, or else why was Michael a miracle baby? She was indeed that callous.) 'He ditched Isabelle, not knowing that she was pregnant –

with Juliette, who was born that year.' As Josephine told it, Isabelle had refused to tell Juliette the name of her father until she herself was dying. This was in 2020, at the height of the pandemic. As soon as it was possible to travel from France, Juliette had come to David Morrow and introduced herself.

Eve, with some effort, kept her voice calm. None of this explained the lovely Juliette's disappearance after the funeral. She brought Josephine back to her question.

'I'm not sure of the details,' (the agent sounded aggrieved at this), 'but my sense is that Juliette was surprised, disappointed, when her father died, not to be a direct beneficiary of his will. She was certainly upset about something. It's hard to understand because she stands to be really quite wealthy when *An English Hero* appears given that David changed his will in January to make her the legatee of his literary earnings.'

Eve, not for the first time in the conversation, was flabbergasted. How could Levine say Juliette wasn't relevant? Why had no-one mentioned Juliette's place in this whole sorry saga? Then again, why had she not asked? The simple answer was that Eve herself had been focused on finding the manuscript, and doing her job, rather than establishing who would benefit from her work. *Cui bono?* she thought, rather smugly dredging up the Latin. She'd also, she recognised, been distracted by both Phoebe and Michael, both of whom had got under her skin in complicated ways. Josephine was still talking, apparently unaware of having dropped a bombshell. Eve looked at her scribbled questions. At least this explained how and why Josephine knew the woman. As literary executor, she was duty bound to make money for Juliette Michel.

'…it's just common sense to keep your will up to date, isn't it?'

Eve had no idea how they'd got onto wills but tuned back in to Josephine.

'I advise all my authors to do so. And he really did have a striking bond with her. The apple does not fall far from the tree.' Josephine pondered for a moment on the vagaries of life, before offering a banal explanation of the daughter's disappearance. 'Perhaps it's as simple as, with her father gone, there's nothing to keep Juliette in England. The family weren't exactly enamoured of her. But her abrupt departure seems a little strange.'

Eve had been thinking hard and fast. Astonished at her own bravado, she suggested one last throw of the dice: a personal appeal to Juliette. She didn't wish to examine her motives too carefully but did find herself hoping that Morrow's daughter had disappeared to a particularly beautiful part of France. She sold the trip to Josephine on the basis of her own persuasive powers. If, and it was a big if, Juliette knew anything about the manuscript, then Eve could be the right person to convince her that it was most definitely in her own best interests for the work to be completed and come into the world. Eve delivered her closing statement with positively thespian intensity: 'I'm a neutral in this war.'

Josephine swift acquiescence in what was, on paper, a ridiculous venture was motivated, Eve decided, by her frustration at her own ignorance, at not being in control. She was as curious as Eve to learn what the hell was going on.

Eve duly received contact details for Juliette. A quick check of the map was extremely pleasing. The young woman lived in a village not far from Toulouse. Eve was so delighted by this that it took a moment to ponder how Josephine had this information to hand when she had only minutes earlier described Juliette as off radar. Perhaps it was simply that, as legatee, Juliette's French address would have been in Morrow's will. And Josephine would have been in touch with her after the funeral, if not before, to discuss the literary executorship.

Then again, it still seemed strange that Josephine knew so much about Juliette if she hadn't been in contact with David Morrow for months. And it remained completely unclear why the young woman was now ghosting the agent. None of it made sense.

No matter. Eve was back on the trail. She believed that there was a strong possibility that Morrow had confided in his daughter over that long Christmas holiday. Did Juliette hold the key to the vanished book? Eve felt a twinge of disloyalty to Michael, but this was outweighed by her knowledge that she had not betrayed his actions to Josephine and, more pertinently, the thought that a train journey to the south-west of France would not be unpleasant in a bitterly cold English April.

X

Eve loved Eurostar unconditionally. She could overlook all its faults: the ridiculously crowded departure lounge at St Pancras (but look at the George Gilbert Scott columns!), the crush to get onto the escalators (but at least there *were* escalators!), the delays and cancellations (but Paris in just over two hours!). Eve had a guilty feeling that she would never cut another human being such slack. Except Rosa, of course. Except Rosa.

For a moment, Eve wanted to be hurtling under the Channel with her daughter, but they'd done a fair bit of that in their time, and right now, she was glad to be on her own. She sipped more coffee, for it had been a very early start and a very expensive train, filled with business people heading to Paris for morning meetings. The caffeine helped fuel what turned into a dash across Paris. She had known it was going to be a close-run thing, even with her stash of Metro cards at the ready, and when Eve simply could not find her train in the bewildering Gare de Montparnasse, she stared defeat in the face. But, at last, she had hurled herself into the first door of the 11:08 TGV to Toulouse and, finding her way slowly to her seat, fourteen carriages away, she breathed at last.

If she ruled the railway world, then Eve would do away with double-decker trains. There was something about them that was, well, wrong. Downstairs was cramped and claustrophobic. Upstairs was a bit too much like being on a bus, and a bus going at three hundred kilometres an hour. Then again, she was grateful to be eating her picnic lunch knowing that she would be in a whole new world by mid-afternoon. She needed to get away. Eve had spent the previous forty-eight hours working, hard, on the job she had been neglecting for the sake of the chimaera of *An English Hero*. Sir Robert's memoirs of a life in pork products had been her primary focus for months now. Just occasionally, she felt a glimmer of hope that together they might just make a silk purse out of it. Stop. She winced. Sir Robert's puntastic humour was infecting her. But it was not him she was glad to escape. No, it was her conversation with Rosa.

They'd sat together on the canal boat which Rosa currently called home: romantic in theory, but downright miserable in a dreary, damp, Thames-Valley spring. Not that Rosa seemed bothered. She was her usual cheerful self and made short shrift of Eve's agonised attempts to get her head around the sugar-baby industry.

'Your generation thought that if you went to college, got a job, got a house, got a family then you were sorted. And look at you. You've said it yourself, Mum. Most of your friends in their forties or fifties, they're not happy; they're trapped, and they don't have any of the things they expected to have – job security, stable family, healthcare, a pension, for fuck's sake. The difference is we know the system is fucked. There's no point in trying to make it work. And, yeah, maybe it's selfish to exploit straight men's pathetic neediness, but we're making patriarchy work for us. For once.'

Eve did not fail to notice Rosa's use of 'we', but this was not the moment to enquire about her daughter's sources of income. Rosa's words were hard to hear, but in her heart, she knew her daughter was right. It's just that Eve wished, so much, she wasn't. The conversation had stayed with her, feeding Eve's nostalgia for the trips that she had done with a less clear-eyed Rosa. It had helped that she was seven. Eve chuckled. Even at seven, Rosa was pretty good at calling out bullshit.

Eve was smiling by the time she reached the best part of her journey. A spring sun shone on an ebullient, southern landscape as the local train meandered west for an hour from Toulouse. It wasn't only the beauty, the slowing of pace. Eve was fascinated by branch lines, an endangered species in her own country, and hardly thriving elsewhere. She had a rather hazy belief in public services, and a less hazy sense that anything that stopped people driving cars was good: branch lines were therefore a good thing. But she also loved the quirky histories of these tendrils from the super-fast main-line services. Someone had the vision for this railway, many more gave their labour to build it, some even lost their lives in doing so. These lines deserved to live on that basis alone.

Juliette Michel met Eve at the station and the two women walked the short distance to her house. To what had been Isabelle's house. At first sight, it was a British couple's wet dream of retirement, all warm stone, terracotta floors, brightly patterned wall tiles, huge stands of herbs, the obligatory blue shutters, and a vine-covered terrace on which to sit with a G&T and watch the sun set. But this was also the house in which Juliette had delivered palliative care to her mother during a global pandemic and somehow the despair and loneliness of those months, years, had seeped into its walls.

The women spoke in English, although Eve could have managed the conversation in French, such was its stilted nature. Yes, her journey had gone well. No, she had not been to this particular corner of France before. Wasn't it superb that, on a good day, one could catch a distant glimpse of the Pyrenees?

Yes, she would be grateful for something to eat. And, yes, if Juliette could show her where she should go, she would freshen up and return for *un apéro*.

Eve was rather enjoying her aperitif on the terrace, the first shoots of this year's vine growth inching their way across the trellising. The season was a good two or three weeks ahead of Oxfordshire and the spring blossom on the trees was almost obscene in its copiousness. Juliette, she noticed, sipped mineral water. The conversation remained awkward, even when, especially when, the French woman brought out two plates of charcuterie. Eve had forgotten to mention that she was a vegetarian and was somewhat dismayed by the amount of meat on display, but there were sliced raw vegetables and fruit as well. Juliette became slightly more animated when she explained her commitment to clean food. Nothing processed. No carbohydrates. No stimulants. As much raw food as possible.

Eve, having raised Rosa, knew just how powerful the forces ranged against young women could be. Clean food sounded so, well, clean, but in Eve's mind it was in fact just another eating disorder in disguise. Juliette, close up and not dressed for a late-winter funeral in Oxfordshire, was, Eve could now see, downright gaunt. It was, no doubt, genetic. Her half-brother Michael was similar in build. But whereas Michael ate heartily when food was put in front of him, Juliette clearly did not. Eve wondered if she was receiving any care or support. The medical world was becoming slightly more able to help the growing army of young women (and not only young women) self-harming themselves in this way. But her concern was a distraction. This time, Eve would not let empathy dilute her professionalism. She was here to find out about David Morrow's work. And she was determined to let Juliette lead the way.

Later, Eve would recognise that, on that early spring evening outside Toulouse, she had been told a strange mixture of truth and lies. Indeed, she would come to question whether Juliette herself could tell the difference.

Her plate of raw food hardly touched, Juliette spoke of her mother's unexpected diagnosis, and the need therefore to leave her own life in Paris. Eve would have liked to know more about her work in the capital, but Juliette moved swiftly on. She had thought she would stay for a short time, to support her mother through her treatment ('chemo – it is a terrible thing, but they said she had no choice'), but this was October 2020. Juliette would be trapped by successive lockdowns and the failure of chemotherapy to halt the cancer. Alone, completely alone, she had cared for her mother as the disease slowly devastated Isabelle's body. Brief visits from nurses, taking blood, bringing morphine patches. Zoom conversations with consultants who gave her mother no hope.

'It took so long for her to die. By the end, I don't know, I wished her dead. She was so weak. I had to bathe her. Put water on her tongue. She could not swallow. It was not a good death.'

To say she was sorry seemed inadequate. Eve's own appetite had gone. She had barely even touched the wine, poured by Juliette. She could not ask about Morrow.

They were both up early, Eve driven by the need for caffeine, Juliette to assuage her demons with yoga. Eve waited until the slender woman arose from her final, superbly held, pose only to discover there was no coffee in the house.

'It is an addiction drug, you know, Eve?' Yes, she did know, but...

Eve felt it was time. She started gently, 'Were you able to talk to your father about your mother's passing?'

Juliette seemed a little surprised at the question but answered easily after a moment's hesitation.

'But yes, of course. It was a great comfort to me to be able to talk with a man who had loved my mother.'

And now for the real reason for her visit. Eve explained the hunt for the manuscript of *An English Hero*. She spelt out, as tactfully as possible, that it would be in Juliette's interest for the book to be published since she had been named as the beneficiary of Morrow's literary earnings. Juliette broke the carrot stick she held in her hand into two.

Was it possible that David Morrow had sent her his files, perhaps as late as February? (Even as Eve asked the question, she realised how unlikely it would be for him to have done so. It was quite possible that Morrow had shared his work with Juliette, but it would be downright strange if she had then not made this known at his death. She had everything to gain, and nothing to lose, by acknowledging that she had the manuscript.)

To cover her embarrassment, Eve started mumbling things about the effects of losing a loved one, that her mind might have been elsewhere, that her grief for her mother would have been triggered once more by Morrow's sudden death.

Juliette interrupted. 'He did send me some files.'

Eve's heart leapt. At last! This ridiculous journey had been worthwhile.

'But I don't think they are useful for you.'

Eve heard echoes of Michael's words: there is nothing here for you. And, once she looked through the documents that Juliette obligingly sent her in a zip file, she understood that Michael had spoken truth. The files were a ragbag of brief notes, founded on poor scholarship, outdated takes, and crass generalisations. The material was as shoddy as she had feared from Michael's assessment of the files he had deleted from his father's computer.

That was crystal clear. Very little else was. Why had Juliette not shared these with Josephine Levine? Had the two women even met or had they simply exchanged business-like messages over the terms of the will? Eve remembered Levine's enthusiasm for the charming daughter, but perhaps the feeling was not reciprocated, perhaps all her talk of the apple not falling far from the tree was just bullshit. Josephine Levine was good at bullshit. And yet, Juliette had agreed to Eve's visit, had been willing to share the material.

Eve risked one question: 'Why did you agree to see me, to show me these, but not your father's agent?'

Juliette thought for a moment. 'I just want him finished, it over.' Juliette's pronouns were a little confusing, but Eve took the point, whether she was referring to her father or the book. 'You can have these. You know they are worth nothing. You are a writer! Even you cannot make them into a book!' There was a hint of triumph, even glee, at Eve's discomfort.

As Eve attempted to make sense of Juliette's manner, while saving the files onto her own computer, her eyes strayed to the young woman's screen. Was she imagining it, or did she see an email pop-up with the words *Est-elle déjà partie?* Was she, Eve, the '*elle*'? And who was wanting to know if she'd gone?

It was, indeed, time to go. Eve made her farewells and began her long but extremely pleasurable journey home. This time, Juliette gave her a lift into Toulouse. Eve was tempted to make a point about her carbon footprint but decided it would be catty. At the station, she at last got her coffee.

She read through Morrow's files once more just in case she had missed something. The historical elements, such as they were, were derivative at best, plagiarism at worst. There was a market for this kind of thing, mash-ups of nineteenth-century historical takes and unrepentantly nationalist hagiography. Morrow and Toby Milton clearly had an eye on that market. But even the sparse soundbites looked stale.

Eve allowed herself to imagine a book that took notice of the new historical findings and questions; that would recognise the significance and power of Sidney's sister, Mary; would explore Philip's sexuality; would expose the failures and horrors of English foreign policy in the later Elizabethan period; would reveal just how colonialism and imperialism were born on the battlefields of Ireland and beyond. Damn her practical, problem-solving mind. Having imagined the possibility of a *good* book, her next thought was how could she, Eve, rescue or redeem *An English Hero*. This was swiftly followed by the less noble thought, *how did Morrow ever get anything published before this?* The answer was dispiriting. He hadn't, really, not for a long time and his early work was, she now understood, indebted to his wife's input.

At last, as her Eurostar slid beneath the Channel, Eve accepted that there was no book and there wasn't going to be a book. Well, Michael would be happy and the Master of Dudley heartily relieved. There would be one less work of hate and one more college building in the world. Morrow's literary legacy would quietly disappear. As Juliette had wanted: he, it, was finished.

XI

Eve arrived at Marylebone to find the station inexplicably closed. Groups of people were collected outside, some on their phones, others striking up conversations with strangers, but most with a very British air of resignation, even those who were probably not British. They waited, accepting, the forces ranged against them. Nothing to be done. Could be worse. Eve was having none of it. She searched, frantically, for an alternative, flipping between travel apps, walking briskly towards a promised Oxford-bound coach. The app gave conflicting information and after ten minutes of standing at what might not have been the right bus stop, Eve returned to Marylebone. The same people were still waiting there.

'Did you need to be somewhere?' asked an older man, solicitously, seeing her return.

Eve felt a little sad saying, 'No, not really.'

Then, with no fanfare, the station reopened and Eve boarded her train.

She had been rather smug at the prospect of leaving a small village in the Gers region of France just after breakfast (if she'd been offered breakfast) and walking through the door of her Oxford home in time for a Thursday night meal with

Milos. Her French connections had even permitted her a quick shopping expedition in Bordeaux, and she had tracked down a 2017 unoaked, biodynamic red that had been on her radar for a while. Any vineyard that took on both the stifling wine-making traditions and the challengingly damp climate of Bordeaux deserved a medal. They also used horses in the vineyards, which appealed to Eve, who liked the idea of animals without actually wanting to have any involvement with them. Now she had missed dinner. She put aside her disappointment about the food, sternly chided herself for even hoping that Ayoub might have been there, and placed the horse wine carefully in the rack for another evening.

Pick up the manuscript, shut her eyes to its content, polish it, take the money, go on a long train journey. *Ha!* Eve expostulated to the pot plants on her terrace, showing the first signs of spring growth. Was it only days ago that she had thought this was what she had signed up to? Now David Morrow's world was interwoven into her very psyche. The visit to the withdrawn, uncooperative Betty had been disconcerting, the conversation with Rachita Solanki mildly shocking, but it had been meeting the graceless Phoebe that had disturbed Eve most deeply, whether because of the mix of vulnerability and prickliness in the young woman herself, the nature of her GFE transaction with Morrow, or the glimpse Eve had caught of this unlikely sugar daddy's last moments.

These three powerful women had thrown Eve off her professional course, drawing her reluctantly but inexorably into considering the life and death of David Morrow, rather than the book he had left. But, even when she returned to *An English Hero*, Eve had only become more entangled. Her visit to Michael had at least confirmed that there was no almost-finished manuscript to find. But it also confirmed just how troubled David Morrow was, and just how much trouble he was in, as man and as author. If Phoebe bore witness to his state of mind in the last hours of his life, then Michael bore witness to the pitiful, grotesque fragments he was producing, and to the misery of the Morrows' home life, in the months – no, the decades – leading up to the man's death.

Both Phoebe and Michael were, in different ways, profoundly troubled by *An English Hero*. Phoebe because the book had not been written: the failure to get the words down was a clear sign of Morrow's inability to function, his distress. Michael because he feared it had been written: a clear sign to this unhappy son that his father had become a force for evil, if that was not too strong a word. Michael and Phoebe were both, however, looking to escape their entanglement with the book and its author. The former wanted no part in bringing evil into the world. Phoebe wanted to play no known part in the sordid drama of Morrow's death at Dudley.

Eve should have walked away at this point, she knew. But for reasons she didn't wish to examine too closely, she had investigated yet another dead end, this time by TGV. It was faint comfort that the trip to Gers had at least revealed the material that Michael had deleted and confirmed Phoebe's account. There was no book. Morrow himself was in a desperate way. And Eve had come to the end of her journey as literary investigator.

She constructed emails to Jonathan Peck Consultancy (explaining why the job was ending), to Toby Milton (explaining that he didn't have a book to publish) and to Josephine Levine (thanking her for her help but confirming that Juliette Michel did not have the manuscript). *An English Hero* was dead.

Toby responded first with a brief email to say he was on the train to Oxford, *spending the weekend with family*, and could she meet with him later that day? She could and so 6pm found her enjoying a rather good pint at one of the many oldest pubs in Oxford and waiting for Toby to appear. He shambled up in his uniform of crumpled linen and ill-fitting corduroy, the image of benign privilege, but he was not in a good mood. Eve listened patiently to his stoic account of having to stay with his elderly parents in their enormous detached North Oxford Victorian pile, ashamed of her cattiness in suspecting that Toby wished they'd sell up, downsize, and hand over the odd spare million to him.

With the second pint, he had moved onto Morrow. 'Never liked the man. I felt – what? – it was a terrible mistake, a misstep, to commission the book, all that money. Yes, it made the news, and not just within the industry, I mean the tabloids got hold of it, which is good, but he'd not written anything substantial for decades.'

Eve felt it was not the moment to mention Morrow's earlier reliance on others, such as his wife, for the substance and let Toby rant. She understood that this was a humiliation for him at Heritage, but it was not the end of the world.

He was talking about the difficulty, now, in recouping the advance paid on signature from the Morrow estate. The money had disappeared. Eve had a good idea as to where it had gone: a room in Oxford, even for a few months, even in a house-share, didn't come cheap and nor did Phoebe's provision of GFE, or whatever package it was that Morrow had bought. But this wasn't her business, and she wasn't going to break Phoebe's confidence. She felt less protective towards Juliette Michel, filling Toby in on Morrow's daughter's prolonged stay with the family in Little Frogford, then turning her wild goose chase to the wilds of Gascony into a couple of entertaining anecdotes. By this stage, Eve was tipsy and Toby drunk, and she had no idea whether he was even listening.

It was a dismal beginning to the weekend as Toby stumbled his way back to the parental home and Eve, sobering up with every step, walked the long way round, putting off the moment of returning to an empty house as long as possible. Normally she relished her time alone. Even though Milos was the most self-contained of lodgers and she could set her watch by his habits and routine, including the regular returns to Essex to see his mother, there was still something special about having the place to herself. Not this evening. She would change into clothes that were halfway to being pyjamas, make herself a cheese sandwich (she'd had halves to Toby's pints but, even so, was feeling heavy with alcohol and needed some food) and try to pull herself together. She didn't want to call Linda, let alone her daughter. Since her early twenties, Eve had prided herself on her independence. But sometimes, not often but still too often, she saw herself as a lone traveller in a speeding boat, vulnerable to that one wave that would tip her into the turbulent sea. It was exhilarating to travel alone, all her victories were hers, and hers alone, but sometimes, just sometimes, she longed for a particular kind of partner. One who would quietly supply an extra engine for the boat or make sure there were paramedics instantaneously available if, when the storm hit, she capsized. He wouldn't physically be *in* the boat, of course. Eve almost smiled.

She called these episodes 'visits from the grey puppy'. Hardly the black dog of depression, but still an unwelcome yapping around her ankles from a beast that demanded attention.

'Fuck off, puppy,' she shouted, safely within her front door. Then, a shock. What the hell was Milos doing here? Too late, she realised that all her travels had confused her. Milos had been down in Essex the previous weekend. He wouldn't be with his mother this Friday night.

She hoped he hadn't heard her outburst, but then a familiar voice said, 'You have a *puppy?*'

Could the evening get worse? Here she was, besieged by a grey puppy in her mind, wearing her least flattering clothes, and Ayoub was back.

Eve went as quickly as possible upstairs, leaving her lodger and his friend to the space. She lay on her bed willing herself to go downstairs, join the guys, have a normal, nice time. She needed a sandwich. But, no, even hunger would not make her move. It wasn't just vanity or shyness. She felt flat, weary, angry. Contaminated by the unhappiness surrounding David Morrow. She had been drawn into his orbit, searched for something that wasn't even there, had never been there. She even felt an unfamiliar resentment, almost scorn, for Milos: what kind of man went home to his mother every fortnight when he was in his mid-thirties? She was living with a loser.

Hugging her pillow to her chest, Eve reminded herself that she had also met great kindness: Michael and Raphael were genuine, kindly people, and Michael had found a way to live his own life with love and dignity. She also told herself that she didn't really know Elizabeth Morrow, so closed off had she become. Eve smiled. Perhaps if she was snowed in with Betty, she'd discover the party-loving artist that David had fallen in love with back in the eighties. Betty Resurgent. And, pleased at the thought, she slept.

The weekend endured, Eve woke on Monday morning clear-headed and clear-sighted. It helped that spring had, at last, arrived. Tulips stood proud and colourful in her flowerpots, and there was a touch of warmth in the sun. She would be out looking for fritillaries soon, an April ritual in the water meadows of Oxford.

Eve collected together the various receipts she had accrued and completed a final invoice for Josephine. She compiled a closing summary of the job for Jon, briefly conjuring Elizabeth Morrow and Rachita Solanki, Michael Morrow and Juliette

Michel (and omitting Phoebe), which she sweetened by an invitation to a Formal Hall some time in Trinity. She left it vague, but the offer was there and she knew how much her boss enjoyed these dinners, driven by the hope he might encounter some wealthy author-aspirant who needed his expensive services. And she put her two-faced notebook away, bidding farewell first to Sir Philip, then to his sister Mary, and last to David Morrow. If only it were as easy to put aside the unhappy people she had met in the last fortnight. With that, she turned to Sir Robert and his membranes, promising herself a long walk in the afternoon if she could only break the back of Chapter Six: Sausage Secrets. She would do her best by *Bringing Home the Bacon: a Life in Pork Products*.

Eve was deep into reworking Sir Robert's reminiscences of his breakthrough (a collagen skin that had the snap of the natural version) into something approaching coherent prose when her phone rang. It startled her. Nobody *rang* anymore; they messaged. She didn't even recognise the number, and immediately felt fear – was Rosa OK? She was relieved to hear Toby's voice, although less than happy to hear the whining hysteria in it.

'That bitch!' (Now was not the moment to lecture him on gendered derogation.)

Eve tried to stay calm but struggled in the face of Toby's fury. Juliette. Josephine. Plotting. Total betrayal.

XII

Quite why Toby was venting to her, she wasn't sure. She had not been the most empathetic of listeners at the pub on Friday, and she suspected she had been a last resort as a companion, Toby's other Oxford chums unavailable whether because of the responsibilities attached to young children or the pleasures attached to weekend homes. Perhaps he had been so self-absorbed that he failed to notice her complete absence of interest in his litany of self-pity. And then Eve realised that he was trying to find out whether she too was a traitor.

'Slow down, Toby. What is Josephine Levine doing and what's it got to do with me?'

It was only rumours at this stage, but given the nature of the publishing industry, Toby was pretty sure that someone was spreading those rumours strategically. The Levine Agency was now representing Juliette Michel, David Morrow's long-lost illegitimate daughter, and was setting the stage for a rights bidding war.

'What? You mean Juliette had the manuscript all along?' It was Eve's turn to be outraged.

'It's worse than that. If Michel had got the manuscript, then it would belong to us, and we'd have been able to publish it – with your help, of course. No, this is something new. They're talking about a hatchet job on Morrow. And they'll get good money for it.'

Already social media was buzzing with the prospect of another old white man being dragged through the gutter. #DaughtersTale was trending. And it would not just be Morrow who would suffer, or even his family, when he was exposed as a serial adulterer, a predatory professor, an academic fraud. Oxford University, and specifically Dudley College, would be under scrutiny for having, at best, turned a blind eye to Morrow's failings, at worst, enabled them.

'I don't like to say it, but Josephine is going to make far more money out of David Morrow dead than she did out of him alive.'

Toby was enraged, cheated of a book and its author, but this was surely absurd.

'Don't be ridiculous – she didn't want him dead!'

'Of course not. All I'm saying is that it was bloody convenient! I mean…'

'What *do* you mean, Toby?'

'All I mean is that Juliette Michel's part in his final months, well, it's now pretty clear she was double-crossing him. All that "I've found my papa" crap. She was just getting the dirt on the bastard.'

Eve was confused as to how Toby knew about 'all that I've found my papa crap' and realised, with horror, that it had probably come from her, via a couple of pints of IPA. All those halves added up. She also grudgingly acknowledged that Josephine had played a blinder. Just how long had she been grooming Juliette?

And then it hit her. Josephine had been relying all this time on Eve's professionalism and tenacity. And probably, damn it, her love of train travel. The agent didn't want to be the person to lead Eve to Juliette. Eve needed to find Morrow's daughter in her own sweet time, and – through Juliette – confirm to the world that *An English Hero* was not going to happen. Something nagged at Eve, in the midst of her fury. Surely Josephine would have realised that Michael would have Morrow's computer. Then again, Levine could count on the very qualities she despised in Michael Morrow (his goodness, his gentleness) to ensure that he would make no moves to get the work published, fragments or no fragments. And yet, and yet – it was Michael who had drawn Eve's attention to Juliette.

But there were far more important things to think about now than who was leading whom down the garden path (or the TGV line). Eve was acutely aware that Toby, and presumably Juliette and Josephine, the new axis of publishing evil, did not know there was even more dirt to be found. The full story of Morrow's death had indeed not come out, but she was damn well not going to drag Phoebe into this mess. Eve muttered a few platitudes, reassuring Toby that she too had completely failed to spot that Juliette was playing her own lucrative game when she visited her in France. She ended the call, silently regretting that she had not asked about that glimpsed message, '*Est-elle déjà partie?*', which, Eve now assumed, was from Josephine, the puppet master. Coffee was needed.

The truth was that Eve had been naïve to the point of stupidity. She had not warmed to Juliette, but she had felt a natural compassion for a young woman carrying such a burden of grief. Talking to Eve, only the trauma of her mother's final months seeped into Juliette's conversation, none of her hatred, her blame, of her birth father. It all made sense when Eve realised what a good actress the young woman was. Juliette's arrival at the Morrows was driven by a profound bitterness, but she seduced, if that was the right word, her father with her charm – and she deceived Eve. Michael! Cursing her own stupidity would have to wait. Eve had to warn him about what would, surely, be all over the tabloids and beyond. A text didn't seem right under the circumstances, so she tried calling him. No answer.

She needed a break from Sir Robert and the Morrow family. Eve grabbed a slab of cake as she went out of the door, her usual ritual, to be devoured on her favourite bench. She strode out hard and fast, attempting to clear her mind of anything but the gentle spring breezes, the touches of vivid green, the noise of the birds. Instead, she could not escape the oppressive noise of the traffic pounding the A34 and her equally oppressive anxiety about the new development.

'It's nothing to do with me,' she repeated, pounding her way through Happy Valley, too wound up even to appreciate the irony of her destination. She would speak with Michael, at least give him fair warning of the storm to come, and then – let it go. Toby had accepted that she was not part of the plot. She wasn't. Who were these people, anyway, who had come crashing into her well-regulated life with their distress, making what should have been a simply professional task into a ridiculously draining psychodrama. But Michael deserved to be warned.

Eve finally got through to him in the evening. He seemed surprised to hear from her and suddenly Eve felt awkward. Where to start? She kept it simple, explaining what Toby had said to her about the prospect of a memoir of his father. It would not be a hagiography. And then the sucker punch: it would be written by Juliette. Michael's 'oh' at this news was heart-breaking.

'Give me a moment, Eve. That's all a bit much to take in after a long day.'

The next voice she heard was Raphael. He sounded on the edge of anger. Eve felt a quick remorse: was this actually any of her business?

'Michael has just come home from the family of one of his parishioners. The guy died this morning. Michael's been sitting with his wife and kids – so he's exhausted. Can this wait until the morning?'

'Yes, yes, of course. I am so sorry, Raphael. I think I've lost sight of what really matters in this whole mess. Give Michael a hug from me.'

But in the morning, it was Michael who called her. They traded apologies, with Eve assuming that he had decided, on reflection, that he needed to hear more about the book.

To her surprise, he didn't: 'I said the same about my father's work – I refuse to peddle hate. Juliette is obviously angry; she thinks it will assuage that anger to write this book. Maybe it will, but I don't need to engage with it or, indeed, her.'

Eve waited for the real reason for the call.

'I may have hated my father, but I also loved him. No-one should die alone. I want to know how and why my father died in the way he did.'

I'm not sure you do, Michael, thought Eve, picturing Phoebe leaving Morrow sweating and barely conscious.

'Michael, do you want the truth, whatever? However painful it might be?'

'Yes, I do.'

So, she told him. To Eve's amazement, Michael's first words, having listened attentively, were, 'That poor young girl.' He paused. 'I can see why she didn't stick around. Why he died alone. But still, something seems wrong. I don't know. The police were involved at the time – they have to be in these cases – and didn't come up with anything. The coroner's report said there was nothing suspicious. I suppose it just felt really sudden. And I was surprised that there was no proper inquiry. There should have been.'

Eve was reminded that Michael was a frequenter of deathbeds.

For a terrible moment, Eve feared that, for all his apparent solicitude for Phoebe, Michael suspected her of something worse than leaving his father to die alone. Would he, could he, insist that the police interview her a month after Morrow's funeral? More likely, she thought, Michael was accusing Dudley College of some kind of cover-up, negligence, whatever. But his closing words were sad, rather than suspicious, let alone vengeful.

'I wish I'd had a chance to say goodbye.'

That evening, Eve attempted to get her conversation with Michael in perspective. It was a great relief to hear that he agreed with her when she explained that she had kept her knowledge of Phoebe to herself to protect the young woman. (Eve did not dwell on the motives of the only other person who knew of Phoebe's presence in Morrow's room that night. She wasn't entirely sure that Rachita Solanki was keeping her counsel for the sake of Phoebe, and she strongly suspected that the Master was primarily concerned with her own position and the reputation of the college.) Michael had then told her that, until this point, his primary concern, apart from just holding himself together in the face of his father's death, was to ensure that *An English Hero*, or what Michael called 'those sick fragments', never came into the world. That threat no longer present, he could now allow himself to consider the reality of his father's death. And he had questions.

Eve felt this was very natural. Like many a bereaved person, he was seeking a narrative to explain an unexpected death. His search was the more urgent because he was a child mourning a father, and a father from whom he had been estranged. Telling Michael about Phoebe should have removed the mystery from his father's last hours. And yet even in possession of what Eve believed was the truth, Michael remained unsettled, questioning, disturbed. His sense that there was 'something wrong' had not been assuaged.

'Of course, he's still in shock – that's why he can't accept that his dad simply suffered a mundane, almost inevitable, heart attack. Shit happens.'

This, anyway, is what Eve found herself explaining to Linda, each with their usual large glass of red wine in hand, and Linda concurred.

'You're over-involved, Eve. He's a grown-up, not a child. He'll get there.' And anyway, what was Eve supposed to do? Don a deerstalker hat, pick up a magnifying glass, and roam the quads of Dudley College looking for clues?

The conversation moved, happily, to other topics, with Linda planning an expedition with Brian at Easter. Only the Isle of Wight, but any kind of travel with her husband became an expedition. He'd been there for holidays when a child and Linda was allowing herself to hope that he might respond. Memory worked in strange ways. Eve's phone vibrated and she made the mistake of glancing at the caller. It was Phoebe.

'Do you mind?' she asked Linda and, after a nod from her friend, took the call.

'Eve, what the...' (a pause; Phoebe resisted the swear word), 'heck is going on?'

The explanation for the substitution could be heard: 'Mummmmy.'

'This French woman called me – she said she knew about me and DM – that she'd pay good money for my side of the story. What does she know? What did you tell her? Two minutes...'

Eve was doing some quick thinking, hardly registering that the last two words were directed at whoever was making whining noises in the background.

'Did she call you Phoebe?'

'Yes, but—'

'So she doesn't know that is not your real name?'

'No, but...' Phoebe, in her distress, had blown her cover.

'Look, Phoebe, this French woman, I know who she is and believe me you want nothing to do with her. Just block her number. She'll find it hard to discover who you really are.'

Phoebe did not sound comforted. 'I don't know why, but I'm frit. Will it all come out? About that night?'

'This woman, she doesn't know; she can't know. I didn't tell her anything, I swear – she's just fishing for a book she wants to write.'

'OK.' That was it. Phoebe cut herself off, leaving Eve staring at her phone. Linda had heard the whole conversation. Eve began apologising for taking the call during their precious wine time, but her friend raised her hand. She had a strange expression on her face.

'Do you remember what it was like when you were her age? She's probably even younger than you were. I'm guessing she's had to go home, with her tail between her legs, home to her parents – and her small child – after her moment of Oxford freedom.' Linda paused. 'She's frightened, "frit". She's lonely.' Linda took a big gulp of wine and said, 'What the fuck is going on?'

Eve had to laugh when her friend, outwardly the most demure and proper of elderly ladies, swore. But twenty minutes later, having told her the whole sorry tale of the previous fortnight, there was no laughter. Worse, Eve was beginning to doubt herself: had she been right to tell Phoebe that Juliette Michel was just fishing? How on earth did the woman know about the existence of Phoebe, let alone have access to her phone number? Her mind raced through more and more outrageous scenarios.

'What if she was there, Linda, there at the college – and saw Phoebe?'

Suddenly it seemed plausible. Juliette Michel skulking around the quads and cloisters of Dudley College, stalking her hated father, seeing Phoebe emerge from his rooms, joining two and two together and making five. Determined to expose her father and his sugar baby, and not just for the truth of their relationship. Sex sells, but so does violence.

Linda was unimpressed. 'Crazy talk, Eve. There'll be a simple explanation of how this French woman found the Sheffield one. You've said that the poor girl was your bloke's research assistant – it would be easy to find out who she was. I mean, you knew.'

'But, but… oh, OK. There probably is a perfectly normal reason.'

Linda, having calmed Eve down, promptly blew all chances of small talk out of the water. She announced that she had changed her mind. Linda still felt that Michael's questions were, most likely, the product of his grief: he saw conspiracy where there was none. He could fend for himself. And he had Raphael. But Phoebe was different.

'Phoebe – we'll keep calling her that since we don't know her real name – needs you, Eve. Forget the rest of them – they sound as bad as each other, to be honest. You can help Phoebe control this – before others make her life hell.'

And so Eve texted: *Phoebe, can I come to see you? I'd like to sit down with the real you – and your child. Explain what's going on. Try to help. I hope you can trust me.* Eve wasn't sure what to expect. She could quite understand if Phoebe decided to block her at the same time as blocking Juliette. But she had tried.

As she got ready for bed, Eve found herself checking her phone, something she usually tried not to do. Instead of a message from Phoebe, she discovered an email from Dame Professor Rachita Solanki. Eve read through it twice, unable to tell whether it was a poisoned chalice or a gift from the gods. The Master of Dudley College wondered if Dr Brook would be willing to shoulder the burden of arranging Dr Morrow's memorial service, which would be taking place in the college chapel early in Trinity Term. Dr Brook understood the sensitive nature of the undertaking and was familiar with the ways of the collegiate university and would, it was felt, offer a safe pair of hands in a challenging time. Goodness, this was smooth. Eve guessed that the Master knew nothing about Juliette Michel's new project. Maybe she didn't look at book-world Twitter, an admirable but foolish stance on a day like today when #daughterstale was all over it like a rash. Eve felt pretty sure that, if she had known, the memorial service would be abruptly withdrawn from the calendar. Eve read on. Dr Brook would, of course, be compensated for her time if she felt she could take this on.

Twist or stick? Eve remembered her mother's piece of (rare) good advice: 'Do the positive thing, Evie. It's better to say sorry for your mistakes than feel regret for things you've never done.' She'd do it, but first she left a message for Jon telling him she'd been approached to organise a memorial service for Morrow, but that she'd like to take it on as a representative of his company, rather than as an individual. She didn't spell out her reason, which was that if – no, *when* – trouble hit, she'd be protected – at least slightly. She did ask Jon to negotiate a fee with the Master, and to go large. Jon got back to her quickly, delighted partly at the prospect of his cut but also at a new vista opening up for his literary consultancy: Memorial Services R Us.

Putting her phone aside, and preparing to sleep, Eve knew that, for her, it wasn't about the money. Or not only about the money. Under the guise of pulling together a memorial service for David Morrow, she would have licence to ask questions. For all Linda's belief that he could stand on his own two feet, Eve would try to learn the truth of Michael's father's final months, days, hours, for the sake of vulnerable, perplexed Michael. And with Linda's full backing, she would find out the truth of David Morrow's final hours for the frightened young woman who was not called Phoebe.

XIII

Eve positively marched to the station and leapt on the train to Didcot Parkway, determined not to dwell on Phoebe's continued silence. She would use the short journey to outline a simple timeline. It was something she did whenever she began a new research project. First, create a skeleton of dates and places. Then, and only then, could you flesh out the life, the work, the story. After weeks of intense engagements with some very powerful, very persuasive, and often very damaged people, it was time to get back to the bare bones. She continued the work on her next slow train, before tucking her double-sided notebook, retrieved that morning from the draw in her desk, into the outside pocket of her rucksack as the train approached her station. Goring and Streatley: she was heading up to the Ridgeway, an ancient pathway that always offered clarity when she needed to do a deep dive into the past. Not her familiar 1590s, but still the past.

The timeline was, in one sense, straightforward to assemble. Eve began with the spring, three years ago, a lifetime ago, before the pandemic, when the 'six-figure advance' had been all over the media. Morrow would have received around £30,000 on signature with Josephine picking up her cut as agent, so nearly five thousand for Ms Levine. Not, in reality, six figures for anyone, but it made a good headline. In public, Morrow was riding high on the back of his time in the USA, a familiar talking head in the UK media. In private, over the coming months, the deadline kept on being pushed back. It was easy to point to the pandemic as the reason, but Eve was pretty sure that delivery of the manuscript would have been delayed even without Covid. She wondered if March of this year had been the final, *final* deadline, whether Toby Milton and Josephine Levine were losing patience with their author.

To this skeleton, written in black, Eve added in blue what should have happened next. If Morrow had delivered on time, in March, he would have received the next instalment of the advance, and then, on publication, the final third. The same applied even with Morrow dead, so long as the manuscript was close to completion. If this had been the straightforward job envisaged by Jon when he brought her in, Eve's work would have ensured that the Morrow estate received both payments. Either way, dead or alive, the complete book would have been with the publishers by early summer, and, by autumn, Eve would have been sipping tepid prosecco at a launch party somewhere in literary London.

Back to black to record what had in fact happened. It didn't take long. *1st March DM dies. An English Hero unfinished.* As things stood, with no evidence of a manuscript, it was Mrs Morrow who was taking the financial hit. Heritage had a legitimate claim against her husband's estate. And against Josephine, presumably, although Eve wasn't quite sure how that worked. The publishers could, and no doubt were, seeking to recoup their advance but from what Eve had gleaned from her various conversations, they were having trouble doing so.

Meaning Elizabeth Morrow would need to sell her house. Was that what she had meant when she said she would not be able to remain living there?

At Didcot, waiting to change trains, Eve had looked at the timeline's starting place and, historian at heart, had been unable to resist taking it back further. She had been told, by Michael, that Sarsens had been inherited by his mother when both her parents were killed in a car crash in the mid nineteen-eighties. Elizabeth's mother and father had only just made the move to Cozens Lane, envisaging a rural retirement. Eve was certain that David Morrow's lecturer's salary would never have been enough, even forty years ago, to buy the place. She was also pretty sure that this meant that he would, even if he had wanted to, have found it impossible to deprive his wife of the marital home in his will. It was hers. Then again, whether one considered his failure to get anywhere close to completing the book or his diversion of his literary earnings to Juliette in the event of his death, he had in effect made it untenable for his wife to remain there. Or, at least, that is what his widow had suggested.

Eve returned to the current year, the dates, people and places proliferating as Morrow's death approached. She had just added Morrow's making of his new will in January, with the most significant change being the insertion of Juliette Michel as his literary legatee, when the train drew into Goring and Streatley.

Making her way through the village streets and across the river, Eve's rucksack was a comforting weight on her back, but she felt heavy with questions. She was perplexed by David Morrow's state of mind in January, the month in which he had changed his will. Without her pen in her hand, her thoughts swirled, uncontrolled. Was he driven by a sense of connection to or responsibility towards his new-found daughter? If so, he was being wilfully blind to his own sorry position. Surely, even as he signed the document, he must have known that *An English Hero* would never see the light of day. Not because of his untimely death, but because he couldn't get the words down.

Perhaps it was that sense of direct connection with the past that Eve always had when walking these ancient paths, but her mind went to Sir Philip Sidney. He made his will because he knew he was dying. And then he made a good death, an exemplary death. So far, so unlike David Morrow. Yet both men's wills had proved to be empty gestures. Although the great and the good had been appointed to oversee Sir Philip's (four earls, his father-in-law Sir Francis Walsingham, his wife Frances herself), there was no money. Walsingham was 'said to have had to pay over £6,000 out of his own pocket towards debts, funeral expenses, and other charges'. Were both men blind, wilfully so, to the reality of their financial situations? Eve thought again she had caught a glimpse of the attraction that Sidney held for Morrow, how sympathetic he would have been to Sidney's frustration with his queen who would not support his visions. Thrift and caution were Elizabeth I's watchwords, and Sidney was not the only courtier to chafe against her rule. Sir Philip's widow's next husband, the Earl of Essex, would die because of it.

Eve forced her mind back to a much closer history, the crowded January of the present year. The month of Morrow's failure to remove Solanki as Master of Dudley in that fractious Governing Body meeting. Or so the Master had it. January: the second month of Juliette's stay at Little Frogford, the month she left. The second, bitter visit of Michael and Raphael. And the month in which Phoebe was conjured through the magic of the internet. Eve was coming to believe that Phoebe was the only person who really knew David Morrow at this time. After all, one of the conditions of her employment was to speak with the man every two days on the phone, or something like that. Once again, Eve marvelled at the nature of the contract that bound this unlikely couple.

Was Morrow clutching at a straw called Phoebe? He had made Juliette his literary legatee knowing there was nothing to leave. Perhaps it was Phoebe who represented a genuine new beginning, a chance for him to make a real difference to a young woman's creative life. Eve tried to remember what people had said about Morrow around this time. He'd shaved off his beard, yes, that was it. He was still a handsome man, in his way, craggy now rather than chiselled, louche rather than exuding health (no Charles Mallam, he), but the bone structure, revealed once the beard was shaved, was good. He was still a presence, whatever that elusive word meant. Eve wanted to ask Phoebe about the beard.

As she began the climb to the Ridgeway, Eve put David Morrow firmly out of her mind but found that someone else promptly took his place: Josephine Levine. The more Eve thought about it, the more she felt unconvinced by Josephine's claim not to know just how badly things were going with her author. Indeed, Eve began to suspect that Levine had quite happily permitted Morrow to spiral to writerly destruction. Possibly even enabled his drinking and delusion. If she realised – no, Eve thought, *when* she realised – that she had sold the rights and taken her agent's cut on a book that Morrow would never deliver, she moved to a plan B: Juliette Michel. Whether the plan B came to her or she came to the plan B was still not clear, but Eve felt almost certain that Josephine and Juliette had been laying their plans the previous autumn. The women must then have had some kind of contact over that winter, poised to unleash *The Daughter's Tale* as soon as Morrow's book was out of the frame. Josephine had been far from honest about her contact with the Morrows, father and daughter.

The death of the author himself rather than his book might have been unexpected, but it would not have been unwelcome. Josephine merely brought forward her plans. In fact, Morrow's heart attack was downright convenient for her, otherwise she was going to have to wait for Toby Milton finally to give up on

112

An English Hero. Which, given publishers' tolerance of some celebrity authors' loose understanding of deadlines, might be a long wait. Eve remembered that Toby had said something similar in the first flush of his fury against the woman.

The most galling thing about the whole sorry story was that Eve had, in reality, been hired to prove there was no book, put David Morrow out of contract, and clear the field for Juliette Michel. Worse, if Eve, in her quest for the manuscript, found more damaging scandal about Morrow, then all the better. What tormented Eve was that she had been a willing pawn in this toxic game of chess. Was her price as low as a train trip to south-west France? It seemed it was.

Simmering with self-loathing, Eve considered, as objectively as she could, Juliette's place in the game. Was she another pawn, a grieving, angry daughter simply being manipulated by Josephine Levine? If so, she had been an easy target, given the strength of her grievance against Morrow, with the agent pouring petrol onto a fire laid by Isabelle, Juliette's mother. Eve felt a twinge of compassion for the bereaved daughter, so bitter, such a good actress, hoping to assuage her demons by revenge, but swiftly tempered it with wariness. Was she so sure that Levine was the one driving this? Perhaps Juliette had sought out Josephine, a sweet vengeance to turn Morrow's agent against him. More to the point, why was Juliette pursuing Phoebe? How did she even know about Phoebe unless (and the thought came unbidden to Eve's mind again) she had been at Dudley College on that first night of March, St David's Day? Eve pulled back from imagining Juliette spying on her father that night, but nevertheless, her quest for dirt through the pursuit of Phoebe was not a pretty sight.

How could Eve find out more about the length and nature of the collaboration, the conspiracy, between Levine and Michel? There must be a way. She crunched through some more miles, envying, as she always did, those lucky enough to live in one of the small farmhouses scattered along the Ridgeway and its lateral valleys, buildings that seemed remote from Swindon or Wantage or Didcot, remote in time itself. Eve needed to stop – both walking and thinking. She found a log and sat down, bringing out her flask of coffee and slab of fruit cake.

Sitting, gazing out over the Thames Valley, on this most ancient of routes, Eve knew that she was obsessing over the two women primarily because she was attempting to salvage her own pride. *The Daughter's Tale* didn't have anything to do with Morrow's life and death, only his reputation. Michael wanted nothing to do with it, and Phoebe needed to be kept out of it. Literally. She must not appear in Juliette's book. Otherwise, it didn't matter.

That clear, Eve returned to the easy task of feeling sorry for herself for being played for a fool. Her only consolation was a healthy bank balance, first-hand knowledge of some particular lovely train lines in the Occitanie and the bottle from that horse-powered estate. And the knowledge that industry veteran Jonathan Peck had been equally duped. Unless Jon was playing a very long game, and she had missed something very early on, the man had been as gullible as she. More walking was needed. Eve's legs were stiffening up. She packed away her flask, trying to focus on the budding trees and the brilliant colours of the occasional wildflower.

But, as Eve marched on, her mind still churning, she remained oblivious to the landscape stretching out beyond her Ridgeway path. She even missed her usual right turn, and unwittingly added another couple of miles to what was already going to be a long walk. Cursing her stupidity, she focused on her map and on simply getting some distance behind her. The ache in her legs and her hunger brought her back to the present. In a small stretch of woodland, she perched on a fallen tree, took out her bread and cheese and apple and had a moment's peace. Physical exhaustion had its upsides.

The final stretch was flat, along the Thames, thank goodness. So far, touch wood, the floods of recent years had not materialised, and the going, though muddy, was not impassable. Calmer of mind, Eve also had a new sense of determination. The prospect of *An English Hero* had disappeared: so too should *The Daughter's Tale*. Eve would wipe the smirk off Josephine's face. She would stop Juliette's hate-filled, punitive memoir. Eve consoled, or deluded, herself with the thought that she would be doing this for others, for the two people caught in the crossfire. If Juliette exposed who was with her father that first night of March, what he was trying to do to her, then Morrow's death would become a salacious story of sex and violence, with Phoebe publicly shamed. Perhaps not dragged through the streets and whipped, but there were ways the tabloids and social media could achieve the same result. As for Michael, he believed he had put out one fire, *An English Hero*, and here was another, possibly burning even more fiercely. Michael, who would always and ever turn the other cheek (and needed someone to strike for him) and Phoebe, who would be collateral damage, at least if Juliette got hold of her.

The fifteen minutes she spent navigating the people and cars and horses of the village brought home to Eve just how tired she was. She could put one foot in front of the other, but she couldn't deal with humans right now. A horsebox rattled by her; a four-by-four swept close – too close; a toddler threw a tantrum on the pavement ahead. And then her phone went crazy. She had been without a signal since the morning. Only one was urgent and confirmed her new purpose. *Can you get here tomorrow afternoon?* She could. Eve immediately booked her train tickets to Sheffield for the next day, entirely unsure that she could claim the money back from anyone.

Back at the house, Milos was deep into Thursday night food preparation, no matter that Thursday night was twenty-four hours away. Eve knew better than to ask him what he was making but cast a quick glance at a bowl of gelatinous gloop on the side and was faintly, and selfishly, concerned that, for once, her gourmet night would be a disaster. She toyed with the idea of dropping a hint about Ayoub ('might be good to get another perspective on your cooking?') but kept quiet. It wasn't just cowardice. Eve recognised, with a heavy heart, that however attractive Ayoub was, she had neither the time nor the emotional energy to even consider getting to know him better. Whatever Linda thought: 'You'll make the time and have the energy when you meet the right person.'

'Yeah, and how's *that* going to happen?'

Eve spent a thoroughly miserable ten minutes getting ready for bed in which she reviewed the demise of all her long-term relationships, replaying conversations in which, if only she had found the right words, things would have worked out. Bollocks to that. Every time she'd tried to talk things through, because 'talking helps', it had still gone wrong. Maybe she should try falling in love with an emotionally available, articulate, generous man next time. With one part of her brain, Eve recognised that she was at the end of her tether, as her mum would have said, and she just needed a good night's sleep. Everything would seem better in the morning. She was asleep within minutes, her book falling to the floor beside her bed, page unmarked.

Two hours later, she was awake. The cast in the Morrow drama cycled through her mind. It had taken till now for her to realise that her hard-won determination to stop *The Daughter's Tale*, admirably focused though it was, did not remotely contribute to her actual goal: understanding the events that had led to David Morrow's death. She had strayed far from her task of skeleton-building. She tried breathing exercises; she tried reading her book again; she made herself a herbal tea. She took out her notebook, still in her rucksack, and stared at the picture of Philip Sidney. Flipped the book to Mary. And gave in.

XIV

There was to be no book, but there was most surely something wrong. Michael's sense was now her own. The books, *An English Hero* and *The Daughter's Tale*, were merely symptoms of a greater sickness, signs pointing towards a greater injustice. For the next three hours, Eve allowed her mind – and her pen – to range over the many encounters of the last three weeks, while adding detail after detail to her timeline. She was now on a quest for the body and soul, the emotions, which would breathe life into the bare skeleton. So much harder, so much less straightforward. And yet she knew that to find the truth of that night in Dudley College meant fully understanding everything that had gone before.

She reflected first on the funeral footage. She felt inexpressibly sad that David Morrow appeared to be a man unmourned, except perhaps by Phoebe (and there could be straightforward financial reason for that) and his GP friend, Nick Goode. Should she add Michael to that list? Michael was grieving, yes, and had a sense of duty and loyalty to his father in his quest to find out the reason for his death, but he was grieving the loss of the idea of a father, the death of a soul, not the absence of David Morrow, a man who had belittled and ignored him.

Eve felt an actual shiver of repulsion when she surveyed the number of people for whom Morrow's passing was convenient, perhaps even a reprieve. For them, his death inspired if not the words good riddance then a private sigh of relief.

Who would have breathed the profoundest sigh? Dame Professor Rachita Solanki was an obvious contender. With Morrow out of the way, she could press on with her negotiations with generous benefactors, Ademola Quad would become a reality, the college's finances would be secure. Yes, Morrow's tawdry book would still come out posthumously, or so Solanki would have believed, but *An English Hero* would sink without trace. In any case, thought Eve, the Master of Dudley was a seasoned political operator and if Morrow and his work needed discrediting then she could wheel out Phoebe, weaponising her knowledge of the young woman's presence on the night of Morrow's death.

Closer to home, Elizabeth Morrow was not shedding any tears for her husband. Eve thought of John Milton's descriptions of unhappy marriage, seventeenth-century style: deadly enemies locked in a cage. It seemed apt for the twenty-first century, with husband and wife trapped by successive lockdowns. Eve knew how hard it was to assess any relationship from the outside, but there had been hints from all sides about the couple's problems. Eve had no doubt that, in this case, smoke meant fire but was uncertain what kind of fire she was looking at. Was Elizabeth having an affair with Charles? Was David a physically abusive husband – and father?

Yes, there was Michael to consider, who, by all accounts (although not Eve's), hated his father. Christmas tended to test families to destruction at the best of times, but Juliette's presence at Sarsens would have added salt to an already gaping wound. And if Michael was in the frame, then so too was Raphael. She could imagine Rapha saying, with an appeasing smile, 'Things happen for a reason.' David Morrow's death had, without doubt, freed his family from decades of unkindness, bullying, perhaps abuse, although now Eve checked herself. She had no evidence of the latter. Then again, abuse took many different forms and could be very well hidden.

Gazing at her notes, Eve baulked at what she saw there. She found it impossible to imagine Michael or Raphael expressing conscious relief at David Morrow's death, even if, somewhere, deep down, it might eventually be welcomed as a blessing in disguise. But with Elizabeth Morrow? Perhaps.

Eve heard the distant chimes of midnight, some college chapel a mile away, and wondered why she never noticed them before. Probably because she was asleep by ten most nights. When had she become so boring? Tonight, though, rest was out of the question.

She turned a new page, still seeking answers to the question: who wanted Morrow dead? Writing *Josephine Levine?* was a far more comfortable process than examining the dead man's dysfunctional family. It was not rocket science to conclude that her author's death would have been if not welcome then convenient for the agent, saving her the trouble of having to wait for him finally to default and for his publishers to get tired of him. Toby Milton had hinted as much. The speed with which Levine had then moved suggested a woman who felt not a single pang of grief for her author. With Morrow dead, her priority had been to establish (through foul rather than fair means – Eve grimaced again at her own gullibility) that *An English Hero* did not exist. Once that was proved, thanks to Eve, Josephine had no further professional loyalty towards the man and could move on to his daughter. Morrow's death was more than opportune: it was a gift to the Levine Agency.

On to the next page: *Juliette.* Eve's pen, which had flowed easily for the last ten minutes, now halted. As she had been throughout when it came to Morrow's daughter, she found herself conflicted. Why did she not have more sympathy for her? Juliette had been through hell and back in the months leading up to, and after, her beloved mother's death. Then, while still grieving Isabelle, she lost the father whom she had only just met and with whom she appeared to have a close, warm relationship. It was a double blow. No matter that, in reality, Juliette hated David Morrow. It may be that her hatred was twinned, complicatedly, with love. Her emotional involvement with the man was certainly not straightforward.

Eve forced herself to ask the same questions of Juliette that she had been asking of all the protagonists. Was his death a problem solved? Did she feel relief? It could well be that Juliette felt that Morrow's death cleared her way towards the book she wanted to write, or that Josephine Levine had persuaded her she wanted to write. If Levine's goal was to make money out of Morrow and she knew she could make more out of him dead, then Juliette Michel's motive was even more stark: revenge. With Morrow dead, his daughter could and would dance on his grave and be well paid for doing so.

Her thoughts, her notes, were taking her in only one direction. Eve had tried telling herself that there was nothing to suggest that Morrow's death was anything other than it seemed: a heart attack waiting to happen. But she had moved imperceptibly from recognising that Morrow's death was remarkably well-timed for some people, a positive relief for others, to considering... *motives*. The word stared back at her, horrified her. Was Morrow's death not merely convenient but contrived? Had someone conspired if not to kill the man then to hasten his end? Eve paused on *conspired*. For a moment, she had a glimpse of a process that had been a long time in the making: someone, cool, calm and calculated finding a way to make sure the problem of David Morrow disappeared.

There was no going back now. Understanding what she needed to do, what she needed to find out, allowed Eve, at last, to sleep. A few hours later, she dragged herself to the station, scribbling a note for Milos to the effect that she was not sure when she'd be back. She was once again grateful, rather than regretful, that she was accountable to no-one, that there was no-one to worry about her, or who needed to be thought of before she packed her bag and headed for the door. She knew only too well how circumscribed the lives of most women of her age and class were: young or teenage children, aging parents, needy spouses, demanding careers. Other than Rosa, Eve had no-one and that was fine. Except her own mother, of course, but she didn't count. 'You are not your mother's keeper,' they had told her in the support group. Yeah. No guilt. None at all. Eve did, however, feel a twinge of guilt about ignoring the arrangements for the memorial service. But the Master and Dudley College could wait. Phoebe was not only the eye of the storm but, Eve hoped, the key to everything, for good and bad.

Eve had two goals in her journey to Sheffield. One was to reassure Phoebe and convince her that Eve had not betrayed her confidence. The other was to have a long-overdue full and frank discussion of what had really happened at Dudley College on the evening of the first day of March.

But before that, she had a three-or-so-hour train ride to continue the work she had begun in the middle of the night. This time, though, instead of shying away from the word, she would look at the evidence, calmly, collectedly. It helped that it wasn't the witching hour. Eve went back over her notes on five people. She was looking for inconsistencies, mis-directions, lies. She set to work as her train pulled out of Oxford.

First, the Master of Dudley. Solanki had stated, categorically, that Morrow was trying to 'fuck' his research assistant, but this did not tally with Phoebe's account of the evening. If it was a lie (and the best lies are the ones with a grain of truth in them, and Solanki certainly believed Morrow was a sexual predator), then it was part of the Master's long game. How far would Solanki go to neutralise the threat of *An English Hero* and perhaps, Eve could not resist adding, its troublesome author? An unexceptional passing, just another dead white man, and the way would be clear for the Nangadef Foundation, the cash injection. Solanki's apparent support of Eve's attempts to find the manuscript were no doubt simply part of a damage limitation project when she believed Morrow's book existed. She had got Eve on side, a safe, feminist, left-leaning pair of hands who might somehow turn *An English Hero* into something that would work to enhance the college's reputation. Morrow himself would be forgotten. And, if that didn't work, Solanki would weaponise Phoebe. The man, if not his work, would be discredited. Again, feminist scholar Dr Brook could be relied on to sympathise with Phoebe and thus deliver on Solanki's agenda.

And now, there was no Morrow and, it turned out, no book. No doubt breathing a huge sigh of relief (one less thing to manage), Solanki had moved swiftly to use Eve again, this time to arrange the memorial service. Eve would provide a final coat of whitewash over Morrow's reputation, and then the college could move on to pastures, and donors, new.

What would Solanki have done to stop Morrow's book? To stop him preying on vulnerable research assistants? Eve felt the Master was quite capable of rationalising any action, whether in the name of protecting the college's reputation or the virtue of young women.

She began casting a highly critical eye over her conversations with Rachita. Was her account of the Morrow-led coup correct? Eve had not bothered to check in with the Oxford gossips about this but made a note to do so. Given how broken

Morrow had been by the previous winter, the rarity of his appearances in college, Eve wondered just how instrumental he could have been. More importantly, she sensed that she had not been given the full, or indeed the accurate, story of Phoebe's arrival on the Master's doorstep after Morrow's death. It was just too neat and, from the little she knew of Phoebe, didn't ring true. Keeping quiet about Phoebe (in the short term anyway) was step one and made sense: no scandal at Dud's and Solanki could position herself, to Eve at least, as an older woman caring for a younger. But had other aspects of Morrow's death been quietly hidden?

Cover-ups and damage limitation were one thing. But surely no-one in their right mind would have removed Morrow simply to make sure that *An English Hero* wasn't published or because he was blocking investment into their college? And if that had driven Solanki, then it had backfired on her. Morrow's death had created the conditions for another book, even more toxic, to appear. Solanki would be kicking herself. She need never have worried about *An English Hero*. If that had been her motive, then Morrow's death was in vain.

Eve was suddenly anxious. Solanki's mantra, oft invoked when mentoring women and POC who sought positions of power, was 'control what you can control'. Dame Professor Rachita Solanki was most definitely not in control now that Josephine Levine's plan B had dropped. Those generous donors would evaporate under the blast of Juliette Michel's exposé. Faced with the prospect of a publication even more damaging to the college's reputation than *An English Hero*, would Solanki find some way to go after Juliette, to try to stop *The Daughter's Tale*? If there was even a chance of that, Eve had a duty to warn Juliette.

'What the hell are you doing, Eve Brook?' Eve spoke firmly to herself. It had been only too easy to build a case against

Solanki, fuelled by her own increasing hostility towards the woman. It was a fiction, created by a mind poisoned by neurotic suspicion. Eve's mind.

Well, if she was going to go down this path, she should do it properly. Eve forced herself to review her conversations with Michael Morrow with the same degree of scepticism. In all fairness, everything she thought about Rachita Solanki applied to him as well, with the exception of the college finances but with the addition of decades of paternal bullying and humiliation. Did she really know how far Michael would have gone to stop 'the hate' his author father peddled? After all, he, like Solanki, did not know the book was a chimaera until after Morrow's death. And now, he too might be spurred to further action by the prospect of *The Daughter's Tale*.

Worse still, there were simpler, more primitive, motives in play when it came to Michael. And Eve knew that when it came down to it, most of the bad things in the world had very basic roots. Michael had witnessed, at first hand, decades of, at best, estrangement, at worst, mental or physical cruelty. OK, Eve had no evidence that Morrow had ever been violent, but abuse can, and does, take subtler forms. She read back over her notes, wishing she had paid more attention to the silences as well as what had been said.

She dimly recalled something that Rapha had said, almost in passing. He'd picked Michael up from York, that was it. At 2am. Where had Michael been on the first of March, Shrove Tuesday? He had certainly not volunteered the information but instead turned her attention to the video of his father's funeral.

The desire to protect his mother, free his mother, might run very strong in Michael, overruling his religious beliefs. Or perhaps he had convinced himself that those beliefs justified action? Eve educated herself, quickly, about the Ash Wednesday service that Michael would have led. It was hard to imagine him speaking the words of the collect ('almighty and everlasting God, who hatest nothing that thou hast made, and dost forgive the sins of all them that are penitent: create and make in us new and contrite hearts, that we worthily lamenting our sins, and acknowledging our wretchedness, may obtain of thee, the God of all mercy, perfect remission and forgiveness…') having sinned against his earthly father, but it was possible. Each day of Lent he would repeat these words, lamenting his sin, hoping for forgiveness.

His sense that there was 'something wrong' could be, paradoxically, an almost-masochistic attempt to draw Eve in, to call her to moral arms, when Michael himself had so utterly lost his way. Eve reluctantly acknowledged that the previous winter would have tested the man in new ways. Had the arrival of Juliette, her displacement of him in his father's affections, the loss of his childhood bedroom, for goodness' sake, finally unhinged him?

'No,' she said aloud, startling the young couple sitting opposite her on the train. She smiled, apologised, and bent over her notebook once more. *They'll think I'm mad. Maybe I am*, she thought. But she was not mad. And part of her not-madness included her faith in Michael. Eve knew that he was a man of strong beliefs. She was sure there were sons walking the streets of England who could convince themselves they were doing the world a favour by removing their troublesome fathers from their earthly existence, even without the added bonus of preventing that father from writing a hate-filled book. But to see Michael in this role? It was absurd. This son, despite everything, did not hate his father. Michael had shown kindness to Phoebe when he had not needed to do so. Michael did have faith. And Michael was the person who wanted to know how David Morrow died, and why he died alone, who sensed there was something wrong.

Nevertheless, she checked her notes one more time, testing Michael's statements against others, sifting what she knew for sure from what she had been told. He had shared nothing of his life after his departure from Sarsens in the new year. And if Rapha had indeed collected him from York station at two in the morning, could Michael have been in Oxford on the evening of Shrove Tuesday? At last something that she could do, and do well. Eve almost enjoyed dissecting the train timetables, proving that Michael could not possibly have been at Dudley College immediately after Phoebe left Morrow lying in his bed and still have made it to York. He could well have been on the last train from London, the 23:00, due into York at 01:30, and presumably delayed that evening. But he would have struggled to get to King's Cross from Oxford in time to catch the train in the first place. Eve permitted herself a wry smile. At last she was living up to a detective role model: Inspector French, the creation of Freeman Wills Crofts, an extremely dull but extremely effective policeman with an obsession with trains and timetables. And alibis. If Eve was truly now a detective, she would question her findings. Was Rapha telling the truth about the York pick-up? Was it indeed possible for Michael to get almost home by another form of public transport from Oxford? Come to think of it, did she know for sure that Michael could not drive? But these questions could wait. She turned to lower-hanging fruit.

It was disconcertingly easy to find the fault lines with Juliette and Josephine. There were so many lies she didn't know where to start – or end. Eve was pretty sure that Josephine had sent the message she glimpsed in France, and that she had been in touch, somehow, with Juliette for months. She was also sure she'd had more contact with David Morrow than she had let on. How did she know he was looking better in January, shaven, more positive? As for all that talk about global interest in *An English Hero*, Eve was disgusted with herself for believing it. Liars, both of them. But lying was not in itself a crime.

That made four. One more to go. And Eve knew that statistics, damn statistics, were pointing her towards the fifth: Elizabeth Morrow. The most common relationship between victim and attacker, where there is a relationship, is a current or former partner. And whilst domestic violence was more usually the prerogative of men, women were sometimes driven to it by their husband's behaviour if not their own demons. Mrs Morrow should be top of the list. It was plausible, inevitable, the stuff of life, the data-driven reality. Eve felt rather sick: she didn't want too much reality. She didn't want to find out what the closed-off woman she had met at Little Frogford might have done, might have been driven to.

So, maybe five was not enough. Eve ran through her notes on the other people she had met over the past weeks. Raphael as the angel of vengeance, pushed to it by Morrow's emotional cruelty towards Michael? Loyal, lovely, loving Raphael taking matters into his own hands. It would be ironic, tragically so, if Michael's quest for truth ended up pointing the finger at his own husband. How about Charles Mallam, committing a *crime passionell*, spurred by his not-so-secret love for Elizabeth Morrow? Indeed, Eve had no idea if there was a Mrs Mallam somewhere, his attic maybe? Or Toby Milton, killing off his authors when they disappointed him? Eve smiled to herself. This was getting silly. But then her smile faded. Phoebe.

Phoebe who was there that night. Phoebe whose very name was false. Phoebe who told one story to the Master of Dudley (if Rachita Solanki was to be believed) and another to Eve about what happened on St David's Day in unsaintly David Morrow's rooms. Phoebe who, more than anyone, had motive and opportunity. Phoebe, whom Eve was meeting in less than an hour.

XV

Eve went back over Phoebe's account of her last moments with Morrow. It looked like, it sounded like, a classic case of a heart attack precipitated perhaps by taking some form of tablet for erectile dysfunction. The Solanki-driven cover-up, if there had been a cover-up, could be justified on the grounds of protecting the college from adverse publicity rather than perverting the course of justice. The Master would no doubt argue that Morrow brought his death upon on himself *morally* and that nobody's interests would be served if a very young woman was thrown to the tabloid wolves. The Master of Dudley's strategies belonged in the pages of a murder mystery. The mess that was Phoebe belonged in real life.

Paradoxically, contemplating that mess brought clarity. If it wasn't Phoebe who tipped Morrow over the edge, then something else, someone else, did. There was just time for Eve to do some research. By the time the train drew into Sheffield, she knew more about erectile dysfunction and little blue pills than she had ever wanted to know. She didn't know whether to be relieved or depressed to find that men are more likely to have heart attacks whilst sitting on the toilet rather than during sexual activity. Not only that, but Viagra was a relatively safe drug. OK, it didn't mix well with alcohol, which still might be the simple explanation of Morrow's collapse after a Formal Hall, a recipe for binge drinking if ever there was one. And if Morrow had an existing heart problem or was being treated for high blood pressure, he shouldn't have taken ED medication but presumably whoever prescribed the pills for him would have checked that out. Then again, Eve discovered that it was a simple matter to bypass medical officialdom and simply order your little blue pills online from the hundreds of websites offering men renewed potency.

Her reading was not in vain, however. The Viagra, if that's what Morrow took, shouldn't have gone so wrong, so quickly. Even if the drug had exacerbated the effect of any yet-to-be-discovered blood pressure medication, then he should only have become dizzy or, at worst, fainted. It was just possible that this is what Phoebe witnessed, but even so, Morrow would have come round. He should have come round. Eve was glad to have something tangible and, she hoped, consoling to take into what was not going to be an easy meeting.

Phoebe had suggested the same coffee shop. At least this time Eve had the presence of mind to bring a flask with her and had replenished her caffeine levels just past Derby. She had also had the presence of mind to grab a bag of Welsh cakes at Oxford station, in theory for her journey home but in reality to demolish as she completed her medical researches on the train's grumbling approach to Sheffield. Fuelled by sugar and carbs, Eve felt full of confidence and positively continental as her tram rattled its way up to Hillsborough. She still managed to get lost in her attempt to find a way through to the coffee shop. Head down in her map app, she found her way blocked, such was the density of adults with buggies, some double with sleepy infants, others dragging recalcitrant toddlers or attempting to stop a small child careering into the busy road on their mini-tricycle, still more standing in clusters, talking. The occasional dog made the going even harder. Eve had hit chucking out time at this council nursery, proudly proclaiming the availability of thirty hours of free childcare and a rating of 'good'.

Eve broke free of the crowd but not before having spotted Phoebe on the other side of the road in conversation with another woman. A child of maybe three or four tugged at her arm. Eve kept walking, just five minutes or so to the coffee shop. It was as quiet as the time before. A couple of minutes later, Phoebe walked in, alone.

The fear Eve had heard in her voice on the phone had gone, to be replaced by a more familiar moody feistiness. Eve ordered coffee and waited for Phoebe to choose her battle.

'This French woman. She's offering me money – for an "interview". "Memories of David Morrow". I thought it might be a trap, or something. You know, that she knew. But she can't know. Only you know. And the head of the college.'

Eve remained silent. Phoebe would do this her own way.

'I talked with my friend last night. And he said I should tell you. Dunno why he thinks you're on my side, but. That night,' (Phoebe almost shuddered), 'I wasn't thinking straight. I did take something from the room, but I don't even know why I did it. DM's diary – you know, one of those twatty little "Oxford Blue" university ones. I found it in my bag when I got home. I had a look at it but there's nowt in there – I mean, it was only February, and he wasn't great for that kind of thing anyway. Mainly initials and times.' She paused. 'I'm in there. *P: 7.*'

Eve guessed what Phoebe's next question would be: 'What's it worth? To the London people?'

Eve chose her words with care. 'I am not a legal expert, but I believe that the diary represents part of David Morrow's goods and chattels and therefore is now the property of whomsoever he bequeathed them to.' She was sounding like a bloody lawyer. 'I suppose if you can prove that David Morrow *gave* the diary to you, then, maybe...' Eve trailed off. She had no idea, in fact, of the legal situation. 'But if you try to sell it – to anyone – you may have to explain why you have the diary – and, as I say, I'm not even sure it's yours to sell.'

Phoebe was thinking, and hard. Eve sipped her coffee (it was as inadequate as last time, but it gave her something to do) and waited.

'OK. You win.'

That hurt. Eve didn't want to win. She sensed she wasn't getting the full story from Phoebe, even now, but she also understood that telling that story was not easy. Particularly to a stranger obsessed for her own reasons with asking questions about your involvement with a book written by a man you last saw dying.

'I'll go and get it. You can deal with it. I'll text you.'

She gathered up her bag, placed her trademark beret on her now peroxide-blonde hair, and left. Still no thank you for the coffee.

Eve wished Phoebe had given some kind of idea of the time involved. Wished she'd had the presence of mind to ask, but also acknowledged that there was a small powerplay going on. Eve would have to wait. She checked the train times back to Oxford. She had time. Especially now that she was a tram expert.

3.30pm accompanied a Google Maps destination.

Eve set out on foot. It was a short distance as the crow flies, but Eve was already wary of Sheffield's hills and gennels. Now she had a new problem, which was deciding on the correct front door. None of the numbers made sense, and her phone seemed to be directing her to a house that looked unlived in.

As she plucked up the courage to knock on the door that she hoped was correct, a woman of about her own age, wearing the baggy overalls and lanyard of a care worker, burst out of an alleyway, looked Eve up and down, and said, cheerily, 'Hello, love – you'll be here to see Colleen. I'm just off, I work four 'til twelve today, but head off round the back – you'll find her in the kitchen with Gracie.'

Another piece of the jigsaw slotted into place. But as Eve emerged from the alleyway to which she'd been pointed, and which had brought her out at the back of the terrace, another dilemma appeared. Left or right? There were houses like this in Oxford; in fact, she lived in one; terraced cottages, two-up, two-down (or, in Eve's case, one-up, one-down in its original form), no front garden, inside bathrooms added fifty or more years after their building. But this business of back-to-back terraces, with a group of houses sharing the access behind, this was new. She listened carefully. Caught the sound of a young voice telling someone all about her day at nursery. Telling her mother, Colleen. Phoebe. Who looked so young, in her parents' house, fixing her daughter's tea, as Eve pushed open the back door.

Eve's first words were, 'Can I help?'

'Yeah, just listen to Gracie for a moment while I do this – normally Mum leaves us our tea, but she had to get into work early tonight for some… dumb… staff meeting or something.' Phoebe (Eve could not think of her as Colleen, yet) had a stronger word than 'dumb' in mind when she started the sentence, and Eve was reminded of their phone call last night.

Eve bent down to say hello to the child that, from a distance, outside the nursery, she had assumed to be a boy. She felt a rare moment of hope for the next generation and their refusal to conform to the gender stereotyping that had deemed her a 'tomboy' for having short hair and wearing dungarees back when she was Evie. Gracie, wearing a T-shirt which announced the virtues of Henderson's Relish, devoured her fish fingers, chips and peas, demolished a yogurt, and was allowed to go and watch a programme in the other room. Phoebe returned, just another tired young woman at the end of the day but with another couple of hours until she could reasonably start the bed-time routine.

Eve was back twenty years in a flash, and not just because she heard the words 'oh the indignity'. *Thomas and Friends* was obviously still going strong. She could not stop herself.

Gesturing towards the empty plate that needed clearing, the toys that needed tidying, the sound of the TV in the other room: 'Twenty years ago, this was me!' As she said it, she realised she didn't know how old Phoebe was. Today she seemed younger than ever.

Phoebe gave her a weary look, but then a rueful smile: 'You love 'em, but… it's reyt knackering.'

'Come on, let me help.'

The two women tidied the kitchen together, in companionable silence, keeping an ear out for Gracie in the other room.

'We've got about fifteen minutes – I'll go and get the diary.'

Eve guessed there would be two bedrooms upstairs, which meant that Phoebe shared with Gracie. No wonder she had relished her brief time as a sugar baby with her own room in Oxford and not a fish finger in sight.

Phoebe was back in a moment, handing over the small dark-blue diary. Eve thought there were more important things to do than look through it at that precise minute, or even to mention that it was an academic year diary, so there would be four or five months of entries, not just the two.

'Colleen?' she asked, tentatively.

'Yeah, Colleen Walsh. Phoebe's my middle name. *Friends.* Family are Irish Catholic. Explains a lot.'

Eve nodded, unsure of the correct response to this half-ironic statement and only belatedly getting the reference to *Friends*.

'How old is Gracie?'

'She was three in November, so she's nearly three and a half now. She got the thirty-hour place from January, so Mum and Dad could manage looking after her while I… while I… went to Oxford. They don't know. I don't want them to know. About why I went. I told them it was a scholarship for my writing. They were really supportive – they know that I wanted to go to uni, but, with Gracie and all, it was just too much.'

How old are you, Colleen? Twenty-one. Twenty-two soon. The age she was when she had Rosa. But she'd been able to complete her university degree, although she still remembered the sheer weirdness of sitting finals when six months pregnant. She'd been strangely confident, until the loneliness of new motherhood hit her. As if it were a film, she saw her younger self standing on the railway bridge, baby strapped to her chest, killing time, under grey autumn and winter skies, no-one smiling or even nodding acquaintance. Maybe her exhaustion sent a message to those who passed her: 'keep away'. Eve knew that the loneliness was not just hers. New pressures had come for new parents now, especially new mothers. The need to have the time and money to sit in a coffee shop, to pay for baby sensory classes, to sign up for Pilates. There was always some kind of class designed to ensure that shameful baby fat was eliminated quickly.

'I remember I didn't want my figure back; I wanted my mind.' Eve risked saying the last words out loud, conscious that she was now twice Colleen's age and, if anything, less clear these days as to what she wanted. Anyway, she was not Colleen. Who had taken her A-levels at the end of her first trimester. Who had to deal with Covid just as Gracie began toddling. Eve counted her blessings.

135

She returned to the present. 'We haven't got much time,' she said, more to herself than Colleen, 'but have you heard from the French woman again – or did you block her?'

'I fucking well did – nosy bitch. And I don't see how she can find where I live.'

Eve was determined to find out just how Juliette had found Colleen's details in the first place (surely not Rachita Solanki? She remembered that the Master had been scrupulous in making sure that Phoebe, Colleen, contacted Eve rather than the other way around) but thought better of pursuing that while her companion was so unnerved.

'What's bothering you, Colleen?'

'Nowt.'

Eve waited, attempting to exude a kindly authority. She wanted to thank Colleen for the diary, though she secretly thought it was an irrelevance. She wanted to say, 'You can trust me,' but knew it was both corny and possibly untrue.

The seconds ticked by, the comforting sound of Michael Angelis's voice filtering in from the front room.

Eve took a risk. 'Is it the Viagra?'

Colleen's eyes met Eve's for a moment, and there was a barely perceptible nod of her head.

'It might help to tell me exactly what happened. You don't have to do it all at once; I can come back later, when Gracie's in bed.'

As she said the words, Eve realised she'd made a foolish offer. Not only was she uncertain about the trains later that evening, given that it was Good Friday the next day, she also didn't want to miss another Milos meal, gloop or no gloop. Fortunately, Colleen seemed ready to talk.

Much of it was not new to Eve. And yet it was becoming less and less clear what, physiologically, had in fact happened that evening. The only certainties were that Morrow had been drinking heavily, but he did that regularly. Colleen thought he took a tablet but became distressed when she couldn't remember the details of the next few minutes. She herself was 'out of it'. Did Morrow make a move on her? Or did he just stumble into her and she push him away? Every time she ran it through, the picture became less clear. She was pretty sure she helped Morrow to his bed and put a pillow under his head. He was fully dressed. And she knows she headed for the bus station and got on the first coach home. To Sheffield. If her parents were surprised to see her sleeping next to Gracie in the morning, well, that was their problem. She told them she missed the little'un.

Eve collected her thoughts. 'None of this is your fault. David Morrow chose to take Viagra, if that's what he did. He was the one assaulting you—'

Colleen interrupted, 'That's what the Master said when she told me he was dead, but he never ass—'

'OK, if he was trying to have sex with you, and you didn't want to, you had every right to push him away. Your push didn't kill him. And,' (Eve paused, realising the importance of getting through to Colleen), 'it probably wasn't the tablets either.'

A small figure wandered back into the kitchen. They had run out of time.

XVI

Glimpsed from the train windows, the long, soft, late-afternoon shadows on the hills and valleys of the Peak District only made the ugliness of so much that she had heard the more stark. Eve took out the little plastic-covered diary, complete with university crest. The only thing she found of interest were the initials 'NG' on 25th February. So, David Morrow had a meeting, perhaps an appointment, with Nick Goode, the college doctor, the Friday before his death. Eve had already decided that the man had some questions to answer about the state of Morrow's arteries and, although she felt rather squeamish at the thought, the functionality or otherwise of his penis. Now she knew the two men had been in contact, maybe even met.

She had spent too much time focusing on who might have wanted to stop David Morrow. She needed to ask a different question. There were too many people with motives. Too many motives indeed. The real challenge was to find out *how* Morrow had died.

If Eve hoped it would be a simpler task, she was wrong. All she had was more questions. Was it merely coincidence that David Morrow died in his college rooms? Had anyone fixed the precise time of death? Eve thought, guiltily, that she hadn't fully interrogated Michael Morrow's movements on the night of 1st March. She now knew, pretty accurately, the time Phoebe had left the college because she'd been able to catch the 21:39, the first of her three buses home to Sheffield. It was not as late as Eve had thought. She had forgotten that Formal Halls usually began and finished early. Which meant more time for Michael to get from Oxford to London to catch that last fast train. After all, Phoebe, on her three buses, had arrived back in South Yorkshire about the time that Michael had reached North Yorkshire. The questions kept coming. Was it coincidence that the death had occurred in a way that might implicate Phoebe? Eve's suspicions of the Master rose up again. A death at Dudley suited Solanki very well. It was her territory: 'control what you can control'. If she knew about Phoebe, and she would have seen her at the dinner, it simply added piquancy, and maybe not merely piquancy. Ostensibly covering up the sexual impropriety for the sake of the young woman (though keeping her powder dry for when she might need to blow Morrow's reputation out of the water), Solanki could have made sure there was a medical cover-up, not too much investigation of Morrow's collapse. Eve wasn't at all sure about the rules, but they had to exist. When did coroners get involved? She tried to remember something Michael had said about this. Did the Master of Dudley have enough influence to make sure that any inquiry was, how to put it, low key? She would have wanted that even without the added motive: her own involvement. And a suspect, Phoebe, to hand on a plate to the police if ever they got too close. Eve barely noticed changing trains at Birmingham, agonising as to whether the location (Dudley College) or the situation (young female in old male's room) were significant to Morrow's death before realising she was still avoiding the fundamental question: what killed the man, if it wasn't a mistimed little blue pill? She still resisted the far more sinister question: who killed Morrow?

Finally, as the train pulled out of New Street, exhaustion kicked in and her head dropped. Eve drifted into a doze, half alert to station announcements. An inconsistency floated into and out of her mind. What was it? It had been the Master of Dudley who had introduced the idea of Morrow as a sexual predator. Colleen's version of events, and of the man, was very different. Had Solanki exaggerated Morrow's sexual aggression because it fitted her agenda? Eve racked her brains and then smiled. Colleen had said that the Master had told her about Morrow's death. It was not as Solanki had it, that Colleen returned to the college, sought her out as a trusted female confidante. No, the Master had sought out the woman who had come to the Formal Hall. Phoebe had not chosen to speak with the Master. The Master had come to her and broken the news of Morrow's death, encouraged discretion, silence. Solanki had dressed up her naked desire to hush up an unpleasant episode in the clothes of pastoral care for a young woman. There was, of course, a plausible explanation as to why she might do this: her concern for the college's reputation. But the Master had lied.

Eve forced herself awake ('we will shortly be arriving at Oxford, Oxford is the next station stop'), gathered her wits and belongings. Her primary task was to organise a memorial service and she would do so. Her primary duty, however, remained to Michael and to Phoebe: to find the facts about Morrow's lonely death, to satisfy the former and to protect the latter. Her secondary goal, born of her long Ridgeway walk, and inextricably entwined with both task and duty, was to stop *The Daughter's Tale*. Eve, when she was being honest with herself, recognised that she was motivated here by an unholy desire for revenge against the two women who had played her for a fool. But thus far, and no further, did her honesty go. It refused to acknowledge that deep, deep down, barely a whisper, was a far more disturbing desire: to find Morrow's killer.

Eve made her weary way home. As she put her key in the door, it was half-past eight. She had missed another Thursday night meal. Or had she? Milos had left her a note, propped on an exquisitely laid table. Apparently, her meal was waiting for her in the fridge. Eve extricated a bowl, waited the requisite twenty minutes for it to lose its chill (Milos had underlined that instruction), brewed the recommended fragrant, large-leafed tea, and then revelled in tastes she had never thought possible. Milos had gone full Japanese-French fusion. He was a bloody miracle-worker.

Eve had feared another sleepless night, but whether because of Milos's cooking and kindness or the hard-won clarity she had achieved over the last twenty-four hours, she slept soundly. The muted sounds of an Oxford Saturday morning – no, it was quiet because it was Good Friday, Eve reminded herself – filtered through her open loft window as she snuggled deeper into her duvet. She loved spring mornings, especially ones fresh like this, being warm in bed while the world and the birds woke up. She allowed herself the luxury of a few more minutes of benign oblivion, then set to work. She picked up her notebook, turned to a completely clean page (this was a new start, after all – she might even need to get another notebook), and wrote a sensible, sober list of questions to ask Morrow's doctor, the man who was also, she remembered, his executor.

The sooner she spoke with Nick Goode, the better. He was surprisingly easy to find, at least an email address, although Eve was aware that it might not be his personal one. Sipping her first cup of coffee of the day, she rather enjoyed spinning a web of words for the good doctor. She was working on David Morrow's legacy, a deliciously imprecise word, and would really appreciate his advice. Urgently. If possible, this very weekend.

To make it easier, Eve gave him her number. Would Goode see the email? It was a bank holiday, after all, and not even termtime. More importantly, would he bite? Yes, he would. To Eve's surprise, he called back only half an hour later. She summoned all her charm. She almost purred. She would really appreciate his input, his *steering*, on a few matters in connection with Professor Morrow's (this was not the moment for strict accuracy concerning honorifics) memorial service. She was reliant on those who truly *knew* the man. All rather hurried, but would he have time to meet the following evening? The moth flew into the flame, although there was a slight pause during which Eve speculated as to the existence of a wife – or husband; after all, she knew very little of the man – within hearing distance.

'It would be a pleasure. Such a loss. Probably best for us to do this somewhere quiet; you know Oxford is filled with old gossips. Come out to my place and we can talk freely – à deux.'

'Where are you?' Eve asked, knowing full well that if it wasn't on a bus route, it wasn't going to happen – and even if it was, she could probably get there but not back of an evening.

Negotiations continued. He was indeed beyond the reach of public transport, making Eve wonder how on earth he got home after booze-driven college dinners, before remembering he probably also had a flat in Oxford, these kinds of people did, with an eventual agreement that Eve would meet Dr Goode ('call me Nick; I feel I know you already; any friend of DM's is a friend of mine; such a loss') in a wine bar in Oxford.

Goode sorted, Eve turned to the problem of Juliette: getting her off Colleen's case and, if possible, convincing her that her book was a very bad idea. She was briefly diverted by the puzzle as to how Juliette had tracked down Colleen. And then Eve saw it! She had been right. Juliette Michel was at Dudley that night. In fact, contacting Phoebe had been a terrible error on her part, revealing Juliette's presence at the college. This was more like it. Eve could hear Linda's voice – 'you're jumping to conclusions, girl' – and told herself sternly to focus on the task in hand. No more crazy.

A second cup of coffee and she had her plan. She wouldn't contact Michael today – it was, after all, Good Friday, and he had other things on his mind – but she could get in touch with Colleen. By Saturday evening, and preparing for her date with Nick Goode, Eve was energised. Both had signed up to her plan. Wednesday, and Eve would have some answers.

Eve looked in the mirror. She'd spent Saturday morning at the hairdressers and hardly recognised herself. She smiled at the memory of her conversation with Digby, the young man responsible for the transformation. When he had asked her if she had anything special lined up for the evening, she had been able to give an honest answer. She was going out for a drink that very night. With a man. She had sensed his relief. At last Eve was behaving appropriately for a forty-something single woman.

What Digby didn't know is that, all those years ago, probably when he was a toddler, it had been a haircut that had radicalised her. Some eager, young, exquisitely made-up woman had asked Eve, trapped in the hairdresser's chair, how she could help.

'So, what's the problem with your hair?'

Eve wasn't sure there was a problem.

'What don't you like about it?'

'I quite like my hair.' It was true. She did. It was one of her good points back then. These days, it wasn't quite as great as it used to be, but that's the perimenopause for you. Undaunted, the stylist persisted.

'Tell me about your regime.'

Putting aside, firmly, a joke about fascist dictatorships, Eve had admitted to not having a regime. To sometimes blow-drying her hair. If it was cold. The young woman was relentless.

'I see you have a natural wave – maybe we could straighten that?'

'I don't have straighteners.'

'They do just the same amount of harm, or rather good, as hairdryers.'

'But I don't normally...' Eve gave up. Not only did she pay five times as much as most men for a haircut, without even a nasal trim or ear singe thrown in, but she was being asked to present herself as a problem to be solved by an industry intent on creating further 'problems' to ensure she returned in six weeks' time. That afternoon in that salon had made Eve a feminist. She began to see the pressure everywhere. A problem is identified (possibly even created) which wasn't in fact a problem at all, and then women were asked to solve it through their labour, money and a hell of a lot of emotional investment. All three, she vowed, she would spend on other things.

None of this emerged while she made small talk with Digby that Easter Saturday in April. Some things were better left unsaid. And she did look rather nice without the split ends. Eve had dressed carefully for her encounter with Nick Goode. She wanted to achieve a balance between sophisticated intellectual woman and vulnerable unworldly girl who needed the guidance and wisdom of an older man. Well, a bit older than she was. As she left the house, Eve surprised herself by regretting that Milos was at his mother's. She'd have liked him to see her looking pretty damn hot.

XVII

The evening began well. Eve thought it might not be the best strategy to go straight into her list of questions: 'Did your friend suffer from ED?' or, 'Did you or did you not make a full investigation of your friend's lonely death?' To her surprise, the conversation took a literary turn: Nick Goode's choice of poet for his eulogy for his friend. Eve remembered that the doctor had made a rather weak pun alluding to lines of John Donne:

'If ever any beauty I did see,

Which I desired, and got, 'twas but a dream of thee.

And now good morrow to our waking souls…'

Out of respect to DM's militant atheism, Goode had moved swiftly past the 'waking souls' and on to Morrow's appreciation of beauty, his desires and dreams, many fulfilled, others cruelly cut off.

'You left out that problematic "got",' Eve pointed out. 'Not exactly the most tactful verb to use when trying to convince a lover of your loyalty, but I suspect Donne would have applauded you. He was the master of the easy slide from the spiritual to the erotic.'

Goode looked at her with genuine appreciation. Not quite

Lord Peter Wimsey rattling off a sonnet of his own making, but Eve would take it.

'That is high praise from a scholar such as yourself. And I am glad you are one of those academics who can enjoy Donne rather than berating him for his attitudes towards women. Can't take a joke, some people.'

Eve wasn't going to go head-to-head with Nick Goode on feminist interpretations of John Donne, but, by God, she was tempted to do so. Instead, deftly she hoped, the conversation was turned to erectile dysfunction, moving from Donne's poetic celebration of penises standing erect to his successor Aphra Behn's exploration of the disappearance of 'vigour' at the most inopportune moments. From vigour to Viagra was a matter of half a glass of wine.

Eve learnt that Goode most definitely did not prescribe Morrow anything like that. In fact, he warned his friend against the bloody stuff when he came back from America where you can buy anything. His reason then was Morrow's alcohol consumption, which was getting out of control. But Goode also recognised that his friend would probably not heed his advice, so he tried to ensure that Morrow took the appropriate blood pressure medication, dropped heavy hints about his heavy drinking, urged him to cut back on salt and all the rest of it. He was pretty sure that the lisinopril he'd prescribed was compatible with, um, anything else DM might have been taking. He confirmed, as Eve had discovered in her reading, what seemed a lifetime ago, that the worst that should have happened is that Morrow would have fainted.

'No, it wasn't that I was worried about...'

Eve snapped to attention. This was getting interesting. Goode had had a phone consultation with DM on Friday of – what? – was it sixth week? He checked his own university diary, identical to Morrow's. Yes, it had been sixth week. DM had been complaining of debilitating nausea. It must have been bad for him to admit it.

Goode, concerned, had ordered a full blood count. Eve immediately joined some dots. She'd had a sixth sense that Morrow had been energised by his friendship, no, his contract, with Phoebe. Perhaps this extended even to giving a damn about his own health. Which meant that he'd seen a nurse that Friday. Goode became more uncomfortable. He had, almost as an afterthought, thinking of Morrow's kidneys, also requested a U and E: 'Urea and electrolyte – and that's what came back showing elevated "K" levels.'

Eve looked blank.

'High potassium levels can kill you. You can get false readings, and DM's weren't off the scale, but it was a red flag. Any higher and I would have insisted he go to hospital. He needed another blood test and, I am now sure, he needed treatment.' Goode had texted his friend, asking him to call him urgently, get another blood test that day. Eve, who still used calendar dates rather than Oxford term weeks, silently calculated that the bloods had been taken on 25th February (thus the NG in Morrow's diary) and that Goode had left him the message urging a further test on the Monday. That was the day before the man's death. His friend had not called back.

As he talked, Goode's tendency to straighten items on the table, glimpsed at the start of the evening and put down by Eve to some natural anxiety at what might look to him like a date, became more and more obvious.

Eve took time out by pretending she needed to go to the loo. Goode had been remarkably frank with her. She knew now that it was possible that Morrow had medication for ED whether from his time in the States or purchased online, and that his doctor didn't think it was a great idea. But she also knew that even if he had taken a tablet that evening, and even that was uncertain, the likelihood of a fatal heart attack still remained low. It was the elevated potassium levels, his (a quick search on her phone told her) hyperkalaemia, that were the key to Morrow's death. Eve was excitingly close to being able to go back to Colleen and reassure her that an underlying medical condition had killed the man. That even if she had stayed, there was nothing to be done.

Close, but not yet there. Perhaps she was poisoned by suspicion, but Eve still felt that she did not have the whole story. But to go back in and accuse Nick Goode of incompetence at best, malpractice at worst, seemed the height of bad manners. But, hell, Colleen deserved the truth.

She'd try charm first, and if that didn't work, go the direct route. To her delight, Dr Goode ('Nick, please, and shall we have a second bottle?') was easily flattered into explaining to an uninformed, wide-eyed listener what happened next.

'In all these cases, you have to understand, we,' ('we' presumably being a charmed circle of doctors, coroners, and college heads), 'are, thank God, able to exercise our discretion. The rules are there for a reason – for the times when there is something really dodgy going on – but the mistake that youngsters make coming up through the system is to investigate everything. Don't know what they think they are going to find – watched too much *Prime Suspect.*'

'The police were already present when I saw DM that morning.' Nick did, to his credit, look a little shaken by the memory of his friend's corpse. 'It was as clear a case of cardiac arrest as I've seen in my...' (Eve could see him revising down the number of decades he'd been a doctor, desperately walking the line between the 'youngsters' who knew nothing of the world and the old guys who needed Viagra), 'years as a doctor.'

'Of course, I might *suspect* that it was related to his use of sildenafil – Viagra is only a brand name, you know,' (Eve did know, she'd discovered this between Coventry and Birmingham New Street the previous day), 'but I hadn't prescribed him the drug and he knew the risks, such as they were. I had attended on him,' (Goode made quote marks in the air on the word 'attended' because it was, like almost every medical consultation at the time, by phone), 'and I knew about the hyperkalaemia. I still believe, if he'd called me, if he'd had more bloods taken, if he could have got treatment, he'd be alive now.' Again, Goode seemed upset.

He rallied, explaining almost to himself that it had been pure chance that the 'K' levels had been found, since most people don't experience symptoms until is too late and their heart health had already been compromised. Eve asked, tentatively, if the end would have come quickly.

'From what I could tell, poor DM suffered a heart attack in his rooms after the dinner, somehow got himself onto the bed, but then suffered the fatal cardiac arrest. He must have lost consciousness pretty quickly because he didn't call for help, but then again, once behind those medieval walls, the mobile signal is pretty useless.'

Eve shuddered. For a moment she felt a profound uneasiness about Colleen. She could, after all, have phoned 999, not given her name, just said, 'There's a man dying in five OB three or whatever at Dudley College.' But Colleen said she didn't realise how ill Morrow was. And Eve believed her. There was also the small matter of avoiding the witch hunt (or slut shaming) that would have ensued if she had been identified as the caller.

Goode was talking, more to his wine glass than to Eve. She tuned in again.

'Of course, the letter of the law says we have to report to the coroner any death that may be linked to drugs or medication, whether prescribed or illicit. And this is where I exercised common sense, Eve – a quality in short supply these days. There was absolutely no need to embarrass everyone, including his poor widow – Have you met Betty? Such a shame – with talk of Viagra and, though I know he had that rather attractive girl to dinner that night, there was no sign of her or any,' (Dr Goode looked rather embarrassed), 'um, sexual shenanigans. That's why the police didn't really bother to search the room. Nothing to be seen. Which just left the raised potassium levels. I'm guessing his kidneys were compromised by his alcohol intake but…'

Eve filed away the welcome information that the doctor knew nothing of Phoebe's presence in the room at the time of his friend's collapse, suppressed her curiosity about the cursory police investigation, and tuned back into Goode's account.

All this he had shared with the coroner. Goode explained, in rather unpleasant detail, just how difficult it would be to prove the significance of 'one potentially dodgy blood test' to anyone's death. This was because the 'K' readings in a dead body would be elevated anyway, because the cells were breaking down. The two men had put their heads together, agreed that a post-mortem would provide no new information. End of story.

Nick Goode looked positively distressed. Maybe he was thinking about the pressure on his own kidneys. The second bottle was nearly gone, and Eve had hardly touched her glass. She felt moved to reassure him.

'Nick, there was nothing you could have done for DM. He should have followed up on that blood test. He chose not to. And if he did take sildenafil, he knew the risks. You had warned him.'

Where she felt less able to reassure the doctor was on the way in which the death had been hushed up. Again, Nick seemed happy to talk about it and Eve realised, with a sigh, that there had been good grounds for her hunch that quite a lot had been swept under the Oxford carpet. She'd sensed this since her first conversation with the Master of Dudley but thought then she was being over-suspicious of the police's backing off so quickly from the case. Michael Morrow had been right. There had been a cover-up.

It was, however, not quite the cover-up she expected.

In fact, it was hardly worthy of the name. Dr Goode had been obliged by law to refer the death to the coroner but not, as he'd already made clear, on the grounds of possible misuse of prescribed or illicit drugs, merely on the basis of the death being unexplained. As he had already made clear, he could speculate about Morrow's hyperkalaemia as a contributory factor, but there was no decisive evidence. More importantly, for Goode, he had done what he could. It was only to be deeply regretted that, despite his GP's best efforts, Morrow had not taken up the offer of a further consultation and treatment.

Eve was pondering Rachita Solanki's role in all this (surely, she was guilty of suppressing evidence by keeping Phoebe's name out of the frame? What had she said to the police, who clearly did not find anything untoward at the scene of death?) but quickly refocused on Nick Goode, pouring himself another glass of wine, and – yes – inviting her out on a double date.

'Fortunately, it turned out to be a formality. There are some nitpicking coroners, so it was a relief to get Dick – Dick Lestrange – do you know him? He's excellent company – perhaps we could all go out to dinner one evening – he has a thoroughly delightful wife; intelligent, attractive, a career woman like you, but also – if I may be so bold – feminine with it.'

Goode made one final adjustment to the salt and pepper pots, now safely aligned, and relaxed his shoulders.

Eve had got, pretty much, what she had come for. It was time to drop the act.

'So, what you're saying is that the coroner saw no reason to question your MCCD,' (damn, she shouldn't have used the acronym because he'd realise she had done her homework and could test any bullshit against actual legal facts), 'because you – and the Master of Dudley – were sure this was a straightforward heart attack leading to cardiac arrest. Elevated potassium levels may or may not have contributed to the fatal seizure, but that was – and remains – impossible to prove either way. It was also possible that sildenafil might have been a contributing factor, given that Morrow may have been intending to have sex with a young woman that evening, but it was unlikely, given the low risk of that particular drug, and not likely enough to require a post-mortem. You believed at the time, and presumably now, that further investigation of David Morrow's death was unnecessary. A belief shared by the police, Rachita Solanki and, fortunately, by the coroner, your friend Dick Lestrange.'

Nick Goode had drunk the vast majority of the first bottle, and had, single-handedly, almost finished the second, and could be forgiven for looking rather shell-shocked as Eve, who had been a convincing drunk up to this point, offered this ruthlessly sober anatomy of his medical practice.

Eve took pity on him. 'I have good reasons for wanting to know the facts of David Morrow's death, but they do not include causing trouble for you. I am truly sorry that you have lost a friend, and I really did appreciate your eulogy at his funeral. You were the only person there who seemed to mourn him.'

'I miss him.' The three words touched Eve. Yes, the guy opposite her was pompous and he seriously needed to go on an unconscious bias workshop or three, but he seemed genuinely troubled by Morrow's failure to respond to his text: 'If only he had got back to me, he'd be here now, taking the Michael out of me…' Goode said, more to his wine glass than to Eve.

She, aware that the evening needed saving, brought the conversation back to the memorial service, her ostensible reason for their Saturday night out. They spent another half hour talking about the best way to celebrate Morrow's life and work.

'He'd have hated that it's in the chapel, but I suppose it's the college's way of acknowledging him.'

Eve belatedly remembered that, in amongst her long list of statements to be confirmed, she had put a question mark by Morrow's involvement with the 'coup' against Solanki. Nick Goode was as good a chance as any to get the gossip on this.

'No, no, I don't think DM was behind that motion in GB, though I wasn't present in the room. I mean, he didn't exactly see eye-to-eye with Dame Rachita but,' (the GP paused, trying to choose the right words), 'DM enjoyed the battle in the moment, if you see what I mean. He was not really one for organising people. Now, I can tell you who *was* behind that no-confidence motion,' and Nick Goode launched into a scurrilous character assassination of a certain eminent scientist.

It seemed a good moment to make her goodbyes. Eve reached for her rucksack and remembered that tonight was a rare outing for her rather lovely crimson handbag, a gift from Linda. Passing the unfamiliar strap over her head, Eve threw out one last question.

'Hyperkalaemia. What causes it?'

Goode seemed distracted, fumbling with his coat. 'Too much potassium – oh, you mean – um...'

Eve waited. She wasn't quite sure what she did mean.

'It's easier to answer for hypo because anorexics can suffer through malnutrition and need to take high doses. But with hyper, it's not that the person has ingested too much – that's hard to do, though I suppose it's possible – it's more that their kidneys can't get rid of it. Which is why it's a red flag for kidney failure.'

Eve walked back through the late-evening streets, stopping only to get an enormous tray of chips from her favourite kebab van. She needed something to soak up the alcohol and this was preferable to Nick Goode's only half-hearted invitation to go on somewhere for dinner. She had, she felt, declined his double-date suggestion rather harshly. She refused to feel bad. There might be a Mrs Goode for all she knew. She kicked herself for not raising the subject herself, but it was all part of her social myopia or perhaps tunnel vision. She blamed her failure to discover even the most basic facts about people to her lack of a normal sentimental education. She'd had lots of good but not exceptional sex when she was a student, one instance leading to Rosa, and then on occasion in the years since she'd become a parent – although not often enough, she thought. But the courtly dance to establish availability extended only to availability for sex, not for relationships. Anyway, people just lied. Before Eve could spiral into despair, the chips worked their magic. She snuggled down under her duvet, content and sleepy. And heard a text land. Eve could not stop herself looking.

Colleen needed her to know something. DM had something wrong with his kidneys – that's why he said that he would not be a 'problem' for her because, in her words, he couldn't get it up. Eve was just too tired to consider where this new piece of the jigsaw fitted in the puzzle and simply sent back a happy, flushed face. As she drifted off into sleep, she had a sneaking feeling that she might have sent an inappropriate emoji. Rosa had lectured her once on emoji and their sexual implications. At least it wasn't an aubergine.

XVIII

Easter Sunday brought two surprises, the first far from welcome. Linda called Eve, out of the blue, and asked if she could come over. Their friendship was based on the unspoken agreement that they met away from their homes: it was an escape for both, a performance of uncomplicated life. So it had to be something bad for Linda to break the fourth wall. Eve threw on her clothes and cycled as fast as she could to her friend's house, getting lost in the maze of cutely named winding streets that characterised the new-build developments that had proliferated on the edges of Oxford over the last twenty years. As if Curlew Lane and Rosehip Court made up for the fact that this was just another housing estate with minimal infrastructure and neither curlews nor rosehips.

Linda had clearly been crying but now her eyes were dry, her voice flat. She seemed almost ashamed of having called on Eve. It was hard to know what to say.

'Do you need me to look after Brian for a bit so you can have a break?'

Linda wasn't responding. Unsure what to do, Eve simply did nothing. They also serve who only stand and wait. Linda roused herself enough to put on the kettle.

'It's Brian. I can't do it anymore, Eve. I just can't.'

The Easter weekend trip to the Isle of Wight had not brought back long-lost memories; it had not offered the couple a chance to connect. Instead, Linda's husband had become distressed, aggressive, confused. They had been forced to leave the bed and breakfast because he was so difficult. Linda had driven them home terrified that Brian might take off his seat belt, might try to get out of the car, might attack her. They had got back the night before. In his own bed, Brian had become calm and then slept. He was still dozing now. Linda had sat up all night.

'I wanted him to die, Eve. I wished him dead. Brian.'

There. She had said it. Eve took Linda in her arms, almost cradling her. They had never been ones to hug, even before Covid, so now Eve was surprised at how frail her friend was, how tiny, how diminished. Nothing like Rosa, the only other human being Eve had held tenderly in her arms for a very long time.

There was nothing to be said, and yet Eve tried: 'You will get through this. We will get through this. One cup of tea at a time. OK?'

Linda began to sob, a grotesque choking sound.

'You don't need to make any decisions right now. Let's just get through the next few hours, get through tonight, and then tomorrow – let's try to get you some help.'

Eve was acutely aware that she was witnessing a form of grief, compounded as grief so often is, by guilt. Brian was not dead, but he was lost to Linda. She had reached the point where she no longer had hope, a point of no return as final as death itself. It was a lonely, terrifying place and all Eve could do was stay with her. Eve wondered when or if Elizabeth Morrow had reached a similar place and whether, if she had, there was ever any escape.

The day unfolded slowly. Linda wiped her eyes, was kind to Brian, who ate some lunch then sat in his familiar chair, looking out at their patch of garden, silent. Eve stayed quietly in the background. She wasn't even sure Brian realised she was there. Linda spoke only twice, to speak of her loneliness, particularly at the loss of intimacy and then, later, with a kind of venom, at the voices that urged her that it could be worse, that she shouldn't complain, others have it harder. The loudest voice came from within Linda's own head.

As evening drew nearer, Eve texted Rosa, having made the radical decision to order her first ever home delivery meal but needing her daughter's advice and instruction about the whole bewildering process. Or maybe she just needed to have some human contact beyond the slow-moving tragedy unfolding in front of her. Rosa replied: *Busy. 30 mins.*

The time dragged by. Eve checked her phone, again, hoping for Rosa's text, when there was a ring at the door. Brian didn't move. Linda glanced at Eve, a question in her eyes. Words were too much.

'I'll go.' Eve opened the door to Rosa, carrying two enormous pizzas, doughballs, and a bottle of red wine. 'Delivery for Dr Brook,' she announced, handing the cartons to Eve, then disappeared, but not before mouthing 'I love you, Mum'.

Linda put Brian to bed. He seemed content. Perhaps he would sleep away his remaining months, years, decades. Eve opened the wine.

She and Rosa had talked long and often about the implications of being a very small family. For all their differences of opinion about pretty much everything, they both celebrated, wholeheartedly, the idea of 'found family'. Seek out a brother, sister, mother, father if the vagaries of biology have not provided you with such or, as was often the case, when the blood brother is no brother at all. Through this long Sunday,

Eve understood, viscerally, that Linda was part of her found family, although whether an older sister, an aunt, a mother, was unclear. And she recognised that she held a similar place in Linda's life, a younger sister, perhaps even a daughter. As with blood relatives, at least in an ideal world, one paid a high price for closeness. You saw your loved one's hidden wounds exposed; you witnessed them at the desperate times; you heard them say the unsayable; and you accepted them and their pain.

Eve had never used the words 'found family' when talking with Linda but thought she might understand. Brian and Linda had one son, Dan, but he had his life in Australia and, well, he wasn't the communicative type. Covid had not helped.

The red wine, and exhaustion, finally allowed Linda to talk. She was facing the truth that her life, what was left of it, was now shaped to the contours of her husband's illness. She was angry and frightened and ashamed of her anger and fear.

'We can't even go away to the Isle of fucking Wight!'

Eve thought it might be a good sign that Linda was swearing again, but she was clutching at straws. She remembered one of the most chilling lines in Shakespeare, a monstrous mother: 'Anger's my meat. I sup upon myself, and so shall starve with feeding.' Linda was right to be afraid of anger, even when it was the most natural thing in the world.

There were many ways for marriages to die. Eve thought again of David and Elizabeth Morrow. The dying, rather than the death, was so often the hardest part. Those who say love never dies, that it endures beyond the body's death, are right, but only if it existed before that body died. If it dies when the body is alive, it is dead forever. Anger and hate live on. Linda must have read Eve's mind.

'I don't want to hate him. But I do hate the illness.'

It was 10pm when Linda brought out the photo albums. Her wedding day, in gaudy seventies colour. Family holidays with Dan, smiling on his father's shoulders, building sandcastles on English beaches. School photos, and not just of Dan. Linda and Brian had both been teachers. Then on towards the present day. The couple's big trip out to Australia to see their son, ten years ago. They had been going to visit again when they retired but then had come the diagnosis and Covid and now it would not happen. The final photos were of the holidays Brian and Linda had taken in the first flush of their retirement. They'd moved from London to Oxford, had spare cash for the first time in their lives, could travel during the school term. They'd managed two trips, and it was on the second that Linda realised that something was seriously wrong. She looked at a photo of the two of them standing awkwardly by a church somewhere in Italy.

'We asked someone to take it – we didn't know about selfies then.' And Linda wept.

Eve held her friend again. She stroked her hair. 'You are grieving. We don't just grieve the dead. We grieve all our losses. And you have lost this,' pointing to the photograph.

Eve left late, having made Linda a cup of some herbal tea promising sleep.

'Tomorrow is another day. Let's talk then and see if there's any help around. You don't need to do this on your own.' Eve's belief in the NHS and social services to offer help was weak at the best of times, and almost non-existent after two years of Covid, but it had to be worth trying. What mattered is that Linda was coming to accept that she was now Brian's carer. Not his wife, friend, lover. His carer. She had been unwilling to accept it, the label. Now, perhaps, she had surrendered to the reality. The first step to getting help.

Cycling home, Eve's thoughts turned yet again to David and Elizabeth. There must have been a time when the marriage was happy. She wondered about the impact on them both of the miscarriages, the stillbirth. It was the 1980s and though things were hardly great now, back then, it was brutal. Deaths not even acknowledged as deaths. Morrow, Eve guessed, was as disturbed and frightened as his wife, but escaped to Isabelle, his work, other women, slipping further and further out of reach. His drinking began to take hold. His son disappoints him. He turns on Elizabeth, mere absence not enough to assuage his own demons. He becomes volatile, anger bubbling beneath the surface. Even if she were compassionate enough to be aware that her husband's wrath was not directed at her, she is such an easy target. And this goes on for years and years and years. When does rudeness become cruelty, criticism become abuse, absenteeism becomes estrangement, conversation become gaslighting?

Eve caught a glimpse of what Elizabeth felt when her husband got his position in America. Relief. Michael has escaped. She has a year of respite, of peace. A year of depression and loneliness, but it is *her* loneliness and depression. She is just beginning to glimpse a world in which she might draw again when he comes back. Morrow picks up where he left off, but now his anger is directed at the world. He has a platform. If he is at home, they exist in the same space, nothing more. Elizabeth thinks she is coping. Then lockdown.

Eve knew exactly why Elizabeth was on her mind after her long day with Linda. Her friend had reached the point where, for a terrifying moment, she had wished Brian dead. Because then she could move on, properly alone. Did Elizabeth Morrow have a moment like this? Not of anger, but of desperation. The words of an English king came unbidden to Eve's mind: 'Who will rid me of this turbulent priest?' asked Henry II, and four knights, over-hearing, rushed to kill Thomas à Becket. The king was devastated. He had not directed the murder. But he had prompted it. Eve could well imagine Elizabeth Morrow

160

standing in her kitchen asking a similar question: 'Who will rid me of this husband who is no husband?' The question was, did anyone hear her?

'Eve!' It was 11.30pm; she was waiting, leaning forwards on her handlebars, at the traffic lights by Folly Bridge, when she thought she heard her name. She was exhausted, longing for home. She should keep going. But then again, her one-syllable name, lengthened deliciously into two: 'Eva!' There was only one person who said her name that way.

'What are you doing here?' was her first, somewhat ungracious, question.

'I've just flown in. Conference.'

'Oh, great.' Eve really wanted to go home, but Giancarlo was talkative.

'How are you? Do you live near here? I'm in an Airbnb,' (he consulted his phone), 'just over this bridge.' Even Giancarlo must have picked up on Eve's air of exhaustion because he was suddenly kind. 'You look bad.'

Eve made a concession for English not being his first language. He wasn't being rude.

'Is there a problem? Can I help?'

Eve felt her eyes prick with tears, but she answered as cheerfully as she could. 'I've been with a friend all day – helping. I'm just really, really tired.'

'Of course, of course. I am sorry. Go and sleep, *cara*. Tomorrow is another day. I'll give you my number.' Smiling at a memory, and Eve knew exactly what it he was remembering, he took a small pack of notecards from his pocket and wrote out his number in the elegant script they still taught in Italian schools.

XIX

Monday proved that it was indeed going to be hard to get help for Linda, not because it was a bank holiday, and not only because Eve was not a blood relation so could not fill in the online forms on behalf of her friend. So much for found family. No, it was more that Linda herself was resistant, given her very natural fear that things would snowball: Brian would have to go into a care home; she would have to sell her house.

It was almost with relief that Eve returned to her double-sided notebook. It was work. Her work. She could actually make a difference. Get something done. She smiled at herself, well aware that, somehow along the line, her 'work' had moved from paid to unpaid, from task to mission. Unless you counted being hired by the Master to organise the memorial service at Dudley College. No matter. She would continue to seek the truth, for Michael, for Phoebe, for herself. And for David Morrow.

The man's death could, of course, be simply explained by too much alcohol and a sexual misadventure. Many people were keen to see it as just that: his comeuppance. Morrow was a hardened alcoholic and, yes, at some point his body would stop trying to keep him alive. But Eve now knew there probably wasn't a sexual misadventure. The more Phoebe had looked back, the more she was unsure as to whether Morrow even took a tablet, the more adamant she was Morrow may have been reaching out to her rather than hitting on her. Reaching out for help, because he was having a seizure.

The evidence she had collected over the past week had done nothing to allow her to go back to Michael and tell him his concerns were unfounded, that he was just finding it hard, as so many people do, to process a sudden death. She had found something wrong. And she now, after her discussion with Nick Goode, had something concrete to investigate: whether and how David Morrow's potassium levels were intentionally increased. But right now, that would have to wait because – forgotten in the emotional storms of the previous days – Eve had another goal in sight. *The Daughter's Tale* needed to be stopped.

It had been *The Daughter's Tale* that had prompted Eve's calls to Colleen and Michael. They had eagerly embraced her plan. Colleen had duly contacted Juliette Michel, as Phoebe, offering to meet her in York, dangling the prospect of the true story of her relationship with David Morrow. York because it was easy enough for all parties to get to: Colleen from Sheffield, Michael (and Raphael, as necessary chauffeur) driving in from Almthorpe, Juliette heading up on the fast train from London where she was presumably being put up somewhere at the expense of Josephine Levine.

The hope was that by surprising Juliette, en masse, they would have the psychological advantage. Phoebe would meet her in a pub, carefully choosing a big table and a quiet time of day. Minutes into their conversation, Michael and Raphael would join them. And then Eve, still fuelled by her righteous indignation at being fooled by Juliette and Josephine, would walk in and take over. That was the plan.

At first, it went like clockwork. Juliette seemed stunned, looking at the unexpected guests ranged around her.

Without even saying hello, Eve barked out her first question: 'How did you find Phoebe?'

However, if she'd hoped to gain the advantage, she failed. There was a plausible answer. It had been quite easy. Josephine had got in touch with a couple of performance poetry groups in Oxford, saying they were looking to recruit new, young, groundbreaking poets for a series. Phoebe's name was mentioned. How could they reach her? A well-meaning friend had passed on her number.

Plausible, yes, but glossing over the real reason for the contact. When Juliette spoke with Phoebe, she failed to mention she was Morrow's illegitimate daughter, had not spoken at all of poetry. She was simply on a quest for dirt on her father.

Eve's next question – 'What did you see at Dudley College on the night of your father's death, the first of March?' – drew only a blank stare of incomprehension. Eve paused, thrown for a moment, before remembering that placing Juliette at Dudley had always been one of her more extreme scenarios. She let it go, moving on to her (she thought convincing) reconstruction of Juliette's thinking.

'Maybe you discovered what your father was doing online when you stayed at his house in the winter, maybe you told Josephine Levine his dirty little secret. You wanted to expose what, in the eyes of a hypocritical world, would be seen as a sordid transaction, your father spending his literary earnings on a girl young enough to be his daughter. Ten years younger than his actual, flesh-and-blood daughter who had received nothing. Or so you realised after the first shock of finding you were his literary legatee. On paper, you would inherit a healthy sum of money. In reality, your father's change of will was an empty gesture, quintessential David Morrow. And you decided you would make money out of your father in a different way: *The Daughter's Tale*.'

Juliette sat, impassive. This wasn't going quite as well as Eve had hoped. She decided to drop the Poirot impersonation and be herself.

'You know, Juliette, making another young woman feel like shit is not going to make you feel better.'

Another pause. All eyes were on Juliette, who was suddenly, for all her poise and elegance, looking fragile. Juliette, who had been filled to the brim with the bitterness of her mother, who had been forced to care for her as she died, slowly, painfully. Alone. Then Josephine entering, stage left, a commanding presence, a woman of a similar age to Isabelle. Offering an outlet for the daughter's grief, anger, an ally.

'Tell us about Josephine. Please. It's time for the truth, Juliette.'

And so, as the pub emptied of its few patrons and the spring sunshine filtered through the grimy windows – and as Raphael brought everyone a round of drinks and some dirty chips to share – Juliette told her story.

She had, in fact, been stalking (she had to ask for the English word – Phoebe provided it) her birth father ever since her mother's death. Her disgust for him was palpable and had only been confirmed when she became aware of his online activities. Juliette had even created an online identity as a way to see what he was looking for, what he was like. The experience sank Morrow even further in her estimation.

That was clear. She was less clear as to why she contacted him, why she pretended affection. Juliette herself seemed confused but regained her poise as she recounted her early realisation that his precious book was in big trouble.

Juliette paused, assembling her story. For a moment, Eve

felt certain that she was still lying and forced herself to check every little thing revealed. But that would need to be later.

Juliette couldn't remember when Josephine got in touch with her. 'She was a woman with a certain something. She was on my side. She, too, despised David Morrow. And she also knew *An English Hero* was a fiction, a fantasy. It was never going to happen.' Josephine encouraged her to continue to get close to her father, to ingratiate herself, and Juliette found it surprisingly easy. Little Frogford became her temporary home. But every minute there was spent hating Betty, Michael, and herself, as much as her father.

It was Josephine who had come up with the idea of Juliette herself writing a memoir. Josephine who had admired her title and put aside her own. *The Daughter's Tale* it would be, not *Good Morrow*. Josephine who had visited her, discreetly, at Little Frogford to keep her vengeful heart stoked. Josephine who joined the dots about the young research assistant dining with Morrow at the Dudley Formal Hall.

Michael finally spoke. If anything, he looked even more thin than when Eve had last seen him and his usual appalling choice of jumper made him look like a man-child dressed by some well-meaning care-home worker. Eve remembered that when Michael had talked about Juliette back in Almthorpe, it had been with uncharacteristic contempt. But his voice was steady and commanding, and his question was a surprise.

'How old are you, Juliette?'

'I was thirty-two in December. There was no celebration.'

'I was thirty-two in March. There was also no celebration.' (Of course there was not: Morrow's funeral would have swept birthday fun out of the window.) 'I am so sorry, Juliette. My father must have abandoned your mother when she was pregnant. Perhaps my mother gave him an ultimatum. Perhaps he couldn't cope.' Michael was genuinely perplexed by the sheer awfulness, the mess and cruelty of David Morrow's life, that late summer more than thirty years ago.

Juliette was almost whispering. 'David Morrow saw me once. I was a few weeks old. He had come to tell my mother that his future lay with his English family. With you.'

So Josephine's version of events was not correct. Morrow knew full well that Isabelle was pregnant. He had held his daughter.

'My mother believed that he was coming to help her. To be with her. He came to say goodbye.'

Eve looked at Colleen, a silent request for permission to speak on behalf of them both. The younger woman nodded.

'Like Michael, I want to say how sorry I am – not just for what you've just told us. But there are two of us round this table who have been in a similar position as your mother. Ten years later in my case. Nearly thirty years later in Col— in Phoebe's case. Time and place make a huge difference, and neither of us have any idea what it would have been like for your mother in a small town in France in the late eighties, but, we want to say,' (Eve took a deep breath), 'your mother made a choice. She could have taken steps to tell you about your father in a different way. She could even have allowed you, encouraged you, to seek a relationship with him. It happens. But she chose to pass on only her bitterness and anger to you. And she did so when she was dying, during a pandemic.' Eve's voice was becoming shaky. 'You had no-one to share this with. I can't even bear to think how lonely it was, isolated with your mother, watching her die, and hearing about this man who had destroyed her life. It was as if your father took the place of the cancer killing her. And when Josephine appeared, you had an ally at last. David Morrow was a selfish, casually cruel man, oblivious to the needs of others.' Eve looked towards Michael to see how he would cope with this assessment of his father. He appeared to nod. 'But he is now gone. Sitting here, now, is your half-brother, who is a very different man.'

Instead of responding to Eve, Juliette spoke to Phoebe. 'Your name is not Phoebe?'

'No, I'm Colleen. I was just known as Phoebe in Oxford.'

'He bought you online, eh? I wondered if one of his women – girls – had… killed him. I mean manslaughtered him, if he had attacked you, and you fought him.' It was a rare slip in Juliette's impeccable English, a sign that she was at breaking point but there was also – was it envy? That the Sheffield girl had done what Juliette dreamt of. Colleen was looking as if she was going to throw up, but, from some well of courage, she spoke.

'Gi' o'er. I didn't kill him. I didn't hate him. I was, believe it or not, fond of the man. We had a deal. He kept to his side of it. It weren't about sex but I don't expect anyone to believe me. He was lonely. And he talked about you – that you were beautiful and clever and reminded him of your mother.'

'Think about it, Juliette.'

The woman bowed her head in acknowledgement of Eve's words, whether in agreement or submission. Eve had no idea where Juliette's thoughts would take her. She longed to be able to leave the pub, to allow everyone the chance to absorb what had been a brutal conversation. And she longed to push Juliette into some kind of promise, that she would abandon her book, tell Josephine to take a running jump or whatever the metaphor was in French. It was unlikely.

Real life was continuing outside the walls of the pub, and real life included Gracie finishing at nursery in under an hour. Colleen needed to get going. So did Michael, but for other reasons. He looked as broken as his sister, and Eve made eye contact with Raphael, encouraging him to get his husband home as soon as possible. She had been amazed at Michael's journey from hostility to compassion for Juliette, guessing at the hours of penitent prayer the man had offered to his God in the days since Eve had first visited Almthorpe. The dirty fries sat, almost untouched, on the table in front of them.

Eve only had a few more minutes but there was one more thing to share. At the end of the previous week, she had straightforwardly reassured Colleen that there was nothing she could have done for Morrow even if she had stayed at Dudley College that night. Eve had since then done her homework, found out more, spoken with Nick Goode. She was going to complicate the picture once again.

'Before you all go, I have to tell you that I believe that David Morrow's death was not caused, at least directly, by any supposed altercation with Colleen or even by his use of self-prescribed drugs.' Eve wasn't going to go into the details of Viagra and its like, primarily because she was increasingly certain it was irrelevant. 'It was a death waiting to happen because of his dangerously elevated potassium levels.'

She looked at four blank faces.

'Trust me on this. I'm a doctor.' The joke fell flat. Eve pushed on. 'The only question that remains is why was that the case? That is what I need to find out.'

A church bell sounded somewhere nearby. Eve sensed a change, however. It was almost as if they were now a team. Not quite the Famous Five, but something had shifted. Colleen was the first to move. She needed to run to catch her train, but she'd be back in Sheffield with enough time to take over from her dad. It was his week for helping out. Before she left, she looked around the table and said one word: 'Thanks.' No irony. Just gratitude. Eve felt her eyes prickle.

Next Juliette, announcing that she would return to London, set up a meeting with Josephine. She had decided. *The Daughter's Tale* was finished. Josephine was welcome to sell, as literary executor, Morrow's clickbait fragments. There was nothing to stop her – except the wishes of the family. And now the family included Juliette. Eve was truly struggling not to cry by now. She blew her nose loudly.

The two women gone, Michael told Eve that what he really wanted was a proper talk with his mother. Raphael immediately offered to drive him (and Eve if she wanted?) there that very evening. If they set off now in the Skoda, they could be at Little Frogford by seven. Over the last few minutes, Eve's appetite had suddenly returned, and she was making inroads into the chips (still tasty despite being stone cold) but she quickly quashed that idea. She persuaded Michael and Rapha not to rush south that night. There was no actual urgency. No-one else knew about their discussions; surely it would be better to have these conversations when they were all less stressed? She persuaded the couple to head back to Almthorpe, make the necessary arrangements, and meet her at Sarsens later in the week, on Friday afternoon.

Before saying their goodbyes, Eve made a confession to Michael. She didn't do it very well, stumbling over her reasons for checking his alibi for the night of his father's death, cursing herself for even using the word alibi. Rapha looked furious, the second time Eve had unwittingly moved this gentle man to anger. But Michael remained calm.

'Eve, you could have asked. I was in London that evening, speaking with my spiritual director ahead of Lent. He's—'

Eve cut Michael off. 'It doesn't matter anymore.'

Making her way back to the station, something Juliette had said was nagging at her strangely. *An English Hero* was indeed a fiction, a fantasy. It would not happen. And Eve felt sad at the thought. She believed there was a hunger for retellings of history that we think we know, for exploring what it is to be English, to be a hero. More than that, she could imagine a book that brought Mary, Sir Philip's sister, into the frame, not merely as the person responsible for keeping his memory alive, but as a woman in her own right, his literary equal, first completing her brother's work, but then breaking new ground as a writer, *her* ground. Mary had done well as a mother: not only the guy she nodded to on her way into the Bodleian, but his brother too. William and Philip were the men to whom Shakespeare's friends and colleagues dedicated their remarkable *First Folio* of the playwright's works. Mother Mary was not alive to see this, but her passing, in 1621, a full thirty-five years after her brother, was marked by a funeral at St Paul's, echoing her brother's final journey. Eve understood that, even if David Morrow had been in a fit state to complete *An English Hero*, Mary Sidney would have been at best a sideshow to the main attraction, but she felt a genuine sense of loss at the book that might have been. She even allowed herself a moment's idle speculation: could she, should she, be the person to write it? No. That was as much a fantasy as Morrow's *English Hero*.

Eve returned to the present and the evening ahead. She had been a little disingenuous when she refused Rapha's offer of a lift back to Oxfordshire. It was not only that she was horrified at the thought of a four-hour journey in the Skoda. She wanted to get back to Oxford that evening. Eve was well aware that she was rubbish at relationships. But she was quite good at sex.

XX

Giancarlo had proved every bit as enjoyable as Eve remembered. They had met at a conference in Italy, Eve talking about the English poet Aemilia Lanyer's origins in the Veneto, Giancarlo talking about homoerotic blazons in post-Petrarchan poetry. Not everyone's love language, but definitely theirs. Eve had made the foolish error of assuming that because Professore Cantini was into queer theory that he would be gay. He wasn't. He most definitely wasn't. And what was even better was that they shared not only a delighted interest in each other's bodies but a love of ridiculously expensive stationery. The exquisite notecard on which Giancarlo had written his number, with his Visconti fountain pen, was his way of reminding Eve that he had not forgotten. Five years on, and Eve was grateful that this uncomplicated, sensuous man had – briefly – been part of her life once again.

Even a dismaying rail replacement bus service, which made her bike impossible to use, couldn't quite dent Eve's mood on Friday. It deposited Eve at Kingham station, and she contemplated the walk to Little Frogford with gritty stoicism. Only four miles. It would give her time to think properly, honestly, over all the various conversations of the recent weeks.

She would find an idyllic footpath across the fields, gambolling lambs, blossom on the trees, birdsong. By the time she turned into Cozens Lane, she was cursing the emergency engineering works, longing for her trusty bicycle, and bemoaning the absence of decent footpaths, let alone space for a pedestrian, on the pot-holed Oxfordshire roads. Rational thought had proved impossible.

The lane was its usual tranquil self. Charles Mallam's house remained worthy of a piece in one of the lifestyle magazines, such was its glow of tastefully managed history. Sarsens was looking a bit brighter and more cared for, but it might simply have been that spring had brought a burst of colour. How long had it been? Only four weeks.

There was even a rather smart car in the driveway. Eve tried to remember whether Elizabeth could drive. Maybe she'd splashed out on a… Eve had no idea and couldn't be bothered to find out the make and model. But it looked expensive.

The woman herself came to the door, equally transformed. A new haircut was the most obvious change. Short, but far from severe. Elizabeth looked glamorous. Eve tried not to stare. Mrs Morrow looked at her visitor with a slight smile on her face, and silver and sea-glass hanging from her ears, catching the light. Eve thought she saw the work of the same jeweller whose earrings Rachita Solanki favoured.

'Where's your bicycle?' was her first question.

Eve explained about the bus replacement service, trying to make light of her long walk from the station. In return, she received detailed information as to what she should have done (two buses would have brought her to the top of the lane), delivered with such intensity that Eve began to question Mrs Morrow's grip on reality.

And then a shock in the kitchen. The founding director of the Levine Literary Agency was sitting at the kitchen table.

As when they had first met, Josephine barely acknowledged Eve's arrival. There was a mere nod of the head in her direction. Elizabeth Morrow, meanwhile, was behaving even more strangely, staring at Josephine, her face a vacant mask. There was no evidence that she had offered her guest any hospitality, not even a glass of water.

Morrow's widow recovered herself enough to make what were in fact unnecessary introductions. Ms Levine had just arrived, five minutes before Eve sweated up to the front door. In fact, she had thought it was Eve arriving. Eve, who was *expected*. There was a heavy emphasis on the last word. Josephine stepped in. An impromptu visit. She felt she had to come down to see Betty. She knew that once the funeral was over it could be a very lonely period, and she wanted to make sure Betty was bearing up under her loss. It was a good story unless you knew Josephine. Eve suspected she was here to break the news of *The Daughter's Tale*. Perhaps she even hoped to get the bitter wife on board. After all, Josephine was well aware the marriage had not been a happy one.

Josephine was saying how lovely the cottage was. It was her first time here. How funny to think that all these years representing David and she had never come to his home, never really spoken with Betty. She could hardly have been more tone deaf, both to the past and to the tension in the room.

Elizabeth interrupted, her vacancy gone. 'You *have* been here before. I recognise you. I have a good eye for faces. I saw you turning into the lane, walking, in the winter. You hold your head like a ballet dancer. No-one comes to Cozens Lane unless they are visiting us or Charles Mallam. Perhaps you are one of Charles's close friends?'

Eve had, until this point, been racking her brains to find a way to get Josephine out of the house before she could destroy Elizabeth's new-found equilibrium with news of Juliette's book or questions about her husband's health. But now, the game had changed. Eve had not expected this. Josephine was vulnerable. She had been caught in a lie and, Eve smirked inwardly, been accused of being one of Charles Mallam's apparent legion of mistresses. Eve knew what 'close friends' really meant. Time to strike.

Eve decided to lob in a grenade, disguised as a polite query: 'Juliette mentioned to me that you'd met with her in the winter. Was it here, maybe?'

'Juliette?' Josephine raised an eyebrow. 'I don't think it was Juliette. David perhaps. Well, yes, all I meant was that I had not been inside the house. Not had a chance to speak with Betty. And, no, I do not know this "Charles".'

Eve should have guessed that Josephine would not capitulate so easily. She knew (from Juliette) that Josephine had been her ally since the previous autumn. She knew (also from Juliette) that the agent had been to Sarsens at some point, but it was an absolute certainty that she would have kept her visit quiet. Now she was trying to make them think she'd popped down to have a chat with Morrow. In the garden. In December. Unlikely, but.

Two strands of thought became disastrously entangled in Eve's mind at that moment. Or that's how she explained her next steps. The first was really quite sensible, the goal being to prevent Josephine talking to Elizabeth and to get her out of the house. The second was not sensible at all. It was the product of far too many nights and days poring over her notebook, picking up and discarding theories about Morrow's death, and her active dislike of Josephine Levine.

In the space of a second, dislike transformed into suspicion, and then into certainty. It proved far more comfortable to suspect Josephine Levine than people Eve actually liked. And Levine's motive was clear as daylight. With Morrow dead, she would lose her share of the advance on signature, but that was irrelevant since she had been convinced for months, if not years, that he would default. The agent was ruthless enough to cut her losses and see that the future was called Juliette – and that the way to a bestseller would be over the dead body of Morrow. It would certainly save on libel lawyers. Eve's mind raced. She became sure that Josephine's surprise visit to Little Frogford was not to offer belated comfort to a grieving widow. She was here to destroy evidence. Or something.

Eve would later wonder what on earth possessed her. The kindest interpretation was that she was not thinking straight due to hunger: it had been a long time since breakfast, and she'd walked a fair way with the promise of lunch. In a move that could almost, but not quite, be explained by Eve's natural clumsiness, she had knocked Josephine's handbag off the table and, under pretence of salvaging it, managed to open it. To empty it. Items scattered onto the flagstones. It might have been easier simply to ask Josephine if she could search her bag. What had she hoped to find? A bottle marked *poisonous potassium*? A note saying *I killed David Morrow*?

'What do you think you are doing?' The words 'you lunatic' could be heard as clearly as if Josephine had said them out loud. It was a good question with no good answer. Eve attempted an apology, all the while consoling herself with the thought that soon, perhaps even later today, Josephine would receive the news that Juliette was no longer on side. There would be no *Daughter's Tale*.

Moments later, Josephine left, offering an icy goodbye to Mrs Morrow, silence to Eve.

Only as the sound of her engine disappeared did the older woman speak: 'I still have no idea why she came to see me.'

Eve thought she knew very well but kept her counsel. She had offered to bring a simple lunch (bread, cheese, salad, fruit) but Elizabeth had written that she should do no such thing, that it was no trouble for her to cook, and that she looked forward to Eve's visit. It was thirty minutes after Josephine's departure, and the conversation was not going well. There was still no sign of food. Eve's ostensible reason for coming to Little Frogford was to talk with Elizabeth about the college's commemoration of her husband. With each passing, awkward moment, and in the absence of Michael and Raphael, she felt less and less comfortable with the real reason: her desire to know more about David Morrow's health. And, of course, her desire to be present when Michael arrived to tell his mother about Juliette Michel's book.

Perhaps Josephine's arrival had put all thoughts of food out of Elizabeth's mind. Perhaps she, along with Josephine, now believed Eve was crazy. Eve tried to put the bag incident firmly out of her mind and launched into her pre-prepared speech about the memorial service. After all, that is why she was supposed to be here, and Elizabeth had seemed happy enough at the prospect of her visit. She was met with nothing but blankness, a return of the woman Eve had first encountered the previous month. Elizabeth toyed with her earrings so much that Eve feared for them and for her earlobes. The message was loud and clear. David Morrow's widow would turn up to Dudley in May – she had to – but she would leave it to Eve and the college to sort things out.

When Eve mentioned Michael's potential role in the memorial service, there was a flicker of interest, but also a wariness. Both increased when Eve described her visit to Almthorpe, being snowbound, getting to know the two men. Was it the warmth with which Eve talked about Michael and Rapha that made the wariness ebb, the interest grow, the tormenting of earrings subside? Eve sensed that Elizabeth wanted to talk about her son. But not yet.

First, two surprises. 'Eve, do please call me Betty,' was the first.

'But, I thought... Charles Mallam said—'

'Charles is Charles. I've been Betty since my childhood. I exhibited as Betty. Betty is my name.'

'OK. Can I ask you something, Betty?'

'Yes, of course.'

'Do you have any food?'

Betty flushed. 'Oh my goodness, that woman threw me, I don't know why. Yes, yes, of course.' She stood up then paused. 'While I get lunch together, I'd like you to look at something.' Betty disappeared for a moment, returning with a small sketchbook, small enough to slip into the pocket of a coat. 'I saw you looking at that picture.' She gestured towards the small charcoal head that had caught Eve's eye back in March. Eve was struck by her complete underestimation of Betty's perceptiveness. She clearly missed very little. She passed over the sketchbook. 'This is what I do.'

While Betty laid food on the table, Eve turned the pages carefully and began seeing the world through Betty's eyes. Each page contained just one human figure, sketched in what looked like charcoal, most sitting, most half-turned away from the artist, almost all old, some looking defeated, but all captured with a strange sense of dignity. It took Eve a minute or two to realise what these figures had in common.

'They're on the bus!'

'Indeed.'

Eve glanced at Betty, having caught another glimpse of her quiet irony.

'Tell me about it,' said Eve. She knew, because Michael had told her, that his mother had been, in his words, a 'brilliant artist', starting to establish herself in the eighties, creating defiantly unfashionable landscapes and portraits, often miniatures. Betty Algarotti. No, she wasn't born in Italy, but her father had been a prisoner of war in Hertfordshire, married an English girl, worked at the car factory in Luton. Eve felt the artist Algarotti re-emerging as Betty now talked about her love of charcoal, its flexibility as a medium, the way in which it hovered somewhere between drawing and painting, the infinite varieties available. Her favourite was the rich, dark, velvety black of compressed charcoal. Its apparent ease of erasure, but the traces it always leaves. She had sat for Auerbach, also a lover of the medium, he'd been supportive, kind. Betty, who was able to withdraw behind a mask, to absent herself – one of the great skills of the artist's model. Charles Saatchi had bought her work, even though (or perhaps because) it was deeply unfashionable. Eve, fascinated, was also busy revising her picture of Mr and Mrs Morrow's early years as a couple. It was she, still working as Betty Algarotti, who was sophisticated, successful, worldly-wise. Older. Strikingly attractive. Creative. Connected.

But, in a tale as old as time, the wife's career had dwindled as her husband's grew, to be completely left behind by the time that Michael was born. The move to Sarsens after the death of her parents had not helped. Her plans to create a studio died with her babies. Betty faltered over the plural, and Eve risked saying that Michael had shared something of what she had been through. There was silence for a moment.

That small portrait that had so intrigued Eve on her first visit was the only trace of Betty past. Now, Eve learnt of her artistic resurgence and its delightfully unlikely source, the bus pass she gained when she had reached sixty-five. Eve remembered that Betty was four years older than her husband. Probably named for the new queen. Little Elizabeth Sidney appeared unbidden in Eve's mind, named in honour of the Virgin Queen, her godmother, a rare moment of royal gratitude to Philip, her father. A father who never held baby Elizabeth, born in the month he headed to fight for the English Protestant cause against the Spanish Catholics in the Low Countries. November 1585. Eve knew how a certain kind of history went. Someone wrote that Sidney 'warmly greeted the little girl' (masking his ever so slight disappointment in her sex with the prospect that now his wife was started on childbearing, a son and heir would surely follow). But those skeletons, those timelines, reveal the truth – he must have 'greeted' his daughter's birth in a letter, because by the time the baby was born, her father was already hundreds of miles away, in the Low Countries, Governor of Flushing. One day, Eve might ask Betty about her husband's journey to France to hold his daughter, Juliette.

Betty, here and now, was talking about her bus pass. It was her permission to roam. Her journeys got longer and longer as her confidence and her hunger grew and as the country came out of the most draconian pandemic restrictions. As Eve turned the pages, the masks ebbed and flowed and finally ebbed. The book was a record of the pandemic as much as anything. Betty would take her seat, an invisible older woman, and draw. The portraits had something about them. A dignity, a sadness, but also a strength – both of line and subject. Eve realised her response was inadequate and began with an apology.

'I am a words person, Betty, not a visual arts person; I don't really know what to say – but I do know I could look at these all day and that I will look at the world, including the people on the bus, differently, having seen them.'

'Thank you.'

The lunch was beautiful. Betty placed a platter of vegetables, the colours and shapes the work of an artist, between them. Two bowls of dips appeared, one another work of art, purple and white swirls. Milos would approve.

'Ta da! Asparagus! The first of the season!' Betty announced with delight. 'This is humus, and this is my favourite –

beetroot… see if you can taste the spice!' And then she surprised Eve by saying, quietly, 'I can eat what I want now, without worrying.'

In that simple sentence, Eve glimpsed the toll of marriage to David Morrow. Her heart went out to the unhappy couple, forced to spend successive lockdowns together, isolated in this remote lane. Every meal a potential battlefield, the fear of producing the wrong food in the wrong way at the wrong time.

'I'm a vegetarian. Have been since my art-school days. David couldn't understand it. Mocked me. Made me cook meat. He insisted I eat meat when I was pregnant. But as soon as that was off the cards, he wasn't so insistent. But still.'

The two women sat in silence for a few minutes, eating. The silence stretched.

'And now tell me why you are really here.'

XXI

Eve, who had been eating an asparagus spear, nearly bit her tongue. She began assembling a series of half-truths, and then decided on honesty. Always, or nearly always, the best policy.

'As you've worked out, it is not really, or not entirely, about the memorial service. I've spoken again with Michael.'

Betty visibly tensed.

'He wants to find out the truth about his father's death. He is sad and upset that your husband died alone. And he feels, rightly or wrongly, that there's been – cover-up is too strong a word – but, let's put it this way, that all the facts have not emerged. Perhaps not been allowed to emerge.'

'Michael has asked you… oh, that is such a relief.'

'Relief?'

Betty had, it turned out, been worrying herself sick. Eve heard more than she wanted to hear about the terrible rows between son and father over the Christmas period. The bad relationship that had become even worse with the arrival of Juliette.

'I knew David strayed,' said Betty. 'I accepted it, or at least thought I did. Michael couldn't.' To their son, Juliette was living, breathing evidence of his father's unforgiveable treatment of his mother. And the twist of the knife was how swiftly the prodigal daughter became her father's confidante, friend, ally. When Michael and Raphael left, after their second visit in the New Year, Michael had hugged his mother goodbye with a strange intensity.

'This is intolerable,' he had said. 'He has gone too far this time.'

'Can you see now why I have been worried? Michael was always a sensitive boy. With an intense sense of justice and injustice. Rapha is good for him, brings him back to the ordinary things. And, of course, he can channel all that zeal into his job. He's a good vicar because of it. But... he's so hurt, so angry... he does take up causes. He was arrested once outside St Paul's for that Occupy thing, ten years ago it will have been.'

St Paul's rang a bell in Eve's mind. Who had also mentioned the cathedral? It took Eve a moment to realise she was collapsing history, and perhaps more dangerously, given the nature of her investigation, blurring what she knew about the distant past and what she was hearing about the recent past and indeed the present. It was the corpse of Philip Sidney that had been taken to Old St Paul's on that February day, well over four hundred years ago. It was the corpse of David Morrow that she needed to focus on now. She tuned back into Betty's agonised and, Eve felt, confusing explanations. Or perhaps not so confusing, on reflection, centred as they were on Betty's understanding of Michael's religious faith, the timing of his father's death, the chance Lent offered for forty days of penitence, and the season's promise of redemption.

Michael's words had, with the powerful irrationality borne of years of unhappy marriage and the desire to protect her son from the worst of his father's excesses, created a worm of suspicion in his mother's mind. For, Eve was convinced, Betty was being irrational. She could not see Michael justifying any act of violence in the name of his religion, penitential season or no. Indeed, Eve couldn't quite grasp Betty's logic. Did she think Michael had stormed Dudley College and confronted his father, precipitating his collapse? Maybe there was no logic, just the maelstrom of grief and, yes, bitterness and in the midst of it all, the words circling: 'He has gone too far this time.' For a moment, Eve saw herself clearly. Was she guilty of exactly the same?

Betty at least was beginning to see her own distress for what it was. Madness. Michael would not be seeking the 'truth' of his father's death if he'd had anything to do with it. She bought herself a few seconds by pouring out more tea and then asked a calm question: 'So, what have you found out?'

Eve began by explaining that, prompted by Michael's questions, she had spoken with the GP who had verified David Morrow's death and then signed the certificate. She touched, briefly, on Goode's sadness that Morrow had made the fateful decision not to speak with him despite being urged to do so. Betty seemed to have lost her bearings again.

'The certificate didn't really say anything. Unexplained or something. I can't even remember what I said to the police. They were very nice.'

Eve ploughed on. This was not pleasant. She told Betty that Goode had asked Eve, for his own peace of mind as friend and medic, to find out if Morrow had shown any symptoms over the long Christmas holidays. This was not strictly true, but she hoped it would be enough to start his widow talking.

Betty claimed to have little interest in her husband's health or lack of it. As far as she was concerned, he was drinking himself to death, but it had been a long time since she'd challenged him on that. She knew that he'd been hospitalised, briefly, during his time in America – something about an all-nighter with his friends and ending up in a rather nice clinic over there. It was one of the reasons he'd turned against the NHS. He'd thoroughly enjoyed having lavish private care at the expense of his insurance company. No, Betty didn't think he'd told his GP here about it, but he might have done.

Eve made a mental note that there were now two people who knew about the sorry state of Morrow's kidneys, Betty and Phoebe. She would need to ask Nick Goode if the information was on his records or whether, more likely, what happened in a small, right-wing campus in the southern United States stayed in a small, right-wing campus in the southern United States.

In answer to Eve's question, Betty acknowledged that, yes, he had brought all sorts of tablets back from the USA. They were probably still in the bathroom. Top of the stairs. Eve, feeling slightly awkward but playing up to her cover story about Nick Goode's concern, looked through the cabinet. There was indeed an array of American drugs, names she didn't recognise like Ultram and Nexium 24hr. She quickly Googled them all: a prescription for the opioid tramadol, esomeprazole, proton pump inhibitors. She deduced that Morrow's gut was troubling him. No shit, Sherlock. But she also noted that most of the medication was out of date. After all, it was nearly four years since the man had returned from the States. And then, yes! A brightly coloured bottle helpfully labelled *Potassium Supplement.* It wasn't going to be that easy, was it? No. The bottle was not only still almost full, but a quick glance at the dosage confirmed what Eve knew already. Even if Morrow had been taking this stuff regularly, his bloods wouldn't have reached dangerous levels, since the legal limit for each tablet was 99mg.

When Eve returned to the kitchen, Betty seemed much more relaxed. Indeed, it seemed she wanted to talk. So Eve listened. She learnt that when Dudley College was open, Morrow could go full carnivore.

'But when he was forced to live here, well, I wasn't going to give in again, so we just had separate meals each night. He managed to make his own lunch, bread, cheese, sausage.' Betty was talking about Morrow's high blood pressure (so she *did* know something about his health), scoffing but not viciously, almost wistfully, at his inconsistency. He knew salt was bad for him so insisted on a salt substitute but, at the same time, cheese and sausage, washed down with red wine, every day? Did he not know they were the killers?'

Betty was talking about her late husband, unloading memories, in a way that was clearly psychologically helpful to her. It was proving very useful for Eve too. She learnt that Morrow had recently lost his appetite, complaining of nausea, of not being able to taste things.

'It might have been Covid, but I think it was the drinking, you know.' It depended a bit on when he had his first drink – if it was at lunchtime, he would pick at his food in the evening. So, it turned out, Morrow had been poorly for a while.

Eve was drawn like a moth to a flame to ask about the appalling Christmas. 'So, turkey for your husband and nut loaf for you?'

'Well, yes, that's pretty much what it was. Although, of course, we had Juliette here as well, and she ate the turkey as well. I do think French people don't really understand vegetarianism, don't you? In fact, that was one of the reasons the two of them got on so well: they used to tease me by eating ever more horrid bits of meat. I don't just mean black pudding but, you know, calf's pancreas and things like that. At least Juliette cooked the damn stuff.'

Eve knew all about Juliette's 'clean eating', or disordered eating as she saw it.

There was no ostensible reason for Eve to stay longer. Lunch was long gone. For the last hour, she had been half-listening for the wheezing Skoda, concerned as to why Michael and Raphael hadn't turned up. Eve glanced at her watch. Betty, alert as ever, reassured her that she could walk up to the top of the lane and catch the Village Connector at 4.13pm. This seemed like permission to stay, so Eve elaborated her tales of Almthorpe life and Betty talked of some of her best bus rides, including, serendipitously, the route from York to Scarborough which 'almost goes past Michael's door'. She even admitted that, for once, she spent most of the time looking out of the window rather than at her fellow passengers. But mostly, she was fascinated by women on the bus.

'Women are rarely allowed the luxury of sitting quietly, at least until they are old. Until then they are responsible for society, keeping the machine oiled, caring for the old and the young, feeding and cleaning, fetching and carrying, conversations about nothing all the time. So I always kept a look out for women just being, in repose. And found them on the buses.'

Eve was reflecting on this, thinking of the parents in Sheffield, talking at the school gate, conversations she had never had the desire to join (which explained a lot about her solitariness) when she realised Betty was talking about Charles, her neighbour.

'Between you and me, he's a bit of a pain!' Betty looked shocked at her own ingratitude. 'Such a good friend, and he was devastated when his wife died, but his idea of life is always to be doing. Driving here there and everywhere in that enormous car of his, charities, societies, clubs, he's on every committee. He spends I don't know how much money on sailing or golf or walking tours, all organised for him, all for and with people exactly like him. He was off as soon as he could – you know, all the PCR tests and whatnot – in the West Indies, some sailing holiday, when David died, and I was almost glad that he was away. I know I should be grateful that he keeps an eye on me, and there have been times when David was at his worst that, well, I was glad to have him next door. Not that David was ever actually violent, but it was a comfort.'

The mention of Charles, his willingness to help, to ferry Betty to any and all appointments in his car when she couldn't get there on her beloved buses, allowed Eve to ask whether Betty had ever learnt to drive. She was still bemused by the rusty VW Polo outside the door. Betty confessed that she had passed her test over forty years ago ('first time!') but had allowed the myth of the anxious lady-driver to grow around her. Eve was so comfortable with the conversation that she felt able to ask if the trauma of losing her parents in a road accident lay behind the decision. But the truth was, Betty hadn't wanted to become her husband's taxi service. David Morrow had failed his driving test and never bothered with cars since. Eve recalled that Michael Morrow also didn't drive, perhaps for a similar reason. But the consequence was the almost wilful isolation of mother and son.

Betty paused. 'Yes, Charles has been so helpful. But there's things he doesn't understand. He struggled to understand why I stayed with David.'

Eve was with Charles on this one but kept silent about her own struggle to comprehend the widow's loyalty.

'And he definitely doesn't understand the buses. Do you, Eve, do you?'

There was a quiet longing in the question and Eve could say, with all honesty, that she thought she did understand. She spoke, briefly, conscious that this was not about her, of her love of long train journeys. The peace that came with being invisible, carried by others, observer not observed. She could have said more. About the way in which packing a bag and heading off on her own proved her self-sufficiency, to herself if no-one else. That being able to cross borders and continents, on the ground rather than in the sky, proved that the world was not quite as broken as it sometimes seemed. But Eve felt a pang. Her travels were a form of escape, not creativity. Perhaps she could learn from Betty. Eve was certainly catching a glimpse of a serenity that currently eluded her. For, sitting with Betty, Eve did not sense anger. She sensed peace. And she thought it had a lot to do with Betty's small pieces of charcoal.

The two women were sitting in companionable silence when Charles himself came in. There was still a Caribbean glow on his cheeks, although Eve, unkindly, suspected it might be from a sunbed rather than the seas around St Lucia. It was almost a repetition of their first meeting. Betty's neighbour was startled to see Eve.

'Didn't see a car – or indeed your bike!' He chuckled, showing he remembered her well, even after nearly a month. Eve was pretty sure that it was the scarcity of visitors rather than her dazzling personality that made her, and her bicycle, memorable. There was a brief mention of the rail replacement service and Eve's fairly long walk, which prompted Charles to offer her a lift – waving his Range Rover and RAC key fob in her face.

'Where do you need to get to?'

Betty was trying to explain about the Village Connector that left in twenty minutes and would get Eve back to Oxford in... 'Only a couple of hours, and you can get a cup of tea in Charlbury while you wait for the S20. They might say they're closing at five but don't you listen to them; they do it for me so they can do it for you.'

But Charles was insistent: 'I'm going to Oxford anyway; hop in.'

Eve had to make a very quick decision. Accept the man's offer or continue to wait for the arrival of Michael and Raphael, obviously delayed somewhere along the way. To wait would mean missing the Village Connector and having to walk four miles in possibly twilight lanes in the hope of a rail replacement bus that might not exist. To wait would mean missing out on Giancarlo's last night in Oxford.

XXII

Careering along in Mallam's extremely comfortable Range Rover – it had been an easy decision after all – Eve tried to make sense of Betty and Charles. She'd been bold enough to suggest that there was something between them to Betty.

'Oh no. He is still in love with his wife.' And Betty had told her of the couple's arrival next door, 'What, ten years ago, it must have been,' and how ill the woman, Marina, had already been. 'She just wasted away. No-one could find out what was wrong with her. No children, of course, though she was younger than Charles. I had my own troubles at the time, and I don't think I was a very good neighbour.' Betty paused, while Eve reviewed her chronology, her historical training kicking in as ever. This must have been around the time that her son had departed for a Yorkshire theological college and her husband for America. 'I didn't really know her – or, indeed, Charles – at that time. Anyway, it all ended very sadly. Marina went into a hospice; she was so frail. He said that they found, in the end, a rare form of cancer. Poor Charles. He was heartbroken. Still is.'

For all Betty's assurances that there had been no romantic connection between Betty and Charles, Eve wondered how it looked to Michael. Seeing Mallam come in so swiftly, apparently displacing his father. Yes, Morrow was a difficult man but he was his father nevertheless. Shades of *Hamlet*, with Mallam as Claudius. Not an uncle, but he might well have coveted his neighbour's widow. Eve rather liked the analogy, not so much for its murderous implications but because she did indeed see Charles as a Claudius-style operator: smooth, controlling, the man of action. Then again, Betty made a very poor Gertrude in this family tragedy: she seemed far more interested in buses and her sketchbooks than she did in replacing her husband with a tanned golfing type in a four-by-four.

Eve smiled at her own thoughts and tried to enjoy her elevated view of the speeding countryside. It seemed strange that Charles had offered her a lift having only just got back to his house, since the enormous beast she was riding in hadn't been in his driveway when she arrived. She voiced her question, disguised as gratitude.

'Public transport is a complete disaster in this country. And I'm always keen to help a friend of Elizabeth. She's looking well, isn't she?'

'Yes. She is,' Eve offered, as neutrally as possible, sensing that Charles was fishing for an account of their conversation.

'She's moving on, don't you think?' Had Charles also moved on? If Betty was no longer, or never had been, a romantic interest, perhaps he had a special friend tucked away somewhere, someone to accompany him skiing or sailing or to RAC ladies' nights. To ask Charles this directly was a question too far, even for Eve, and she wasn't that interested in any case, so she brought the conversation round to the memorial service and expressed the hope that it wouldn't be too painful for Betty.

Charles was adamant. 'Elizabeth is made of strong stuff. She'll thrive now that Morrow is out of the way.'

It was an interesting way of putting it. Eve couldn't resist prodding the man. 'I was talking with Betty about her husband's health – or lack of it. It seems that his cardiac arrest was precipitated by an underlying health condition, exacerbated by his heavy drinking.'

'Wouldn't surprise me in the least.' There was a hint of smugness in this man of Morrow's age who clearly took as much care of his health as he did of his car (immaculate) and his house (similar). 'What was it? High blood pressure? Liver failure?'

'No, hyperkalaemia.'

'What's that?'

'Elevated potassium levels.'

'Well, I've not heard of it, but it sounds unpleasant. But if I know David Morrow, even if there *had* been something he could do about it, he wouldn't have done it.'

They had reached the broad expanse of St Giles and Eve asked to be dropped by the Lamb and Flag pub. She feigned a meeting at the Bodleian Library and strode purposefully in the direction of Broad Street.

Charles's parting words had been: 'I can see there needs to be a memorial service, but then I think it's best if we just let Elizabeth get on with her life.'

Eve remembered, belatedly, that she had not told Betty about Juliette's book, something that was guaranteed to ensure that Betty did not get on with her life. Well, she was certainly not going to tell Mallam. In any case, Eve now believed, she hoped, there would be no book, so long as Juliette had not capitulated to Josephine. *Don't think about Josephine.* She couldn't prevent a flashback to the bag incident, and Eve felt her cheeks burn. She glanced over and saw the Range Rover waiting at the lights by Martyr's Memorial, then, as they turned green, roaring round the corner into Beaumont Street. Mallam disappeared from sight. She again wondered at his chivalry in offering a lift and his final words, which had more than a hint of warning in them. Had he feared she had upset Elizabeth? He didn't sound like a man in love, but he was extremely involved in his neighbour's life. Then again, everything in his upbringing, from the minor public school to the job in the city, would have taught him never, ever, to let emotion – from love through to hate – show. Some of his age and class and wealth didn't even feel it in the first place.

Musing on men, Eve reached home. She still had an hour before joining Giancarlo at the post-conference drinks reception. And after that, she had a pretty good idea what would happen. How shallow was she to distract herself from matters of life and death with some enjoyable and uncommitted sex? Very.

But later that night, Eve admitted to herself that while no-strings sex was great, with the lack of strings came a lack of conversation. The boundaries were clear, Eve herself had set them, but she was longing to talk with someone. She was feeling overwhelmed, confused, uncertain. What about Rosa? For all her maturity, she was still so young. *Don't dump on your kid*, Eve told herself, determined not to visit the sins of her mother upon her own child. And in any case, some of her thoughts would be difficult for Rosa to hear. The spectre of Thomas à Becket rose again. How could a mother bear the words 'this is intolerable'? What would she do to make life tolerable for her son? No, Rosa was out of the question. Linda was, understandably, preoccupied with her own quest for support, her own despair. And Milos was Milos. She couldn't, she wouldn't, imagine sharing her problems with him. And, in any case, she felt sure he would question why on earth she was spending hours of her time, money, energy, and intellect on something that wasn't anything do with her. He would never understand quite how involved Eve had become, emotionally, with Phoebe, Betty, Michael. With David Morrow, who, from being a cartoon monster, now seemed simply a broken, desperate man, struggling with unacknowledged alcohol addiction, intelligent enough to know he was hated by those who had once loved him, to know that he was a fraud, a failure, but without the ability to change.

For Eve knew that she was uncertain, not because she needed to know more, but because she was nearing the endgame, ever more conscious that she might yet be in pursuit of one of the very people to whom she had grown attached. She was close to understanding not merely who might have wanted Morrow dead, but how he had died.

Eve spoke with Nick Goode the next morning. She began apologetically, hoping he would forgive her phoning him up on a Saturday morning after her almost thank you for what had been an almost date the previous weekend. He was surprisingly gracious when she explained, nervously, that she had at last seen a glimmer of the truth about David Morrow's death. She told him about her visit to Betty Morrow and asked him if he had known about DM's hospitalisation in the US, maybe four years ago. He hadn't known and was both surprised and aggrieved.

'If he'd been on a bender so bad that he ended up in hospital, the renal compromise would go some way to explaining the elevating "K" readings, but still…'

'Yes, but still, there needed to be something else,' said Eve. Nick Goode listened as she admitted to doing a quick check on Morrow's bathroom cabinet, her hope (was it a hope?) that he might have been self-medicating with dangerous food supplements.

'He wasn't. In fact, he was cutting down on salt because of his raised blood pressure, admittedly a futile gesture given the amount of alcohol he drank and his almost complete lack of exercise. The lisinopril you prescribed could only do so much.'

Hoping that Nick wouldn't think her completely mad, she got to the crux of the matter.

'Something Betty said made me think. What if his salt substitute was in some way faulty or contaminated?'

Goode sounded dubious. Eve pressed on relentlessly. She had been over this in her head now a hundred times. What would it sound like when spoken out loud?

'And I am now wondering if someone contaminated it. If – and I should admit that it is a big if – I have deduced correctly, whoever tampered with the potassium chloride was doing so with a clear goal in mind.'

Goode started to say something, but Eve was determined to finish.

'That goal was for David Morrow to suffer a heart attack, preferably at a profoundly humiliating moment – the belief being that a triple whammy of sildenafil with sexual activity and hyperkalaemia would trigger a collapse.'

Goode was silent. Eve checked to see if their call had been cut off, which might have been a blessing, but, no, he was still there.

'Nick, isn't there a way we can check it? If I'm wrong, I promise never to mention it ever again. And whatever happens, I will get on with the memorial service and make sure it is a good and proper celebration of David Morrow.'

Her priority, she said, was simply to test the salt substitute that was still sitting in the kitchen at Little Frogford.

Goode, after what seemed a very long time, agreed. 'If you can get hold of it, then I can get it analysed. Call in a favour. I hope you're wrong.'

Eve was effusive in her thanks. Her hands were shaking as she ended the call, and she decided against another cup of coffee. She was well aware that she had not been completely frank with Nick Goode, but thought, maybe feared, he was smart enough to join some of the dots.

If the SaltSwap had been contaminated, it was obvious to anyone who had easiest access to it: Betty. A desperate wife, pushed to the edge. There were other easy-to-draw, logical conclusions. Whoever did this knew that Betty was protected because she ate her own food (and used proper sea salt). It was not looking good for Mrs Morrow. There was more. If someone did contaminate the SaltSwap, did they do so knowing that Morrow's kidneys were already compromised? As far as Eve knew, Betty and Colleen were the only people who knew about the binge-drinking hospitalisation. Goode claimed not to. Knowledge of this episode immediately made the plan more deadly, the goal not just a humiliating collapse in Morrow's college rooms but a fatal cardiac arrest. Eve knew that her analysis was skewed by her involvement with the protagonists and forced herself to recognise that the case, for in her mind it was indeed now a case, would come down to some lab results and logistics. Not personalities. To a simple question: who had access to Sarsens over the winter months?

Not Colleen, despite her knowledge of Morrow's compromised kidneys. Not Dame Professor Rachita Solanki, Master of Dudley, and Toby Milton, Morrow's publisher, neither of whom had, as far as Eve knew, been anywhere near Little Frogford over the winter.

Then again, she had only found by chance that Josephine Levine had made the journey, although why she had been there was another matter. So perhaps Solanki and, yes, even Toby Milton also needed to be checked out. Eve was ashamed of how much she wanted Solanki still in the frame. Then there was Charles Mallam, conveniently next door. Until he went off to Barbados or wherever it was. Who knew what he really felt about his neighbour, David Morrow? If Eve had to guess, based on the conversation in the car the day before, if he thought of the man at all, it was with mild disgust. No. Unfortunately,

Eve had to accept that the three people, in addition to Betty, who had motive and ample opportunity to do whatever they wanted, whenever they wanted, with a box of SaltSwap over the Christmas holidays were family: Michael, Raphael and Juliette.

Raphael's view of his father-in-law was not completely obvious, in part because the man was so utterly charming, all of the time. Only when Eve glimpsed his fierce protectiveness of Michael did she also catch a glimpse of what Raphael believed he was protecting his husband from: his own father, alive or dead. There was nothing complicated, no need to guess, when it came to Juliette and Michael, and the knowledge gave her very little comfort. There was most definitely bitterness, anger, hurt – although she hoped that in at least Michael's case, these were balanced by compassion and forgiveness. Maybe one day, Juliette would reach the same place.

But Eve also felt it would be madness to suggest that one of them took steps to harm David Morrow, even if the most benign interpretation of events was being considered. There was one simple reason. She believed that all three would have had compassion for what could only be called the collateral damage. They would not have known her name, but the plan surely relied on Morrow making a sexual attempt, and that would involve a vulnerable woman. No, the person Eve was looking for cared only about one thing: humiliating, punishing, and, when it came down to it, removing David Morrow. Anyone caught in the crossfire was irrelevant.

Damn *Hamlet*: the play ran like a mindworm through her always and forever. This time not Claudius, but Ophelia, a green girl controlled by a couple of alpha males – make that three if you add boyfriend Hamlet himself: she didn't stand a chance. Even Gertrude doesn't want to see her when Ophelia cracks in despair, becomes suicidal. Eve was haunted by Ophelia's apparent passivity, her relentless 'I know not, my lord'. To know nothing was, in the end, no protection. Eve was not only haunted by fiction. Linda's desolate confession about wanting Brian dead nagged at her, unnerved her. Eve was convinced that almost every person involved with David Morrow would have had a moment like Linda's at some point in their lives. But she was equally convinced that only one person acted on it. The question was: which one?

With a guilty start, Eve realised that she had not checked in on Linda for a couple of days. She risked phoning and was not encouraged by her friend's weariness.

'He's the same. Just sleeping a lot.' It was turning out to be very, very difficult to speak to anyone in the health service. Someone was due to call Linda at some point. She was still waiting. It was unlikely that Brian would be seen in person. Eve felt dismayed but determined. She would help her friend, somehow.

XXIII

Michael phoned Eve later on Saturday morning. 'Sorry, sorry, sorry, we got held up with a parish matter, God give me patience, and we didn't get to Mum's until evening. She said you'd been there, got a lift back to Oxford with Charles Mallam.'

Eve reassured Michael that it was fine. She felt as clear of mind as she had done since Jon texted her back in March. She knew, for sure, that Morrow's elevated potassium levels were like a ticking bomb. She did not yet know, for sure, whether someone could, whether someone did, plant that bomb.

From her conversation with Nick Goode, Eve now understood that whoever poisoned Morrow was running only a small risk of discovery, in part because of the fallout from the pandemic. The laws around verification of death had only just returned to something like normal. The horrifying spread of Covid, the desperate attempts to avoid contact and infection, had led to a change in the regulations. Non-medical professionals were permitted to verify death, using remote clinical support. This was still the case when David Morrow died.

It was sheer chance that a doctor who had actually spoken with him, actually requested blood tests, was also the person to verify his death. Nick Goode was the only reason that 'hyperkalaemia' appeared anywhere on the death certificate. Anyone else would have been satisfied with 'cardiac arrest' and then contributory factors (alcohol?) or the suitably vague 'the precise medical cause of death has not yet been ascertained'. Then again, anyone who knew the Oxford collegiate system might guess that it would not be a complete stranger who signed off the death. And anyone who knew the Oxford collegiate system might also assume that any head of house worth their salt would ensure that nothing untoward appeared on said certificate. So, even with Nick Goode in the picture, planting your bomb to go off at Dudley was an intelligent move.

The only dangerous, uncertain element was the timing of the explosion. Otherwise, Eve grudgingly acknowledged, the plan was almost foolproof. Everyone knew of Morrow's tendency to drink himself under the table, his reputation with 'the ladies'. It was pretty much guaranteed that he would do something to exacerbate the situation, and he was more likely to do it at Dudley than anywhere else. Even if the elevated 'K' levels were found, as they had been, they could be explained clinically – as Goode had in effect done this very morning – as a sign of Morrow's incipient kidney failure.

Even after her conversation with Nick Goode, Eve found herself wanting to believe that this was indeed the beginning and end of the story. Weakened kidneys. Elevated potassium. A heart attack. No sinister hand at work, drip-feeding Morrow potassium.

But it would not do. She needed to be sure.

Eve gave Michael her instructions. She was fortunate in that the couple were already suggesting dropping in to see her in Oxford on their way home later that day. All they had to do was scoop up the SaltSwap and bring it to her. She would do the rest.

They arrived early afternoon and Eve basked, just a little, in their appreciation of her home. Such was their interest, Eve gave them a quick tour, including her loft space with its small but perfectly formed shower room. She didn't show them Milos's room, of course, on the first floor. She'd never been in there herself. For a brief moment, she recognised that this was not entirely normal, but then dismissed the thought as irrelevant. It was how they lived. It was fine.

Eve herself had been in the house for twenty years to Milos's two and took great pride in her beacon of stability. House prices were already becoming stupid by the time she graduated and she, unlike most Oxford graduates, had a small baby to consider. But in one sense she was lucky, if that was the right word. Her dad had died that year and, long separated from Eve's mother, he surprised both women by leaving his daughter a substantial legacy. Substantial enough to put a deposit on a one-up, one-down terrace house, no front garden, but a rickety kitchen extension which extended out into a water meadow. Yes, it was prone to flooding. Yes, she had to share a room with Rosa, or sleep on a futon mattress, which doubled as a sofa, downstairs. Yes, the front door opened straight onto the street. And, yes, it was in a terrible state of repair. But it was hers. Somehow, through thick but mainly thin, she had continued to pay off her mortgage. She would have been nearly done with it if she hadn't gone wild when Rosa was – what was she? – twelve or thirteen? The loft conversion was a dream come true – her own room at last! – but had required a remortgage. Another reason to stay in her university post.

Michael and Raphael were tactful enough not to ask too many questions about Eve's mother's response, both to her ex-husband's largesse and to her daughter's thrift. She had shared enough with them in Almthorpe to know that Eve had to learn, and young, that her mother could not manage money. There had been no need to spell out why.

It really had worked out well, though. It was not just that property prices had become even more crazy in Oxford. Her house was, she was told by keen estate agents eager for their cut, worth five times as much as she paid for it. No, it was more that, as soon as Rosa moved out, which was as soon as she had finished her A-levels ('not much point in a degree these days, Mum,' and she might have been right, given the fact that her university experience would have been swallowed by the pandemic, delivered through a screen), Eve redecorated then rented out her room.

It helped with the remortgage payments and let her swerve career. The first incumbent of Rosa's room did not last long. The woman wanted a friend. Eve wanted a lodger.

Two months later, by mutual agreement, she left. Milos had appeared like a gift from the gods in midwinter of that year. Three months later, Covid hit. The two of them had coped, brilliantly, with lockdowns. The perfect non-couple.

Raphael wandered round the kitchen as if in a dream. 'You have some amazing stuff, Eve!' he announced, gazing with something approaching adoration at the knives.

'Oh, not much of it's mine. Those belong to Milos. He's the cook. I am just the eater.'

'Oh, I think I like Milos already.' Raphael smirked, and Eve was not entirely sure to whom the innuendo was directed. But she blushed anyway. Eve turned the conversation as quickly as possible.

'So, how did it go yesterday?'

As Eve asked her question, Milos let himself in to the house. And headed straight for his room, having clocked that she had company. Michael hardly noticed, but Rapha gave Eve a very strange look.

'Mum was on good form. She said she'd had such a good talk with you, that you seemed to understand her.' Michael smiled so warmly at Eve that she felt her eyes burning. Blushing. Crying. What was coming over her? 'Of course, she fed us – it's amazing what she's got stashed in her freezer – and she even had a glass of wine.'

Eve tucked that one away for later: she'd not spotted that the house had been cleared of alcohol, presumably Betty's response to her husband's dependency.

Michael was taking a suspiciously long time to get to the point.

Rapha stepped in. 'Michael didn't want to upset his mother – it helped that you'd been there earlier and told Betty that Nick Goode wanted, for his own peace of mind, to find a reason for the elevated potassium levels. She said you'd asked about Michael's father's health over the winter—' Rapha still couldn't quite say David's name.

Michael interrupted. 'Mum was a bit funny about it, to be honest. I think she thought I was accusing her of something, got all flustered then did her blank thing, saying she couldn't remember much about those last few months. I thought I'd just leave it, since you'd had the conversation. It felt more important just to spend time together, now it's just the two – sorry, Rapha, three – of us. Without Dad. It will take time.'

Eve wasn't going to mention Betty's revelation of her fears about Michael and was just glad that mother and son were rebuilding the bridges destroyed not only by Morrow's death, but by his many years of bullying behaviour towards both.

'So, did you manage to bring it?'

'Yes,' answered Raphael, digging into his bag. 'We didn't say anything to Betty. We just enjoyed a walk into the village in the spring sunshine. If she notices – and she probably won't – we'll simply say that Dr Goode wanted to check an idea out.

That maybe the SaltSwap was a faulty batch. Yeah, I know it's weak.'

Eve took the container, feeling both absurd and troubled. Michael seemed to feel the same.

'Take it to your Dr Goode. I'm not sure I want to know what's in it.'

XXIV

The University Parks were looking nothing short of resplendent when Eve met up with Nick Goode and handed over the SaltSwap. It was the first full day of term and Goode was busy with his college duties and could only escape for a few minutes at lunchtime. Eve, to show her gratitude for his help, had offered to provide a simple picnic in the park, and she found herself rather enjoying it and, even better, forgetting the actual reason for their meeting. Nick Goode was more relaxed than she had seen him. More importantly, he did not accuse her of madness and did confirm that he would get a toxicology report. Given that it was First Week, everyone was under the cosh, but he would do his best. This was said as he rushed off, having lost track of time.

'You'll be getting me into trouble, Dr Brook!' Eve wasn't quite sure whether this was flirtatious or a hint that Goode rather resented the way she was using him. She was better at deciphering sixteenth-century secretary hand than twenty-first-century conversation. It was one of her many blind spots. She'd often look at animals or birds and wonder if they were mating or fighting. It was so hard to tell. She felt the same about humans.

Walking home, Eve debated sending a message to Juliette, from whom she had heard nothing, but thought better of it. Pressurising the woman wouldn't help. But she could not quite dispel the fear that she had backtracked since their meeting in York. Another fear, a second cousin once removed of the first, was more nebulous but also strangely enticing, because it refocused the case on *An English Hero* and away from David Morrow's family. If the book, not the man, was the target, if someone had taken drastic steps to ensure that Morrow's work would not appear, that same person might take equally drastic steps to ensure the silence of his daughter. Someone who was motivated, powerfully, to avoid or prevent bad publicity. Someone like the Master of Dudley College. Someone who believed in controlling what you could control and who would justify the hiding or the warping of the truth in the interests of her college if not herself. Someone who had downright lied to Eve about the woman she now knew as Colleen Walsh. And who was much harder to see now that it was First Week.

'God knows what she was doing with him. Then again, Carrie must have seen something in Boris.'

Rachita Solanki, like Josephine, was not proving an easy nut to crack when Eve was finally granted an audience on Wednesday. Eve knew, from Colleen, that the Master's version of events was false. Rachita had sought out the woman she knew as Phoebe. It was not the other way around. When challenged, however, there had been no apology for lying, and certainly no confession of worse sins.

Solanki stated, calmly, that she had seen a young woman leave Morrow's rooms in a state of distress. She looked coolly at Eve.

'I was concerned. More about the girl than about Morrow, but still. I looked in.' (Eve guessed that the Master of a college would find little problem in opening closed doors.) 'The door had been left open.' (*Damn, this woman is a mind reader*, thought Eve.) As the Master told it, she saw Morrow asleep on his bed. She left him, shutting the door behind her. She had made a mental note to speak with her aberrant fellow in the morning when he had sobered up.

Eve was keen to ask whether the Master had seen any evidence of medication in the room. She was still trying to work out the truth of Colleen's increasingly hazy memories of DM taking a tablet of some kind shortly before he collapsed and Nick Goode's assurance that, having taken a good look round the room in the morning, there was no evidence to suggest he did. But the Master was in imperious form not brooking interruption.

In the cold light of day and hearing the news from Nick Goode (who had been summoned by the scout who had discovered the cold body of David Morrow), Solanki decided not to mention that she had seen him sleeping the night before. She had a quiet word with the porters about the CCTV cameras and, funnily enough, there was nothing to see there when the police asked to review the night's events. Now, to Eve, she implied rather than stated that Dr Goode had told her that Morrow's heart attack was unsurprising, given his way of life. She implied rather than stated that her least-favoured colleague had brought his death upon himself. The Master, with a responsibility towards the good of the whole college, was not going to complicate matters by bringing the girl into it. It was at this point that Carrie and Boris were invoked.

Rachita took her silver hairpin out, held it up to the light, then slowly coiled her hair onto the crown of her head, and inserted the gleaming metal. She'd missed one strand, which fell fetchingly to her shoulder. Maybe she had intended it to.

Eve found herself dismissed. She hadn't felt able to mention Juliette's book. Did Solanki even know about it? Did she know it wasn't going to happen? (And why had Juliette not been in touch? It had been a week.) And where was the Master's cat? Eve had developed a hearty dislike of the Master of Dudley and therefore had to remind herself that there was absolutely nothing to suggest she could have been responsible for Morrow's hyperkalaemia, even if she had wanted the man dead.

The toxicology results came through the same day. Goode texted her, cautiously, suggesting they meet up to talk further about 'that matter we discussed'. Eve was still fuming after her meeting with the Master and felt like throwing her toys out of the pram. There was no way she was going to do a memorial service for the woman, the college, or even for David Morrow. But her sulk evaporated with Nick's news. The levels of potassium in Morrow's SaltSwap were well over the legal limit. They'd found the smoking gun. Depending on the condition of Morrow's kidneys, it would not have taken long – weeks not months – for the potassium levels to build up to the levels found in the bloods taken in the last week of February. So, not only a smoking gun but a time frame: the long Christmas vacation at Little Frogford. There was one more thing to find. Where could that extra potassium have been sourced from? Was it ever prescribed? She listened to Goode, made notes. No flirtation now, just a sense of two people trying to look calmly and honestly at something terrible. But no closer to understanding the human source of the terror.

XXV

The rain poured down, water levels rising in the meadow behind her house, but Eve hardly noticed. She moved between reassessing, adding to, removing the data in her notebook and walking away from her desk to force herself to gain perspective. For weeks now, she had seen the true picture of David Morrow's death as a giant jigsaw puzzle. Each new piece of information needed to be fitted in, a decision made whether it was part of the background or central. Where did the shooting of a seventeen-year-old in Liverpool or a rusting VW Polo fit? Peripheral, she was now sure. What of the Nangadef Foundation or a replacement bus service? Also, she believed, not significant. And yet, even though Eve had only a handful of pieces left to fit in, the picture did not yield its secret. Perhaps the puzzle was of a different kind. Years ago, Eve had become obsessed with fiendishly difficult cryptic crosswords. She couldn't remember when she had stopped lulling herself to sleep with Azed. Solving one across or twenty-three down sometimes involved a particularly cruel challenge, whereby you had to work out which part of the clue comprised the definition and which the cryptic key. Sometimes you didn't even *have* the definition in the clue but had to deduce it from another clue. Eve picked up her notebook once again. She looked at Philip Sidney on the front and his sister on the back. Or was she on the front, and Philip on the back? Of course, it was no longer about a four-hundred-year-past English hero and his brilliant sister, but a different, living story and cast. But what had she missed? Whom had she missed?

Eve was not good company for Milos on Thursday evening, but then again, she was not sure he noticed. The food was, as ever, delicious, but for once it did not work its magic. Eve was haunted by Betty's words, 'I can eat what I want now, without worrying.' She remembered Juliette picking at her raw food. What would it be like to have every meal policed by your partner? What would it be like to have every meal policed by the demons in your own head?

'Milos, I'm sorry. I have to go check something.'

If he was offended at Eve's abrupt departure from the kitchen, he did not say so.

Twenty minutes later, Eve returned downstairs. It had been relatively easy to find the location of the document she needed. She had a name and a date. She had paid out her thirty-five pounds. She had read, with some dismay, that it would take two working days to receive the document. If only she had joined the dots sooner. It was now 8.15pm on a Thursday. The earliest she could hope for was Tuesday.

The kitchen was empty, and, of course, clean. She would thank Milos, apologise, in the morning. Then she spotted the glass of dark, darkest, chocolate mousse, with a single mint leaf decoration. And a note. *Hope you found it. Keep going.* Bloody hell. This deserved more than a thank you and an apology. But how could she do something for a man who appeared to have as much use for gifts as he had for praise or gratitude? Her only hope was that, if she offered Milos the French horse wine, he might get pleasure from creating a biodynamic feast around it.

Friday brought some welcome news from Juliette, and, surprisingly, in person.

'Can you believe, I have never explored Oxford! Little Frogford is so far from everywhere.'

Eve remembered not to suggest coffee or alcohol and found a juice bar that would, she hoped, suit Juliette. Over a glass of green, Eve heard about Juliette's meeting with Josephine. She had no need to have been so worried. Indeed, the whole episode was an anti-climax. As Juliette told it, the world had already moved on from David Morrow. Certainly, Josephine Levine had done so. He was old news, already replaced by younger, bolder and nastier voices who were making people like him and Jordan Peterson look positively nuanced. Eve thought of the headlines around some body-building guy with a huge teenage following and felt dismayed. But Juliette looked better in herself and, taking a risk, Eve suggested that Rosa join them. The two women seemed to be getting on fine, which allowed Eve to get back to her comfort zone: propped up in bed, with a book for company, Radio 6 playing, looking out over the water meadow.

Sunday at least provided the distraction of May Morning. No matter that there was a very English drizzle, to go with the very English morris dancers, the very English crowds (no pushing, no shouting, just murmurings of 'sorry'), and the very English public-school boys endangering their lives by jumping, drunk, off Magdalen Bridge, police cordon or no police cordon. No matter that the sunrise was barely perceptible. It was only after descending from the rooftop of a friend's house on Folly Bridge Island, where they had sung a mix of madrigals and ABBA to rival the best efforts of the Magdalen College choir boys high on a tower at the other end of the High Street, that the full horror of the situation returned to Eve's mind. Rosa and her eclectic friends did their best, insisting Eve join them for a picnic on Port Meadow. None of them had had any sleep, having partied all night, ready to welcome in the May dawn, and Eve could only marvel at their stamina. She lay on a rug, a watery sun having cast off the drizzle and providing a modicum of warmth, and listened to the quiet buzz of conversation and laughter around her. She thought of Milos, with his mother in Essex, missing this. But then again, she couldn't quite imagine him getting up at 5am to join large crowds who wouldn't get anywhere close to the actual action of May Day. Her eyes closed and she fell into a doze, marvelling that her daughter had the gift of making friends.

Bank holiday Monday morning and Eve lay, exhausted, on her bed, half watching the clouds move across the skylight above her head. She dutifully took three deep breaths, then three more. Invariably, it would surprise her just how effective this was, how unaware she was of her own tension until it began to ebb away. But today, nothing was working. She couldn't shake the headache that had started on Friday. Painkillers, coffee, stretches, drinking lots of water. As she exhaled, again, Eve heard a key in the front door. She tensed. Waited.

It was Milos, back early from Essex. Eve couldn't remember the rules by which Milos lived, the deal he had with his mother. Maybe she'd never known or asked.

Eve abandoned her breathing and joined Milos in the kitchen, accepting his offer of a cup of coffee. This was usually the beginning and end of their morning interactions, but to Eve's surprise, Milos not only shared that he was walking over to Binsey to buy asparagus from the farm there but suggested she go with him. The expedition proved to be strangely calming and comforting. And educational. Milos identified every single plant and bird that they passed by as they walked upstream along the river. Asparagus in hand, Eve suggested they walk back past her favourite wine shop, and she'd buy something special. Now was not the moment for her cherished horse wine, but it was her way of saying thank you for the chocolate mousse. Back home, it was at last warm enough to sit out on Eve's tiny terrace, so they nibbled steamed asparagus with a lemon dipping sauce, sipped from a bottle of Bacchus (not, in fact, the best wine she'd ever tasted, but it was local and created, like the asparagus, on the banks of the Thames just a few miles south of Oxford), and watched the evening light on the water meadow. Her headache had gone.

The post dropped through the letterbox at twelve noon on Tuesday. She opened the envelope, almost shaking, and took out the document. Yes. It was as she had thought. She spoke, hurriedly, with Nick Goode, ostensibly to check that her conclusions were sound, but in reality to feel less alone with her terrible knowledge. It was a time for honesty. She had risked asking Nick why he had been friends with a man who had behaved so terribly to so many people.

'It's really hard, Eve. I am not sure I can explain. I didn't *like* him, though he could be good company. But, I don't know, maybe it's a doctor thing. I felt a duty of care towards him. I suppose I could see how troubled he was. I remember once – we were both a bit drunk – he talked about his wife. He knew he was a bastard to her. Didn't stop him, but he knew. And then he told me about the miscarriages, the stillbirth, how helpless he felt at the time. I know this doesn't excuse him. He was vile about his – well, I won't use the word he used – but his son. OK. I don't know.' Eve had pushed Nick Goode well past his comfort zone. He sounded bewildered, distressed.

'Look, I'm sorry. It was a dumb question. And I completely get that you felt a duty of care towards him, despite or because of his destructive behaviour.' After all, was this very different from the sense of duty that had driven her to try to help Phoebe?

Eve phoned Dudley College. She had to speak to the Master. It took a lot to get past Michelle, now most definitely a guard dog for Solanki.

'You have five minutes. And this better actually be a life-or-death situation.'

Eve spent two of those minutes explaining to Rachita Solanki why she felt there were grounds to reopen the police investigation of David Morrow's death. The Master, unsurprisingly, was unpersuaded.

'You were not here when Morrow died. The police came that morning. Everything was above board. I made sure that it was. If Nick Goode is going back on that, then...' Solanki's tone made it clear that Goode would find life in Oxford unpleasant. And not just Goode. There was little point in reminding the Master that she had admitted to Eve, in this very room, that she had seen Morrow that night. 'Sleeping'. And not mentioned this to the police.

For all her talk of involving the police, Eve knew in her heart that there was very, very little to go on. If only to salve her conscience, she tried calling 101. She was urged to refer matters such as fly-tipping and dog-fouling to her local council. A pause. 'Our officers are extremely busy and unable to take your call at this time. Please leave a message.' She left her name and number but no message. What could she have said? 'I'd like to speak with someone about a possible murder?'

No. It was up to her. Eve's next conversation had to be with Betty Morrow. It proved to be neither happy nor easy. Indeed, how could it be anything but painful? But it was done. The trap was set.

XXVI

Friday, and Eve was back at Little Frogford, the toxicology report in her bag, and butterflies in her stomach. She knew the truth. She also knew she could not prove it.

Betty sat in her usual place, a steaming pot of tea on the table in front of her, a small jug of milk, mugs at the ready. Her hands played with a stub of charcoal, black smears appearing on her fingers, on the table, on her earlobes. No earrings today. Eve sat opposite. Between the two women sat a jar of SaltSwap and a small blister pack of blue pills. The older woman looked at Eve with an expression that the younger could not read. Was it hope?

'He will come.'

Betty was right. Eve heard the door open, the sound of footsteps, and continued to talk about the beautiful spring weather, so different from her first visit to the house.

'Charles?'

The man stood rooted to the spot, silent, gaping at the table. Betty's use of his name, a question, roused him, but only for a moment.

'I saw... I saw that...' And he lapsed into silence again.

'Sit down, Charles, before you fall over.' Betty said it almost kindly. Eve watched as this odd couple assumed their usual places, Betty over the tea pot, Charles at home in his favourite chair. She was the third leg, the gooseberry to their intimacy. Eve remembered why she was here. To shatter that.

Betty broke the awkward silence. 'Charles, you remember Eve? Of course you do. You gave her a lift back into Oxford whenever it was, a couple of weeks ago.'

Mallam was rapidly pulling himself together, although he could not quite take his eyes from the table. It was time.

'We know what happened. We know you were responsible, but we don't know why.'

Eve watched, unaware that she was holding her breath until the answer to Betty's question came: 'I did it for you.'

'You hastened the death of my husband for my sake.'

'You weren't going to leave him. That pathetic son of yours was not going to stop him. That Solanki woman wasn't going to fire him – she could have got rid of him. She knew what he was. He had to be stopped.'

Eve expelled her breath. They had their confession.

'This place could be beautiful. It's been allowed to decline.'

Eve nodded, imperceptibly, to Betty. They two women had agreed that if Betty felt she needed Eve to speak, she would suggest a cup of tea. There had been no mention of tea. Betty could handle this herself.

'Until you said those words, I might have believed, agonised over, you when you said you did it for me. But that's not true, is it, Charles?'

He had no answer. Perhaps he realised he had already said too much. He stood up abruptly, seized the container and tablets, put them in the pocket of his Barbour, and was at the door. He turned to them, summoning all his years of complacent privilege and hurling it at them in his final words.

'You can't prove a thing. Morrow died of natural causes. He was probably fucking, or trying to fuck, one of his appalling

217

bits of skirt. Needing these pills. Should have taken better care of himself.'

The profanity was the most shocking thing, coming from the mouth of this man of such smooth respectability. Mallam waved the foil pack at the women. Eve couldn't resist a very well-concealed smile. She and Betty knew it was a pack of Phenergan, an over-the-counter antihistamine treatment. Not Viagra. But she couldn't allow Mallam to walk out of the door. She and Betty were ready for this.

'Did you think we'd be that stupid? *That* is not the container that has been in this kitchen, which was used for all David's meals, the container for whose contents I now have a toxicology report. It may only be circumstantial evidence, but we could make your life very miserable. There are fingerprints on the container I removed from this kitchen.'

Eve pressed on, mentioning her 'preliminary conversations with the police'. This was a stretch. She had left her message. It was a rather one-sided conversation.

'There will be a clear trail once the police know *what* they are looking for and *who* they are looking for.'

'You wouldn't?'

The question was to Betty, and she answered. 'I would. My pathetic son is right. Vengeance is mine, sayeth the lord. It was not yours, Charles Mallam. You stepped in on my behalf without my consent – consent that I would never, ever, have given you – to remove David, my husband, from my life, from my son's life, from his new-found daughter's life, no shriving time allowed. It was not yours to do.'

Charles Mallam was visibly caught between fight and flee. It was not a pretty sight. Eve told him to come and sit down again. He did. Obedience to a certain kind of woman went deep in him, and right now Eve was that kind of woman: strict, in charge, just like Nanny. Betty poured a cup of tea, and Eve saw, as Charles picked up his cup, that his hand was bleeding, so tightly had he been gripping his keys.

'There is another way. There is something you can do. It's time for you to do the honourable thing.'

If this had been a Golden-Age mystery, then Eve would have been offering the murderer the chance to blow his own brains out before the law put a noose around his neck. She'd never liked those endings. Nearly a century on, this mystery would end differently, and honour would take a different form.

Over a nice cup of tea and a biscuit, Eve set out their terms.

XXVII

Two days earlier, she had taken the first train out of Oxford. Cycling through the Cotswold lanes, Eve was astonished at the riot of spring colour appearing around her. Why did spring always come as a surprise? She spotted Betty sitting on a bench under an oak tree in the centre of Frogford Parva, a mile or so distant from Cozens Lane, at least if you took the footpaths. As arranged, Eve rang her bike's bell, the sound more cheerful than she felt, then carried on past Betty to loop round the back of the pub to a recreation area, empty at this time in the morning. Betty strolled towards her, and the two women greeted each other as if this meeting were entirely a matter of chance. Jane Austen knew better. They were undoubtedly surrounded by a neighbourhood of voluntary spies who would ensure that nothing untoward occurred to disturb rural England's complacent stability. But they could at least try to have a conversation unheard.

Eve did not begin with Marina Mallam. First, she explained what she now believed had happened. It meant admitting that Michael had taken his father's SaltSwap on his last visit. Betty flinched. It meant admitting that Eve had got it analysed, meant explaining what Nick Goode had found. It meant taking Betty through her thought processes, or most of them, over the previous days: her search for a source of potassium, her discovery that it was prescribed for people with eating disorders, her focus on Juliette, with her painful thinness, her clean eating.

Eve was not handling this well. Their fiction of being two women stopping for an idle chat (they really needed a dog) was crumbling. Betty's eyes were full of tears. She blew her nose loudly.

'Let's walk a little.'

Walking made it easier to talk of Marina Mallam.

'She didn't have cancer. She was suffering from anorexia. She was already ill when they moved into Cozens Lane. For a time, I thought that perhaps Charles didn't understand his wife's illness, that he genuinely believed she was dying from an undiagnosed condition, believed she needed palliative care. It all gets a bit tangled up with the pandemic and I thought I'd never ever be sure of the truth, since pretty much anyone could sign off a death certificate in those chaotic early months. They didn't need to have attended the patient. But Marina Mallam's death certificate gives anorexia nervosa as cause of death, not cancer. She died "with Covid" not from it. So someone at the nursing home knew what was wrong.'

To Betty, Eve could admit that she had joined some dots and made a picture, but that she was still unsure she had joined them correctly. This was one of the reasons she had not taken more steps to involve the police. She couldn't know, but she believed that the source of the potassium was the spironolactone tablets Charles Mallam's severely anorexic wife had been prescribed.

Eve felt compelled to reassure Betty. 'There was nothing you could have done. And anyway, you were dealing with a lot yourself.'

Marina Mallam had declined as David Morrow departed for the USA and Michael for theological college. Betty had almost entirely withdrawn into herself.

'I'm not sure of the details – I've got most of this second- or third-hand – but I get the impression that Charles didn't, in a strange way, want his wife to get better. Or couldn't acknowledge the nature of her illness. Anyway, she died.'

Eve did not dwell on how she had gained that impression. She didn't want anyone to know too much about the conversation she had with someone at the RAC Club in which she'd implied (never stated) that she, a literary consultant, was in the earliest stages of exploring resources for a celebration of the life of Marina Mallam.

'It always helps to get the friends' memories, a sense of her social group. The family, you know, the family, feel it's time.' Eve didn't say which family.

She'd come away from the RAC with a name. Sophie Winters was delighted to get a call from a journalist, doing a piece on the hard yards done by women behind the scenes at male-dominated London clubs. Eve heard a lot about charitable foundations, balls and fund-raisers, where most of the actual work was done by what Sophie called the WAGs. Eve mentioned she had a photograph of Sophie and a couple of other women from an event in the autumn of 2019. This was true: she was looking at it on her screen. Eve paused as if she was reading their names for the first time. This was not true. Catherine Onions and Marina Mallam. Would they be willing to talk with Eve?

'Cat? Why not? But she's in France most of the time these days, got her residency or whatever it's called, in time; she's clever that way. By the way, if you get in touch with her, it's Oh-nyons. Not the vegetable.'

Eve winced, not at the pretension but at the remembrance of her own willingness to rush to France in search of Juliette.

Sophie's voice turned solemn. 'You clearly don't know, but Marina died. At the beginning of Covid. She obviously wasn't well, I think it was cancer, that's why she came out that night, but still, it was a terrible shock.'

Eve remembered that the picture of the women was at a fundraiser for a cancer charity.

'I'm so sorry.' Eve was. 'Were you close?'

'Well, to be honest, no. Charles – that's her husband – would usually come to events on his own. We all felt for him, but we didn't want to ask too many questions. When Soho Farmhouse started up near him in the Cotswolds, I thought I'd get to see her a bit more – I mean, it wasn't as far to come as London, but…' Sophie's reminiscences sputtered into silence.

Eve thanked her and promised to run the piece by her before it came out. Which would be never.

Charles Mallam remained something of a mystery to Eve, but she tried to put into words the glimpses she had had of his mind.

'I can't truly get into Charles Mallam's head – I'm not sure I want to – but my sense is he became slightly obsessed with what he viewed as your husband's sins. He's a man who likes to be in control – of himself and of others. He believed, perhaps even hoped, that David's binge drinking, his elevated blood pressure, his other activities,' (there was no way Eve was going to have the Viagra conversation with Betty, even if she had claimed to have not cared about Morrow's straying), 'would lead to his death. When that didn't happen, he began to think it would do no harm to speed him on his way. In his own mind, he would think he was doing it for you. As you said, he couldn't understand why you stayed with him.' Eve paused. She was determined to be fair to the man. 'In his favour, if that is the right word, he didn't know that your husband had been hospitalised in the States for kidney failure, on the back of a particularly brutal night of drinking.'

But there had been something ruthless in his methods. He must have known that spironolactone should be taken in tablet form, so that the body digests the medication safely, slowly. Yet still he had ground up his wife's tablets, added them to Morrow's SaltSwap, knowing it was a quick, dirty and potentially lethal way to get high levels of potassium into the man's bloodstream.

Eve privately saw Mallam as a dangerous prig, someone with an unhealthy preoccupation with virtue, especially for men. Charles Mallam was a good man. That there were bad men made him, made men, look bad. He wanted to humiliate, to punish, Morrow. He was judgemental of what he perceived as his neighbour's sexual profligacy. Judgement turned to obsession with the arrival of Juliette, a living, breathing instance of Morrow's corruption.

There was a kind of logic to Mallam's strategy. He probably assumed that Morrow wouldn't collapse in his own home because he had never brought his women home with him. Ideally, he would be humiliated in his college rooms, *in flagrante*. But the reality was that Morrow *could* have collapsed at Sarsens, with Betty in the house. He would probably have survived, if she could have got an ambulance to him in time. Then again, dialling 999 was a whole other kind of lottery.

Betty was determined to be forgiving. She argued that his wife's death might have reset, or rather skewed, his moral compass. Perhaps he knew not what he did.

Betty and Eve had talked long enough for the playground to fill with parents and children. What they wanted was for Mallam, challenged, to defend himself from their accusation, to attempt to bolt, and thus reveal his guilt. Eve floated the idea that they sabotage Mallam's Range Rover: surely it was as simple as putting sugar in the petrol tank? Betty went one better: she would get her friend, the community bus driver, to block the road. The two women looked at each other and shared a wry laugh. They were being thoroughly foolish. In the end, there was nothing, except Eve's precarious chain of circumstantial evidence, to show that Mallam was responsible for Morrow's hyperkalaemia. And even if that could be proved, it would be another leap to argue that the man was responsible for Morrow's death.

With this sobering knowledge, they nevertheless decided to make one attempt to surprise Charles Mallam into an admission of guilt. If it had failed, then there promised to be some very awkward moments for neighbourhood relations.

But it had succeeded. Mallam's ego had overwhelmed his better judgement. The miracle had happened. And Eve had been ready for it.

XXVIII

July in Oxford. Dudley College shone with such wealth and privilege that the stones hardly needed burnishing by the rays of the English high-summer sun. The students had gone, leaving behind only a record of their rowing prowess, chalked up on the walls of Leicester Quad, and a handful of discarded bikes in the cycle store. More discreet acknowledgements of the college's good fortune were scattered throughout the quads and gardens: inscriptions recording generosity towards the creation of theatres, artworks, libraries and sun dials. 'Forever Duds' appeared on a number of them, from an early twentieth-century colonial with a life of service 'to Africa' to an early twenty-first-century undergraduate who had taken her own life. A small army of gardeners, a battalion of sprinklers, had created perfection. The striped, green lawn. The riotous borders. And a small army in the college kitchens had provided a buffet, which was shrivelling in the sun, despite the best efforts of the waiting staff. Eve reckoned that vegetarianism or veganism was the safer path for everyone, not just her. The prawns looked dangerous.

People clustered in small groups, keeping to their own: heads of colleges, pro-vice-chancellors, a scattering of emeritus professors. Not many people under fifty. Almost all white, but the Master was not the only person of colour on the green lawn. Dame Professor Rachita Solanki basked in the late-afternoon heat, her hairpin flashing as she turned her head, politely attentive, to the three or four people around her. The Nangadef Foundation had shown up. Change was coming. The Master had prevailed. Morrow and his book were gone. Charles Mallam's plan had, Eve believed, relied on Solanki's unconscious complicity. She could have got him medical help that night. She did not. She could have insisted on a full investigation of his death. She did not. Yes, Solanki knew what Morrow was: a problem. And she had been quite content to let someone else solve that problem.

'Splendid, absolutely splendid. A send-off worthy of the man.' A grey-faced, red-nosed, older man congratulated Eve. She was surprised. She did not realise that her organisation of the belated memorial service was common knowledge. Perhaps he just meant it as a general comment. Eve smiled, remembering the readings, including one from twenty-two-year-old poet Colleen Walsh. The woman seated in the row behind her had judged it, 'A bit dark, don't you think? Isn't this supposed to be a celebration? It's not a funeral, after all.' Her neighbour in the pew seemed more eager to speculate on the poet's youth and her relationship to the dead man. Eve tried not to listen. Now, grateful though she was for the man's kind words, Eve thanked him and then pretended she had seen someone she knew.

Which was, in fact, not untrue. Colleen had, in her words, 'got the fuck out of here' (as she had always said she would) during the final Amen. She had good reason. Her sister Siobhan, having completed her degree in Transport Studies, was starting a graduate trainee post with one of the Yorkshire railway companies. Eve was more thrilled than Colleen about her little sister's career path but was sure that the party to mark Siobhan's success would be a good one. Only Michael remained

227

at Dudley. He stood in the shade of a mulberry tree at the far end of the garden, in full Anglican regalia. Up in Yorkshire, he had tended to dress down. Here in Oxford, he had chosen full pomp, as well he might. Somehow his thin frame gained gravitas from the robes, rather than being swamped. He had led this memorial for his father's life with a quiet authority. One of the most moving moments came when Juliette read from one of Lorca's poems, the last line of which was printed as the epigram for the order of service: 'A wall of difficult dreams divides me from the dead'.

It was all part of his, and Eve's, determination to retain a sense of honesty about David Morrow's problems and his legacy. She wanted to thank Michael for his help. But as she walked over, Eve watched Raphael watching him, protective, proud, anxious. She turned away when she read the couple's body language: keep away.

Eve looked around. There was no-one else. Betty, who had sat, a quiet defiance in her, in the front row as the memorial service unfolded, had also left as soon as she could. She was still not ready to talk about her marriage, even to those close to her, let alone to a full chapel. Juliette too had left early, but Eve had been pleased to see the young woman sitting close, or close enough, to Betty. Juliette wore – of all things – a veil. Eve had to admit that it was a superb look, but it was not quite in the spirit of this 'celebration' of David Morrow's life. Only later, in the ladies toilets, after the service, catching sight of Juliette's desolate face, her eyes red, her face pale and yet flushed, did Eve recognise that, for Juliette, the memorial service for one person had offered a chance, as it so often did, to grieve for another. There had been no possibility of any kind of ritual farewell for Isabelle, and Juliette had been fuelled only by anger during Morrow's chilly March funeral. Anger had protected her from grief, drowned out the pain. It was a useful emotion that way.

And now at last the tears were coming. Eve touched Juliette on the shoulder, left her in peace, and took herself out to the lawn, sure that Juliette too would not stay to exchange platitudes in the Warden's Garden. If anyone noticed the absence of David Morrow's neighbour, Charles Mallam, they did not say.

Eve realised there was no reason for her to stay. She would see Michael and Rapha soon. They had invited her up to Almthorpe to stay for a few days, and she had eagerly accepted, keen to get to know both men better. And, having discussed it with Betty, she was keen to tell Michael the truth about his father's death. Betty would speak with Juliette, when the time was right. But for now, Eve would leave Michael and his husband in peace. She thought of interrupting the Master, but any intrusion upon the important work of fundraising would not be welcome. Everyone she knew, everyone she had grown to care about, had left.

So Eve went home.

XXIX

Three Months Later

Dudley College: the Nangadef Centre is formally announced by Dame Professor Rachita Solanki. There will be a competition to find an architect, someone from the global majority, so woefully underrepresented in this ancient university. Dudley will retain its name but will move confidently into the twenty-first century, with an overhaul of the college's portraits (fewer dead white men) and a new mentoring initiative at a handful of inner-city schools. There has not been quite enough time to ensure that the first 'Mary Sidney Scholar' can start their research in the current term, Michaelmas, but there are hopes that, come Hilary, the selection process will be completed and the fully funded, three-year, post-doctoral position will be taken up by a suitable candidate.

A bookshop in Sheffield: the publication of Colleen Walsh's first collection of poetry is being celebrated. Gracie is allowed to stay up late, her nanna in attendance. Colleen's dad even sheds a tear. This is a night for all the Walsh family, and they are determined to enjoy it. They do. Eleven copies are sold, four of them to Eve. It is a triumph.

An art gallery in Shoreditch: a private view of a new, remarkable series of charcoal drawings from Betty Algarotti. Yes, Algarotti who worked with Auerbach. Yes, she's still alive. Eve is there, seeing a glimpse of Betty in the nineteen-eighties, or what she could gather she looked like from the grainy photographs in which the artist would often be hidden by a group, or be captured turning away from the camera. But her intensity was unmistakable. So too her short, fierce, dark hair, her lips dark red against her pale skin. Tonight, Betty, with short, fierce, grey hair now, again wears her trademark crimson lipstick. Across the room, a slender woman with the posture of a ballet dancer holds court by the drinks table, claiming to be one of those who just *knew* that Betty was the more talented of the Morrows. Betty glances over towards the speaker, Josephine Levine, and takes another sip of her sparkling water. Her face is unreadable. An agent speaks to her about a book: 'Betty's Buses, perhaps?' Betty appears to ignore him. She surveys the room. The orange dots are proliferating. She cannot wait to get home. Her newly built garden studio is waiting for her.

A portacabin, somewhere in Yorkshire: Michael Morrow sits with Monica, the director of a charity doing groundbreaking work with adult survivors of abuse. They are discussing the best use of a surprising, but extremely welcome, and extremely generous, anonymous bequest. Michael knows that there are those who will say that they do not want him anywhere near abuse survivors, whether on the grounds of his gender, sexuality or employment with the Church of England. That Michael knows this is part of his strength. He will find a way to serve. He doesn't know that Betty, who had chosen the charity to be the recipient of the proceeds from the sale of her neighbour's house, had expressed the hope that Michael would be involved. Eve remains conscious that she may never know the truth of the Morrow family's life, the nature, extent, impact of David Morrow's behaviour on his wife and son. But Betty's choice of charity tells its own story.

A care home in Oxford: Brian sits in what they call his favourite chair, looking at what they hope is his favourite tree. He does not respond when Linda comes in. He does not know her any longer, and it is not because she is wearing a mask. Linda finds it harder and harder to sit with her husband. She asks one of the carers, yet another kind, plump, very young, dark-skinned, masked woman working far from home, if Brian has spoken at all. Done anything.

The woman shakes her head, touches Linda's arm. 'He is not unhappy.'

'But I am,' Linda wants to scream.

Back home, she makes herself a cup of tea, picks up her library book, and loses herself in its pages. In the morning, another night endured, she sees an email, sent at 2am. It is from her son, Dan. He wants to come home. *See you soon, Mum*, he writes.

Cozens Lane: two young children play hopscotch in the lane, dressed as if it was 1954. Their parents watch, delightedly. 'It's been so good to escape London. Children can be children here. Free to play in the street!' they say to their friends trapped back in the mean streets of Clapham or Ealing. The price tag for this freedom had been high, but not that high, given the owner's eagerness for a quick sale. They had not known then that Betty Algarotti, the artist, lived next door, but they now pretended they had, especially when talking to their new friends at The Farmhouse.

The station master's office at Malton station: graduate trainee Siobhan Walsh is presenting her research on the York-Scarborough line's viability in a post-Covid transport era. She is well prepared, articulate, and (as her line manager says) easy on the eye. Siobhan hears him and later, in the loos back at head office, makes another voice note in her phone. One day, she will bring these guys down.

Eve's kitchen on a Thursday night: Milos, white shirt, black jeans, is cooking, focused on his culinary rituals. Thankfully something, someone, is unchanged by the dramas of the last six – no, eight – months. Although even Milos is not immutable to time. Is Eve imagining it, or does he have a touch of grey at his temples? Ayoub is laughing. Juliette is perched on his lap. Rosa is opening a bottle of Lebanese red. Milos plates up. Ayoub and Juliette bounce between French and English, linguistic puppies:

'Michel?'

'Ha! Someone like God. You see I know the Hebrew!'

Rosa glances anxiously at her mother, but Eve cannot even remember what it was like to feel, let alone display in public, such noisy affection. She feels old but that is a comfort right now, not a burden. And the food is even better than usual, and Milos does not seem discomfited by having to serve an unusual number of people on a mismatched selection of plates.

The evening ends and Eve lies again on her bed. She has not booked her trains to Turkey.

'Erdoğan's regime,' she says solemnly, if asked why not, or, less grandiose, the need to prepare her teaching for the new year, but these are excuses, not reasons. She has not even jumped on a train to Italy, despite Giancarlo's warm invitation to share his bed, if not his life. She's not quite sure why she is spending her time and money on household repairs rather than adventurous rail journeys or uncomplicated sex. What has she become? Maybe Rosa has the right idea; maybe property ownership has been a terrible mistake; maybe she should sell-up and become a peripatetic cat-sitter in other people's houses. It seems to be working for her daughter. Remembering the words of Rebecca West that she shared with Linda, Eve knows that she has, it seems, the gift of helping others to 'add good things' to life but also knows that she is unable to help herself.

For although *Bringing Home the Bacon: a Life in Pork Products* has come into the world, to Sir Robert's great pride and delight, Eve has not revisited her own research on Penelope Devereux, Philip Sidney's 'Stella'. That moment on the train home from York, when she imagined writing a counterblast to Morrow's take on history, had been just that: a moment. She doesn't quite understand why it is not the path she has taken, but she takes pride in clearing the way for others to do so. In the end, it had been ridiculously easy. Where better to celebrate Philip Sidney's sister, Mary, Countess of Pembroke, than Dudley College? The woman was indeed a daughter of Dudley: Mary Dudley was her mother. The Earl of Leicester, Robert Dudley, he whose name graced one of the quads at Dud's, was her uncle. That was enough for the traditionalist. For the more forward-thinking, Eve crafted a proposal packed with buzzwords (synergy, intersectionality, traction) and hinting at the rich seam that might be uncovered if the Sidney family's involvement in Ireland, understood as a dry run for English imperial ambitions in the New World, were to be properly examined. Eve had clinched the proposal with a quotation from John Donne, who described Mary and Philip as Miriam and Moses: equal but different, both worthy of study, both worthy of an honest, radical reappraisal. For all her pride in her eloquence, though, Eve knew that the Mary Sidney Scholar's smooth progress through meetings of Governing Body was helped by the promise of an anonymous donor who would match any external funding. No-one needed to know that the money was a small fraction of the proceeds from the sale of a rather lovely house in Cozens Lane. The best use of a much larger fraction of the proceeds were currently under discussion by Michael and Monica at the Women's Refuge. And there was enough left over for Charles Mallam to start again, somewhere else. Eve wasn't a monster.

She herself had quietly contributed, because it didn't take much, to the publication of Colleen's poetry collection. Betty's resurgence, the Shoreditch Gallery, the talk of *Betty's Buses*, was entirely due to the artist herself. Eve was more delighted at this than anything.

Betty was inspirational, but Eve could not follow her. It would take more than a few months to let go of what had become, in her mind, the Morrow case. There was a great sadness in her as she understood, fully, that she had been chasing not one but three phantoms through the spring and summer: *An English Hero*, *The Daughter's Tale*, and, just as illusory, her own work on Penelope Devereux. Now the second Queen Elizabeth was dead, joining the first as history. Autumn was here, winter was coming, and there were to be no books. Morrow's manuscript had proved to be irrelevant to his death.

Put simply, two men had fought, although only one of them was aware of the battle. One's death had been hastened, to borrow his widow's word, on the first day of March. And Eve had learnt, that morning, that the other was also dead.

Charles Mallam had removed himself to a Provençal village, replicating his life in the Cotswolds but with added sunshine. He did not lack for female company and his tennis game improved immeasurably. No-one could explain why, one day in late October, he piled his clothes neatly on a remote pebble beach and swam out to sea never to return.

This would not do. Eve picked up her phone and looked at a text that had arrived a couple of days previously. She had been ignoring it. *Can I take you out to dinner? I would like to share just*

one toast to David Morrow (imperfect human like all of us; well,
maybe a bit more so than some of us) and then we can talk about
John Donne or, if you would prefer, Aemelia Lanyer? N x.

She decided to say yes.

About the author

Anna Beer is best-known for her bold feminist non-fiction based on original research, including the groundbreaking *Sounds and Sweet Airs: The Forgotten Women of Classical Music* (2016). A regular contributor to TV, film, radio, and concert platform, Anna was lecturer in English Literature and Creative Writing at the University of Oxford for many years and remains a Visiting Fellow at Kellogg College. *Death of an Englishman* is her debut novel.